COFFIN & CO.

COFFIN & CO.

NJAMI SIMON

Translated from the French by Marlene Raderman

Black Lizard Books

Berkeley • 1987

Coffin & Co. was originally published in France as *Cercueil & Cie*
by Lieu Commun. For information please contact: Le Bureau du
Livre Français de New York, 853 Broadway, Suite 1507, New York,
N.Y. 10003.

Coffin & Co. is a Black Lizard Original published by Black Lizard
Books, 833 Bancroft Way, Berkeley, CA 94710. Black Lizard Books
are distributed by Creative Arts Book Company.

ISBN 0-88739-049-8
Library of Congress Catalog Card No. 87-70592

Manufactured in the United States of America.

Chapter One

The Dew Drop Inn, on the corner of 129th and Lennox Avenue in Harlem, was a place where you were sure to have a good time. There in a part of the neighborhood nicknamed The Valley, blacks in their Sunday best came in little groups to have some fun. The music made the jukebox shake, mixing with the incredible hubbub of the bar and the improvised dance floor between the counter and the room where men and women of all ages pranced about. In the shadows, a little withdrawn from all the action, two old men sprawled before glasses of cold beer, lamenting the passing of a time when, instead of Michael Jackson, the voice of Big Joe Turner made black hips sway. This part of the black islet had been baptized the Coal Bin. It was even more dilapidated than the rest of the district, though once it had been the domain, the kingdom of dreams, through which these two black cops pursued their scuffles and adventures. Retired now, the only things left for them to do were drink, hum a bar of "Sometimes I Feel Like a Motherless Child" in a throaty baritone like Louis Armstrong, blubber about past glories, and prove by way of a few sharp words that two old lions could still terrorize the rats.

"Shit, man, we have to do something," sighed the one whose face looked scalded with violet scars. "Anything but sit around here rotting! I'm sick of bar-hopping like a couple of morons."

"Right on," the other answered. "I feel exactly the same. I'm not going to end up like all these niggers!" His glance across the bar took in a row of two-bit pushers, armed thieves, worn-out whores and the bloodshot eyes of men who hadn't slept since their last fix. The solution for these burn-outs, these lost souls, these addicts, was one and the

1

same: live and let die. Above all, survive and protect your miserable hide through thick and thin.

"Come on, let's split," grumbled the one with the marked face.

His partner fell into step behind him. The bartender didn't charge them for their drinks as they left. Having tough guys for guests made a good impression, even if they had hung up their badges.

Their black sedan sat parked on the Lennox Avenue sidewalk. Every hood in Harlem knew the car. The men climbed in. The key had not yet turned in the ignition when a young man with a radiant face tapped on the windshield. He was built like an athlete and held a large ghetto blaster balanced on his shoulder. He sported the red cap of a Queens baseball team. W. Jones Dubois, riding shotgun, opened his door.

"Get in, kid. You shouldn't be hanging around here at your age." Dubois was forced to shout over the music that escaped the radio, drowning his words.

"Turn that racket off!" shouted Smith in a voice loud enough to shatter the car window.

Looking contrite, the young man turned down the volume and edged across the seat behind Dubois. "You're just not with it. Bruce Springsteen's great."

Any spade'd make that kind of music has got to be crazy. That kind of racket's not our style, boy."

"Springsteen's not black."

"That's even worse," Smith snapped.

The car rumbled off toward Central Park. Smith drove slowly, as if they were still making the rounds. Indifferent crowds moved along the sidewalks, knowing that in this neighborhood prayers were never heard. Night fell, sharpening the keenness of dark eyes. Smith burst out laughing. "Not the time to put out the whitebait now."

"No," his partner somberly agreed as the old Plymouth turned sharply left onto 126th Street.

Without slowing down, the car passed the police station where a new, young lieutenant had replaced the legendary Anderson. It continued in the direction of the Harlem

2

River. Decrepit buildings rose toward the sky with hideous grandeur. His face pressed against the window, Dubois had the disagreeable sensation that pincers were twisting in his gut. And yet he felt certain that he knew Harlem better than anybody. During long years of service he had wallowed about in this filthly place; even so, with sixty years behind him, he was disgusted by his helplessness before it. To think that shit was the natural element of black people! The tires screeched at the intersection of First Avenue and Harlem River Drive.

"So, Gravedigger, you got the blues, or what?" asked Smith. The nickname stuck to Dubois like skin.

"Sometimes I think America isn't really our country, and that's why we're all living here like wolves. Otherwise, it just doesn't make sense."

"You're both out of your minds," scoffed little Cassius.

Jones Dubois turned around laboriously. "You should have watched "Roots" when it was on the tube, Feather-brain."

"This is where I live," Cassius shot back, "and this is where I'm gonna make it. I don't want to spend my life dreaming about another city or another country, waiting for the white man to do something for me. I'm going to take what I can get right here."

"Swing low, sweet chariot," Smith smirked, making fun of his friend.

The Harlem River cut the black ghetto in half. To the west lay Harlem, to the east, the Bronx. The Plymouth followed the river for a moment, before re-entering the heart of the forest of girders, buildings, gutted cars, billboards and burnt-out neon signs. Smith drove aimlessly, waiting until the last possible second to make his turns.

"So, kid," Dubois went on, "why aren't you at Columbia today?"

"Weren't any interesting classes. Besides, I wanted to break the news to you myself."

"It's not up to you to decide if a class is interesting, kid. You got to swallow everything they give you. You got to work hard if you're going to be secretary of state. Twice as hard as any whites," he said.

3

There was a moment of silence as each one meditated on these words.

"What's this news of yours, anyway?" Smith finally asked, not about to be distracted.

"I can't talk about it just like that. Let's go some place quiet. It's serious."

"You eat yet, kid?"

"No, man! I'm hungry. As long as . . ."

"Clam up," Smith cut him off. "We haven't eaten yet either. You can tell us your story over a big plate of chicken feet and green peppers. That way when you open your trap, you won't be able to close it again."

Mama Dodge's place was located in a narrow alley between Park Avenue and Lexington. The two men knew they could find a full plate here at any hour of the day or night. The restaurant was actually a stall, just large enough to hold three tables, and Mama Dodge reigned over them as indisputable mistress. Seeing the two giants get out of their car, she walked over to them.

"Been awhile since I seen you here," she said.

She tossed a murderous glance at a customer lost in contemplation behind an empty glass. "This isn't a hotel. You better move along now."

Though Mama Dodge was not herself a poet, she played the muse to local graffiti artists. With a bust that several bras could not contain, large hips still nicely rounded, and the legs of a wrestler, Mama Dodge had made an impression on more than one man. The customer she'd called to stood up, paid and left without a word. Mama went over to the table, pocketed the change and wiped the Formica with a dirty towel.

"Come sit down," she said graciously to the three men in the doorway.

Noticing the young athlete, she turned to the two men, laughing. "So, the old couple's managed to make a brat. Is this one of yours?"

"Sort of," Smith answered. "He's the son of all the oppressed niggers on the planet. One day he'll be somebody too."

Mama Dodge pouted and looked uncertain. There were

some bets she preferred never to make. Since the men were not there to debate this question either, they quickly sat down at the empty table. A spicy odor, strong enough to make a corpse howl, wafted through a beaded curtain from the kitchen.

Seated before the detectives' favorite dish, Cassius' tongue began to wag as Smith had predicted it would. The hot sauce made his gut burn and brought tears to his eyes. The tears blurred his vision. Enormous drops of sweat pearled under his two companions' hats. Everything conspired to make the scene appear to drip, as though the room were losing its mascara. Smith noisily licked his fingers.

"So?"

The student rubbed his eyelid with his dirty hand, then wiped his mouth, which was smeared with sauce. Dubois downed a large glass of California red. Little Cassius smiled mischievously. Mama Dodge pushed aside their empty plates and set down full ones, then she tossed her guests an anxious glance. They in turn showed a lively admiration for her cuisine by smacking their lips and grunting loudly.

"I know everything," the kid announced, once Mama, reassured, was at a distance.

"What do you know? You're still young enough to be in knickers," Smith interrupted good-naturedly. "Right, Gravedigger?"

Smith turned to the kid. "You'd better let go of your mama's tits or you'll stretch them out until she wraps them right around your neck."

"Cut the crap," exploded Little Cassius. "Don't talk to me like that. It won't work anymore. I know who you really are. I know you've never laid eyes on Chester Himes, and that you're not Coffin Ed and Gravedigger Jones. All those stories you've been spreading around Harlem are just a bunch of b.s.! I'm just as much a super-cop as you are. Books written about you—that's a lot of crap. The books exist, but you don't," said the kid.

"What's this little bastard going on about?"

Smith's voice broke; a rattle came out of his mouth. In spite of himself, his fingers tightened on the chicken leg he

5

was sucking. Cassius gloated. He had his revenge. At nine-teen he could make them walk on tiptoe. He no longer bought the scorn or lessons of these phony heroes. He didn't dare turn the other cheek now. Instead he felt like breaking Jones' jaw. As for Smith, he could eat his words about short pants. Dubois put his hat on, covering his shaved head, which looked like a relief map of the earth, complete with mountains, continents and valleys. He didn't dare look up at his accomplice.

"Don't look so glum," Cassius went on. "You've been having a good time for years. And anyone has the right to take himself for a Napoleon."

"Or for Cassius Clay," Smith said, giving him a hard look.

Caught out though they were, Smith and Jones were still old foxes. A sense of reality did not escape them for long. Once over the shock of this initial revelation, they wanted to hear more. Maybe the kid was just bluffing.

"Whatever gave you that idea?" asked Smith.

Cassius smiled a tender smile filled with emotion. "One of my buddies at Columbia is African," he said. "His parents live in France. They always send him piles of books. This month he received the latest Chester Himes. When he told me about it, I realized you've been fooling everyone around here for years."

"What's the book about?" asked Smith, a little anxious.

"Coffin Ed and Gravedigger both die. Cold, stiff, buried. They can't be up to too much now," Cassius said.

"What kind of joke is that? You'll see this stiff lay you out flat in a minute, just as soon as I finish off this plate."

"You can do whatever you want, but not those two, at least not anymore. Himes is the one who wrote it. You can bet they're not munching on chicken feet today. They're too busy pushing up daisies."

Smith let the chicken bone fall to his plate. It landed with a dull thud, like a stone fragment falling from a statue. Mama poked her nose out of the kitchen.

"Hey, you two, what's the matter? You look like you've seen a ghost."

"Nothing, Mama," Cassius said. "Something's stuck in their throats."

Unconvinced, the woman shrugged, then stepped over to an empty table armed with her dishtowel.

Jones drew a heavy breath. "Where can we find this book?" he asked.

"You'd have to go to Paris," Cassius replied.

A gleam lit up the old combatant's eyes. "You mean it's not for sale over here?"

"That's right," said the kid.

"Do you think many people have read it yet?" Smith asked.

The two detectives' mental wheels turned in tandem. For years they had strolled in step along the sidewalks of their city, copying and aping two models they had accidentally found one day between book covers. Together they saw a gap in the clouds, a light at the end of the tunnel.

"Maybe Boubacar, but he never lends his books. So, I don't think so. I haven't even read it yet myself. Anyway, I don't know enough French yet to understand it."

Smith retrieved his bone from the sauce and commenced to chew, softly crushing it between his jaws. The shadow in his eyes hadn't disappeared yet, but a shaft of sunlight struggled to replace it. Jones observed his friend. It seemed as if they hadn't seen each other for days. Smith's forehead was furrowed with deep lines.

Cassius felt a little guilty for having broken faith with these two old fools. He imagined them now as blind orphans, groping their way along like lame birds, jeered at, surrendering to the madness of the town. But why would real detectives want to act like movie stars, strutting their stuff in Harlem, posing as heroes when they were only sorry cops? He saw that they acted even more like children than he did, taking refuge in a world they had invented, unable to admit to their vanity. They're too old to start over now, he thought, I should have been more careful. He pushed aside his plate and stood. The meal they had bought him now took on a bitter taste.

"I'm gonna go get my sound machine."

"It's open," said Dubois, worn out by now. His eyes followed the young man's silhouette.

7

Planting her feet before the table, Mama Dodge interrupted his train of thought. They could see that she was anxious to hear the news, but the ex-cop merely took out a bill and handed it to her.

"Thanks for everything, Mama."

Smith was already standing. His face looked more sullen than ever. The customers at their tables watched them leave with a mixture of fear and admiration. They were celebrities here; a writer had even immortalized their greatest exploits in the ghetto. Out on the sidewalk, they discovered Little Cassius on the curb staring into space with his cassettes resting on his lap. He turned around to them.

"I swear, no one will find out about this. I know how to keep my mouth shut."

He tried to speak in a casual tone but neither Smith nor Jones replied. Jones opened the passenger door and slipped inside, reappearing with the giant ghetto blaster at arm's length. Smith was already taking his place behind the wheel as he handed the radio to Cassius.

"Step on it, Gravedigger," he said.

Little Cassius heard this and felt heavy. He had exposed their game, and still they went on using borrowed nicknames. Sooner or later they would take a fall. There was no room for clowns, however sad-faced, in the world waiting just around the corner. As the car pulled away, Little Cassius raised his hand in a gesture of farewell.

The most mundane details of the passing scenery caught the old cops' eyes: graveyards of abandoned cars, a shapely girl leaning on a fence, torn-up pavement, plumes of smoke that now and then unleashed layers of coal dust as if they too were taking breaths of air.

The car rolled past a section of Park Avenue called Blood Alley. They left Fifth and Marcus Garvey Park behind and turned back onto Seventh. Smith glanced at Dubois and saw at once where they were going.

The intersection of 125th and Seventh had been Harlem's Mecca during the epoch of the Black Muslims and Black Panthers. This was where they had paraded at the height of their power, with black berets clamped tightly on their heads and rifles pressed firmly to their chests. Even today this was a privileged nexus where current styles and new ideas circulated freely. Mr. Grace's bookstore was a meeting place of local black intellectuals. Grace himself was a small gentleman with shiny skin and a foxy manner. The shop was crammed with books, piled to the ceiling in stacks. To move about one edged between these chancy precipices in single file. At Mr. Grace's you could find any work related to the Cause, from near or far, whether it dealt with music, dance, painting or politics.

The Plymouth pulled up quietly beside the bookstore window, and the two old men pulled themselves out, their backs bent over by black thoughts. For forty years these two ordinary cops from a rotten neighborhood had linked their lives to two imaginary characters, whose existence they had substituted for their own. In every hovel, inside the smallest gambling den, card dealers all trembled at the sound of "Freeze! Hold it right there!" According to them, Chester Himes had become a sort of bard or *griot* canonizing their livelier adventures. But with this latest book reality was taking its revenge, coming to claim its due. The usurped titles, the borrowed risks, the myth of two extraordinary lives, had to be restored to the fiction from which they had departed.

This was a hard blow for the two companions. Since their retirement they had lived in an enchanted past, shamelessly mixing actual adventures with dreams and fiction for the benefit of spellbound audiences. Admitting to the death of Coffin Ed and Gravedigger Jones would be to admit to their own disappearance. If Himes buried them before their time, they no longer preceded history and would be revealed for the plagiarists they were. They could not conceive of an existence where mockeries flowed freely from the mouths of punks, whores, and junkies, a world wherein they commanded no respect.

These two cunning fellows invented new memories from book to book. They had tacitly agreed after thirty years of municipal service to fight to preserve this aura to the end. Without it, their lives would lose the color, strength and eccentricity they had taken so much pleasure in ever since they had discovered an author who had elevated their

9

heroic doubles into legend. They entered the bookstore, alert.

Mr. Grace was working in his small office at the back of the bookstore. The old man removed his glasses and carefully refolded an accordion-like catalog. He smiled at his two regulars. Dubois and Smith searched his face and found it empty. There wasn't the slightest clue in his expression or his attitude. There were only the usual features, permanently animated by a kind of interior joy which the two ex-cops had never managed to figure out.

"What gives me the honor of this visit, Inspectors?"

Dubois and Smith removed their hats. They did not dare look the old fox in the eye. Did he already know? Smith took the plunge.

"Well, Mr. Grace, we've heard Chester's just published a new book . . ."

"And you'd like to know if it's in yet?" finished the bookseller. Well, no, it's not, but I can tell you when . . ."

He stopped. His eyes twinkled.

"How is your friend Himes?"

The two cops bragged to everybody about their close ties with the writer, mingling accounts of their own adventures with those of his characters. They suddenly wondered if Grace was making fun of them.

"You will be getting it in then," said Dubois.

"Getting what in? Ah, yes, the book. Of course. It'll be here in a few weeks, maybe even in a few days."

The little man began searching through a pile of old papers littering his desk. He fished out a sheet and waved it under their noses.

"Here's the order form. Yes," he said, setting down his glasses and deciphering the paper. "You really heard that, Chester Himes . . . Wait a minute . . . Here!"

It was as if instead of the form, he were brandishing the actual book. Dubois and Smith looked at each other. Mr. Grace, the only black man in Harlem for whom they had ever felt a degree of respect, coughed and began to clean his glasses.

"Sit down," he addressed his visitors.

He pointed to a green velvet chair. It was a sort of cross

between an armchair for a very large person and a loveseat. The two detectives complied, firmly embedding themselves, hip to hip, between the armrests. After a long moment of silence, the bookseller smiled warmly.

"I know why you've come to see me. I have to tell you that I've been prepared for this moment for a very long time. We're about the same age, right? We just want a little peace until the day of our great voyage. I know just how you feel. I haven't read the Himes book, but someone told me what it's about. And I imagined your reaction. It's just that now, nothing can stop the machine. You have to resign yourselves to it. Absolutely nothing has changed for me though."

The ex-cops stared at the ground as if they were hoping for a sign. Dubois lifted his distracted eyes to Mr. Grace.

"Our whole world's caving in on us."

"I know," said the bookseller philosophically, "but what can you do about it? Anyway, you will have a slight respite because the book I'm going to receive will be in French. Not too many people in Harlem will be tempted. And those who do know French don't know you two."

Dubois and Smith stood up. All was not lost. Smith wanted to say something, but the bookseller stopped him.

"If you're wondering what I'm going to do, don't worry. I've been guarding your secret for nearly thirty-five years. And, you know, I've always found you more likable than your heroes! If you had been Coffin and Gravedigger, I might have sent you somewhere else to buy your books a long time ago. No. I won't breathe a word! Save your explanations for the others. A word to the wise is sufficient."

Dubois and Smith overflowed with apologies and thanks. Like two sleepwalkers, they left the place where their glory had been born and where it ran the risk of being irreparably tarnished. Dubois sat down behind the wheel. They headed south toward Central Park, skirted Grand Central Terminal, left the road which led to Little Italy and headed west toward Greenwich Village. Dubois ran several red lights and almost crashed into a taxi, double-parked on Fifth Avenue. Suddenly Smith seemed to wake up. He tapped his companion on the shoulder.

"Let me out here, man; I have an errand to run."

Dubois silently looked him over, then pulled the car over to the sidewalk to let Smith out.

"Don't bother to wait for me. I'll find my own way home. I'll call you tonight."

Dubois nodded and drove off without asking any questions. The street was swarming. He was surprised to see so many whites, then, coming to his senses, he realized he wasn't in Harlem anymore.

Smith waited until the black sedan had disappeared into the traffic, then hailed a cab. He gave the driver the address of Mr. Grace's bookstore. Although Grace didn't have any coordinates on the European continent for Chester Himes himself, he did manage to find the address of his Paris editor. Smith thanked him timidly a second time and returned to the waiting taxi.

That night he went home weary. He suddenly found the silence that reigned in his oversized apartment disturbing. He removed his hat and his trenchcoat, remembering a time when the house was filled with his wife's screaming and his children's racket. He turned on the television and thumbed the buttons on the remote control, unable to settle on a program. He was in the bathroom in his underwear when the doorbell rang. He hastily grabbed his bathrobe from a hook, forgetting to tie it shut, and went to the door.

Dubois laughed, leaning in the doorway.

"Is this how you dress for your guests now? Is this supposed to be the latest style?"

Smith waved him in without answering.

"I have an idea I think you're going to like," said Dubois mysteriously. But put some clothes on your back. I can't stand to look at you like that. I feel like I'm at some kind of scar exhibit."

"Fix yourself a drink. I'll be right back."

Smith removed his robe as he walked toward the bathroom. He glanced up at the broken window, patched with newspaper, and shrugged. For some time now he had been letting everything go. Why fix things? For whom? Since the death of his wife, life without her companionship was like whiskey with no ice. There were only memories, and even those were threatened. As he mechanically slipped on his trousers, he read the yellowed headline for the thousandth time:

DON KNIGHT, BLACK MILLIONAIRE, BUYS INTO BLACK BEAUTY SUPPLY FIRM

The celebrated businessman proposed to open a business in Paris. With the help of professional training courses, the working girls from Pigalle would be transformed into experienced hairstylists and beauticians, provided they were black. Don Knight's favorite dish, it was reported, was *escalope a la crème et aux champignons*. When in Paris, the magnate bestowed his favors not on the palaces of the Right Bank but on a discreet German-owned establishment, the Hôtel du Vieux-Colombier.

The article was accompanied by a photo showing a handsome fifty-year-old athletic looking black man, exhibiting all his teeth. Smith finished dressing and joined his companion in the living room.

Dubois stood somberly waiting by the bar. He was still wearing his trenchcoat.

"It's not too late to stop this, Ed. It was pickling my brain until Mr. Grace gave me an idea."

"It's been eating at me too, Gravedigger," Smith replied without adding any details.

"We're going to go see Himes and convince him not to translate the book. We can at least try. After all, he owes us that much."

"Yeah," said Smith. "We can at least try."

Chapter Two

Charles-de-Gaulle Airport. Despite the late hour, a crowd of travelers was still bustling in the first floor lobby. The pale neon lights, those suns that never set, made the white skin they tainted look unhealthy. White people looked afflicted by an incurable disease. An impeccably coiffed woman trotting behind a cart with a small leather trunk enthroned in the center turned suddenly around. She was startled by a burst of thundering laughter. The echo made it still more impressive: Jones Dubois was greeting France.

"Can you believe it, Ed? We're in France!"

For the first time in thirty long years, the two partners had left the territory of the stars and stripes for a little dilly-dallying.

Ed Smith couldn't believe it. He walked along on a sort of magic cord, afraid it might break at any moment. A taxi pulled up in front of them. The driver, bundled in a gray overcoat, was pressed against the wheel. A Gitane dangled from his lips. He watched them collect their bags and open the door.

"France seems pretty nice," said Smith before climbing into the taxi.

"Où que je vous conduis, messieurs?"

"I beg your pardon?"

"Where you go, please?" insisted the driver, resigned.

Dubois took control of the situation. He exhumed a small dictionary from his pocket, which he had lightly skimmed on the airplane, and began feebly leafing through it.

"Hotel . . . Paris," he finally uttered in a pure Harlem accent.

"Ca va. O.K. Compris," said the driver, who was used to this sort of thing. He put the car into first gear and drove off slowly.

Smith smiled.

"And we thought the Plymouth was small," he commented, beaming. "What do you think about this one? Think maybe she'd move out just a little bit if we put a third cylinder in her?"

"Stop complaining. You shouldn't criticize things here," guffawed Dubois. "This isn't home."

He tried humming a few measures of "La Marseillaise," but the look he encountered in the rear-view mirror dissuaded him.

Each man leaned his head against his window, absorbed

by the play of passing lights. The taxi passed the Porte de Bagnolet.

Taking advantage of a red light, the driver turned back to his fares.

"C'est quoi le nom de votre hôtel? Name? Hotel?"

He tried hard to detach each syllable, but every attempt seemed doomed to failure thanks to the cigarette plugged between his lips.

"I can't just pick one out of thin air," the driver mumbled to himself in French. "Damn!"

Smith and Dubois looked at him blankly. The driver rolled his eyes. A concert of honking horns informed him that the light had been green for several seconds. Suddenly Smith, seized by inspiration, remembered the only French name which lingered in a corner of his memory.

"Hôtel du Vieux-Colombier," he said in execrable French.

Pleased with this discovery, he repeated himself several times, as if charmed by the sound of his own voice.

"The one in the sixth arrondissement?" asked the driver.

"Well?" intervened Jones, as he continued twisting his last few hairs. Smith gave him a hard look.

"Yes, sir, yes," he assured the driver.

The car drove on, while in the back seat the two cops lapsed into a contest of circumflexed eyebrows. When they imagined that they had arrived, they undertook the task of extricating themselves from the Peugeot. Dubois handed the driver a five-hundred-franc note and waited patiently. The change stacked up in his open palm. At the reception desk, Smith asked him how he had calculated the exchange rate so fast.

"I didn't calculate anything," he answered. "I just waited!"

The new arrivals showed their passports to the receptionist. He was a pale thin young man. When he realized his Oxford English was of no use with these two zombies, he straightened up a bit. They persisted in expressing themselves by gesturing and demanded two adjoining rooms. Three minutes after they went upstairs, he saw them rush by again. They hurried outside without dropping off the key. What a couple!

They were tall and stocky and had the same square

15

jaws, short-cropped hair, and graying muttonchops. What aroused the curiosity of passing Parisians was not so much their large physiques but the way they dressed: the customary felt hats they wore day and night, their long trenchcoats opening on colorful jackets. While this ensemble might create a good impression in Harlem, it raised a lot of eyebrows in the sixth arrondissement. Although eccentric clothing was not lacking in the Latin Quarter, it wasn't often sported by giant black men, curious about everything. Their ungainly appearance caused passersby to step aside, clearing a path for them through the crowds at rush hour. From time to time Ed Smith changed course slightly in order to barely graze a woman passing in the crowd.

"I like this country, man," he confided to Dubois. We're right in the middle of a white neighborhood and people aren't looking at us like we've got the plague."

"You're right. They're not afraid we're going to stab them in the back."

"It's mellow here."

They walked into an O'Kitch near the fountain in the Place Saint-Michel. They thrust open the door with a surge of enthusiasm, and the customers froze on the spot. Although they took pleasure in their strange new surroundings, Smith and Dubois welcomed anything that reminded them of home. They had heard about filet mignon, that culinary speciality of the Seine, but failed to run it down each place they went. Now they grimly settled for two enormous hamburgers.

"You come from America?"

Screwing up his eyes, Jones turned to face the stranger who had addressed him. He was one of those African specimens who had been around, a sort of figure commonly seen in the capital but who seemed exceedingly exotic to Jones Dubois, especially because of the bone necklace he was wearing.

"I heard you speak English and I just wanted to talk with you about America."

"Where are you from?" inquired Smith in his gravelly voice.

"Africa. My name is Zigaman Fâ, Doctor of Mentalo-scopic-Kinesis.

16

"Doctor of what?"

"Mentaloscopic-Kinesis. It's a science created to overcome the old ways imposed through the ages by the whites."

The ex-cops smiled knowingly at each other. There were plenty of these doctors hanging around the streets of Harlem. Its was best to get out of the way when they took out their black bags. Even so, this one might prove useful.

"Say, Doc, you must know a lot, right?"

"That depends on what you want to know."

"We'd like to find a good place to eat. You get what I mean?"

Zigaman Fâ closed one eye and placed a long finger to his pink lips. His face lit up.

"I know exactly what you mean."

When they stood, Zigaman Fâ propelled a tall girl with amber hair and a pale complexion in front of the two Americans and introduced her to them. She was a twenty-seven-year-old student named Sylvie.

Sylvie was the proud owner of a *deux-chevaux*, which had been repainted by hand and which she piloted like a Formula 1, lockjawed at the wheel, eyes riveted on the horizon. They drove to Mère Sophie's restaurant. She was a buxom woman from Zaire. She welcomed the doctor and his troupe with a meaty laugh, which shook her body from her toes to her flimsy brassiere, the straps of which were visible through her loose *boubou*.

The restaurant was steeped in the odor of burnt fat, which carried Smith and Jones back across the ocean to Mama Dodge's. Mère Sophie drew her whiskey from a large cask on the counter, filling wine bottles with it. She made it a point of honor to warn her clients that she didn't serve any nonalcoholic beverages. Coffin and Gravedigger's tall tales fascinated the neoscientist, although he did not entirely understand them. The conviviality of the detectives, combined with the obvious charms of Zigaman Fâ's well-endowed companion, created a most relaxed atmosphere. When the two Americans had paid the bill, which fixed catfish at the price of salmon, Zigaman Fâ opened up

17

his arms as if to reunite two continents in his embrace.

"If there's anything you need while you're in Paris, let me know. I'm always in the cafe on the Boulevard Barbès after seven."

He handed them a dog-eared card before giving Sylvie's car a little slap. Pale as a corpse, she drove off more than a little drunk.

As they climbed into bed, Smith and Jones began to feel the effects of jet-lag. Unless it was simply the effect of Mère Sophie's whiskey.

Chapter Three

The key turned in the lock just as the light went out in the stairwell. Amos Yebga kicked his apartment door shut.

He was a young man with an attractive stature, a dark and velvety complexion and long black eyelashes, which gave an almost feminine touch to his angular face. He was wearing a maroon suit with a light shirt, no tie and black moccasins. In the ten years of his journalist's profession, he had never felt so bored by his routine. This job was worse than the rut of a civil servant. You sat behind a desk, turning out articles on any subject so long as they were about Africa and . . . hop! On to the next one! He had even given up playing the gadfly, no longer interjecting his perpetual accusations during the editor's conferences, such as, "We're becoming a bureaucracy! We're turning bourgeois!" These objections had only raised polite smiles on the faces of his indifferent colleagues. Yebga had been dreaming of other things while wearing out the seat of his pants on the bench at journalism school. It seemed to him at that time that the profession he was embracing incorporated adventure, danger and risk. He had chosen to exile himself to France, because Cameroon was not ready to confront its own corruption. Since then, he had had to change his tune. It was as though all his accumulated hopes were about to fly away. He was almost thirty-five, an age of reckoning, he thought.

Furious, Yebga tore off his jacket and hurled it onto a piece of furniture that adorned the vestibule. The living-room light switch was just to his right. He flipped it on. A warm light inundated a spacious room furnished with discretion. At the bar, he poured out his usual evening drink. Then he settled into an armchair beside his answering machine. Sipping his whiskey, he played back the messages.

Legs stretched out onto a carpet of exotic motifs, he listened to a series of voices chopped up by static on the tape:

> —Hi Amos. There's gong to be a party at my place Saturday night. If you can drop by . . .

> —Hey, man, it's Bill. I finished developing the photos. So let me know when you need them.

> —Hello, Mr. Yebga. I'm taking the opportunity to call you back regarding the book project you spoke to me about. It would be good if you'd contact me as soon as possible. The idea interests me.

And so on.

Yebga had not set foot in his house for three days. He felt a certain pleasure hearing these mixed voices of friends and mere acquaintances. He paraded all these callers through his mind, thinking they made up a strange group. They reminded him of his own vagabond life. With each beep tone, a face or a shadow materialized in his memory. He stood up. The urge to hear "Body and Soul" by John Coltrane moved him. The voices continued their deaf litany:

> —Amos, it's George. Could you loan me your apartment for the weekend?

> —Hey, man, I have a little problem. It's urgent. I'll call back later.

Paris white and Paris black. This was success for a black man.

19

Yebga crouched in front of the stereo cabinet. He did not listen closely to the last message until he had adjusted the stereo. Something had clicked in his head. After the joyful, calm, composed voices, this one seemed harsh. The caller was unknown to him. What exactly had he said? Confused, Yebga retraced his step and pushed the rewind button:

> —Hello. My name is Salif Maktar Diop. Some friends told me you could be trusted. I have some things to tell you. They must be put in your paper. Be in front of the Café Escurial on the corner of the Rue du Bac and the Boulevard Saint-Germain at five tomorrow.

The reporter dreamily played back the tape several times. Then he emptied his glass, looked at his watch. There was definitely no time to spare. He was going to be late to his girlfriend's again.

Neither Ed Smith or W. Jones Dubois slept very long. Early the next day, they were in the street, their felt hats covering their migraines. Last night's menu, which had fallen to their legs, made them feel like they were wearing lead socks. They were afraid they might miss something. They planned to spend a part of Thursday visiting Paris and the other looking for Chester Himes. One of them selected from his wardrobe a suit the color of fresh butter. The other opted for a midnight blue ensemble. Neither of them neglected to put on their eternal cop trenchcoat. They thought that Paris was cleaner, safer and better organized than its New York counterpart; however, this did not prevent them from getting lost. On their way to the Champs-Élysées, they ended up at the Porte de Vanves. It was maddening that nobody seemed capable of giving them directions. Even blacks scurried off, arms waving as if a full brigade of Harlem cops were chasing their black asses down the street.

"And you fed me that line about how you knew this town like the palm of your hand," mocked Smith, jabbing his friend in the ribs. "Where'd you pick up your French name anyway? The way things look around here, you'd have thought we'd walked here from Harlem. We didn't need to take a plane to see this.'

"Things have changed since the war, boy," answered the other. "And as for giving you a line, don't forget I don't have anything to show you here anyway."

A fare-hunting taxi rescued them from confusion and finally dropped them at "Champseeleezay" after having circled the city many times.

The joy of rediscovering the handsome neighborhoods extinguished the two detective's mistrust, and they strolled the avenue for more than an hour, forgetting that they had not come to Paris to play tourist. They had themselves photographed in front of the Arc de Triomphe, wolfed down a series of Italian courses at Pino's Pizza, which would have inflicted indigestion upon any other stomach, but which just sufficed to quiet their hunger.

It was five o'clock when Smith seized his friend by the arm. The men returned up the Seine on board a tourist boat. They were the only people who dared face the open air of the immense rear deck.

"We've got to go see the publisher," Smith said regretfully.

The charm of foreign adventure fell away instantly. The monuments, the ancient stone arches, the voice of the tour guide who chattered about the curiosities of the city, the promise of pleasant evenings described in the brochures, all this vanished into thin air. Dubois bitterly recalled the motive of their trip to Paris, and the scenery around him lost its colors in a flash.

Seated on the terrace of the Escurial, Amos Yebga surveyed the horizon, staring at all the passersby. He stood up to stretch his legs. He had been seated for more than an hour, watching the play of intersection lights and breathing exhaust fumes. What could Maktar Diop look like? Who would recognize the other and how? And furthermore, how had Diop picked his coordinates? This was the first time in his career that Yebga had received this type of message. Until now, he made himself valued more for his deductions than for his investigations. Maybe Maktar Diop was an African opponent who was going to offer him ultra-secret documents. Then why speak to Yebga? He would give anything to make his editor, Glenn, see him with new eyes, rather than regarding him as a desk man, a man of routine, an intellectual. In fact he was a man of action. Often his colleagues begrudged him his diploma. Papers do not make you a reporter, they would say, it's the terrain. He was weary of waiting for a chance to put his feet on it. Maktar's call had arrived in the nick of time. It awakened hope. But it was better not to let himself be dazzled by this. Anyway, Maktar Diop was not going to show up now, Yebga was certain of it. He tried to convince himself he had only come to meet Diop out of professional conscience.

Yebga left a twenty-franc note fluttering on the table. He set out with a halting step toward the stoplight on the boulevard. He noticed two giants heading toward him. It was obvious these guys were smashed. They looked haggard and kept walking into each other. Even their exaggerated boxer's gait was not enough to steady them. Yebga saw them glancing about distractedly. The graying hair on their heads and cheeks evoked for him a confused image of his own grandfather from Yaoundé. He had died when Yebga was ten. Lost in memory, he starred unconsciously at them. They drew near, banging into the table next to where he was standing. For a handful of seconds, Yebga even thought they were going to speak to him, but they turned away at the last minute.

"Hey, sista," yelled the one with the scarred face, addressing a young woman from the Antilles. She in turn almost got herself run over trying to dodge them.

They spoke in English, apparently convinced this was the language blacks used the world over. Yebga's eyes shone with amusement; these two guys looked like they had just landed from the moon. Their long trenchcoats, felt hats and gala clothing called to mind the archaic uniforms of the Congolese sappers. They flailed their arms about like drowning men.

"Yes, can I help you?"

Doubtless the guy who addressed them was from the political science department, with this display. He stopped, a large smile smeared across his face.

"Wow! Hey man, we're in luck," sighed Dubois. "I thought no one in France spoke English."

"Yeah," added Smith. "And there's only a little ocean between us."

The two blacks stood planted side by side on the sidewalk. The stream of passersby elbowed each other trying to avoid them, not without occasional complaints. Yebga watched them exhibit a sheet of crumpled paper under the eyes of their new savior. What could they be looking for with those faces like half-reformed dunces or hoodlums? Ex-marines or racketeers from Harlem come to get themselves fleeced in who knows what den of thieves.

But how touching they were, cheek to cheek, intently watching the future young professional point a long finger toward the Rue de Bac.

Yebga did not linger over this scene; he mechanically turned the pages of his Bloc Notes, looked at his watch. When he looked up again, the men had disappeared.

Yebga combed the boulevard once more with his eyes for the sake of his conscience, then went home, worried, feeling morose for no real reason.

The first thing he did was to listen to Maktar Diop's message again. No doubt. He had not mistaken the time or the meeting place. One thing was certain: this nigger's voice oozed with fear.

Chapter Four

As she set her book down onto the pulpit of her desk (a book her employers would have doubtless classified as a war novel), the receptionist gave a start. She stared at them, one after the other, incredulous. One sported a blue tie sprinkled with yellow designs. It stood out from a white shirt. His trousers, an abundant piece of clothing, were worn to an almost threadbare brightness and fell too far onto his enormous shoes. He smiled in a disquieting

23

manner, like one of those guys who, not satisfied just to steal the cash, looks ready to work you over in the process. His white teeth shone like pearls. He removed his hat with the folded-down brim and articulated a few words. The bewildered woman decided to interpret these as a greeting. The other man was a giant of about the same size. He was swathed in clothing the subtlety of which was comparable to that of the statue of Louis Maine in the middle of the Rue du Départ. Imitating his companion, he raised his hand to his headgear.

"If you're making a delivery," the receptionist forced herself to speak, "use the other door. The one on the left as you exit."

What could these two be doing at Gallimard? They had probably never opened a book in their lives, except the Bible!

The two men were black.

Dubois spoke.

"We would like to meet Mr. Chester Himes," he announced, somewhat strained.

If the two men spoke English, it was because they were Americans. And if they were Americans, they couldn't be deliverymen. What were they then? From the corner of her eye, Marguerite tried to get a better look at them. Boxers maybe, with those faces, singers, or retired killers for hire. She couldn't decide. She was only aware of a pressing need to get up and call someone. Taking advantage of the fact that she barely spoke English, Marguerite rose.

"Moment, please. I don't speak English. Somebody come. Wait."

She had a Belleville accent, but Dubois understood. They watched her walk toward an office that was separated from the reception area by a glass partition. Ed Smith ogled her buttocks as she fled.

"What an ass, man. I wouldn't say no to that."

Jones Dubois gave him a reprimanding look.

"Just kidding, partner. But don't you think she's well put together for a white chick?"

The receptionist returned shortly with one of her superiors. She was an older woman, who appeared incapable of lust.

24

"These two gentlemen must have an appointment with an editor. I think it's for their memoirs," said the young woman. "They're boxers or something like that."

"Hello, sirs," said the woman with a good university accent. "What can I do for you?"

"We want to see Chester Himes," answered Jones Dubois.

"Chester Himes?"

"Yes. The writer. Are you his editor?"

The woman looked embarrassed. She looked at them strangely, stammered and said, "Wait a minute, please."

She picked up the telephone from the receptionist's desk and dialed a number. The receptionist looked on from behind a glass partition. Smith and Dubois heard her speaking in French. So as not to appear as if they were eavesdropping, they looked away, inspecting their surroundings. To their left was a long corridor dotted with a series of numbered doors. Their eyes met those of a man of about fifty. He was wearing a coal gray suit; a white turtleneck sweater stood out from under his jacket. The man wore glasses with thin gold frames. His austerity reminded the two associates of certain white pastors they had had the opportunity to meet back in the United States. He was engaged in intense discussion with a little bald man. This one had quick eyes and was shabbily dressed. His manner reminded them of a rapist or a devotee of morbid tales. In the lobby, next to the entryway, a glass case housed books and photographs. Among those exhibited, Dubois and Smith recognized a guy with a vicious smile and graying temples smoking a pipe and a blond wearing an overcoat reminiscent of turn-of-the century sailors. The two men had just stepped back into the office as the woman cupped the receiver.

"What are your names, please?"

"Edward Smith and W. Jones Dubois."

The woman relayed this and hung up.

"Please be seated," she said, motioning to some maroon armchairs behind the two men. "Robert Warin will be right down. He will be able to help you."

The two associates complied. The young receptionist, now reassured, furtively tossed them ambiguous glances in which the two former cops would have been able to read a curious mixture of fear and interest if they had raised their own glance above the waist of their hostess. The legend of the black male lives on!

Dubois and Smith didn't have time to wonder how a guy like Chester Himes, writing the books he wrote, could survive in an ambience of whispers, kiss-ass smiles and boudoir shadows, a thousand leagues from the lures of the "Big Apple." Presently a man came down the stairs into the receptionist's office. He exchanged a few words with her before approaching the two men. He was about fifty. Dubois and Jones admired his elegance.

"Gentlemen."

He held out a carefully manicured hand. A shadow briefly crossed his face. Then he resumed an attitude of calm self-confidence.

"Are you Ed Smith and Jones Dubois?" Warin spoke impeccable English.

"Yeah," answered Dubois.

"This is incredible," muttered the man, noticing Dubois' face. "You correspond exactly to the image that I had of Himes' characters. Coffin Ed and Gravedigger Jones were however created by Chester Himes. Do you know them?"

The two partners eyed him suspiciously, then looked at each other. They had to maneuver quickly. Smith made a slight sign, and Dubois knew instantly that they had to lie.

"Excuse me," the editor began again, "but it's so crazy. . . . How did that happen to you?" he asked Dubois, pointing to the red mark on his face.

"Vitriol. Harlem niggers aren't choirboys."

"And you are inspectors in Harlem?" continued Warin, ready to hear it all now.

"We were," said Smith bitterly. "We finished up as sergeants."

"Now we're good for pulp," added Jones Dubois.

Warin sat down in an armchair next to them. The look they gave him was like that of a starving child standing in front of the window of a delicatessen.

"And why do you want to see Himes?" the editor asked suddenly.

"To speak to him about his latest book. We don't much care for the blow he's given us," answered Smith.

"Blow. What blow?"

"We made an agreement at the beginning of this whole thing," said Smith. "We give him our characters, we tell him about our adventures, but he has to consult us before he publishes them. In the last book, he finishes us off. And we don't agree, if you know—"

"Are you saying that you're Coffin Ed and Gravedigger Jones?"

"Well, we are and we aren't, but it's a long story." Dubois swaggered.

There was a moment of silence while the two ex-cops heard the pounding blood rush to their temples. If Warin knew the truth, their cover would be blown. The editor attempted to organize his thoughts. His eyes continued to shift from one to the other.

"Too bad Duhamel isn't here anymore to see this," he muttered to himself. Then to the two cops, "If I understand correctly, Himes used you to model his characters after, and he didn't consult you before publishing the book where you both die. That's why you want to see him."

"You got it," confirmed Smith.

"Alas, he isn't with us anymore! I know he's living in Spain now, near Alicante. But I can't tell you much more. I'm replacing Marcel Duhamel. He knew Himes well. But I can call his new publisher if that would help you."

The telephone conversation lasted a fairly long time. From time to time, Warin looked suspiciously in the direction of the two giants. Finally he hung up and removed a card from his inside jacket pocket. He asked the switchboard operator for a pen and scribbled a few lines on it. Smith and Dubois stood up. They were holding their worn-out hats in their hands.

"Here," said Warin, handing them the card. Everything is here. It seems he's seriously ill."

"Don't worry," said Dubois, putting on his hat. "We'll take care of him."

The two men shuffled toward the exit. Warin looked at the door for a long time after they had disappeared. He realized only then that if the two giants had really been close friends of Himes', they would have known both his address and the state of his health. On the other hand, Warin wasn't a cop. To each his own! He shrugged his shoulders and went back up to his office like a sleepwalker.

Chapter Five

A mos Yebga moodily rushed into the editing room at the *World*. It was aptly nicknamed "the kitchen" because it was constantly bathed in the smells of cooking from the restaurant downstairs. Due to a change of ownership, the odor in the editing room had changed from that of the familiar and tenacious french fries to the more delicate aroma of curries. Although more delicate, these curries had the insidious effect of imposing their flavor on the bottles of mineral water the secretaries passed around from desk to desk with the looks of disgruntled wine-makers. On his good days, Glenn claimed it was unthinkable not to take such "influences" on the political drift of the paper into account. On these days the editing room turned into a surreal place; rows of blacks seated before pens commented on the most exotic smells. On bad days Glenn threatened to skin the cook alive.

Yebga was late. He was furious about his failed meeting and the importance he had wrongfully given to the words of some nigger who was probably dead broke. He regarded his colleagues with less affability than usual. They in turn displayed the restlessness of the imminent deadline. The conversation rambled on. People scurried about, called out to each other or pretended not to recognize one another because their concentration was pressed to the point of incandescence. Always this African tendency to gesture instead of taking action! Yebga sat down at an empty desk. He tried to calm himself as he slipped a sheet of paper behind the platen of his typewriter. After fifteen minutes all he had typed was: "Chicken with Ginger," then, "Uncle Tom's rice, Tom, T.O.M." He crossed out his lucubrations, ripped the paper from the typewriter, rolled it into a ball and heaved a deep sigh. Then he stood up. Henry Mangane, the foreign politics columnist, couldn't contain his laughter.

"Hey, Amos, you stuck?"

Yebga stared at him coldly. Mangane was wearing sunglasses, but there was absolutely no need of them in the faintly lighted room. These were doubtless a gift from Willy, the paper's black music specialist.

"You said it, man," Yebga pronounced. "I'm stuck." Then appearing sincerely interested, "You think those glasses will protect you against AIDS?"

Mangane pushed his typewriter away, shrugged and took a pack of chewing gum from his pocket.

"Here," he said, handing a piece to Yebga. "Have a hit of menthol. You'll experience life's coolness. It clears the mind."

Yebga accepted and sat chewing it dreamily on the corner of his desk. Mangane removed his glasses with a dry gesture and pinched the bridge of his nose before continuing with his column.

The *World*'s editorial room resembled a long corridor flanked on both sides by a series of identical desks. There was a door at either end. One led to the elevator, the other to the assembly room. Three tables away from him, Yebga recognized Pierre Lioné, a fifty-year-old with oiled hair. Pierre had a reputation for being well versed in African politics. He was debating passionately with Moussa Traoré, an immense man from Senegal. Traoré was gentle to the point of appearing servile. Yebga couldn't clearly make out their conversation, but he judged by their mimicry and by certain cries of despair which pierced the brouhaha, that they had launched into one of their eternal debates about the O.A.U. Traoré, beside himself, waved a bundle of papers under Lioné's nose (probably his article). Lioné, in turn, interrupted his yells with forced laughter. Yebga followed the scene without retaining any of it save the impression that Traoré always carried on too long, whether it be a compliment, a comment or an article. This was a charge Yebga did not risk incurring today. As for the rest of it, there were only the usual old problems stewing in the same old pot:

the O.A.U., neocolonialism, cooperation, the one-party system and so on.

Yebga decided that from here on he would judge the importance of a subject in direct relationship to the influence that it held on his own life. Enough debates hollow as a butterfly's cocoon. Smiling coolly, he crossed the room, passing the two antagonists, and arrived at a door riddled with thumbtack holes. A black Bakelite plaque read in gold letters: "Editor-in-Chief." Yebga nudged the door with his fist so that if necessary, it would appear he had knocked before rushing into the small square room.

The office was almost entirely empty. The only evidence of activity was a pile of papers littering the desk and an immense globe. Robert Glenn lifted his eyes to Amos. He removed his glasses and stared at Yebga for what seemed like a long time. Glenn was fat and bald and had a lively expression.

"Have you finally finished?" he asked.

Yebga scratched his head.

"That's just the problem, Robert. I can't seem to write. You'd better use something else instead."

Yebga stood in front of the desk. There was a long moment of silence while he concentrated on the smoke rising from a cigar sitting on the edge of an ashtray.

"O.K.," said Glenn, sighing. "If it suits you."

"Thanks. Thanks a lot, Robert."

Yebga had already turned to leave when the editor-in-chief's voice stopped him.

"Damn it! Is that all you've got to say to me? If you can't write, at least try to talk. For Christ's sake! What's wrong?"

Amos turned slowly around.

"I don't really know. That's the trouble. I'm just not with it. I don't know."

"Then take a break. Take a week off for winter vacation."

"Yeah."

Yebga shrugged and slid out the door. Glenn continued to stare in disbelief. He retrieved a cigar butt from the ashtray and took a big puff, pivoting his chair toward the window. If he had to take care of these guys' love lives in addition to everything else!

In the stairwell, amidst the sound of clattering dishes, Yebga found himself face to face with someone he realized he should have thought of sooner. Rodolphe Mukoni bragged about how he knew every African in Paris, including those in the underworld. He was tall and thin with a jovial face. Yebga grabbed him by the arm.

"Hey, what's the matter with you. You look like you're in trouble, brother!"

"Do you have a minute?"

"I'm just dropping off a story. Then I'll have all the time in the world."

"O.K. I'll wait right here."

Mukoni disappeared into the elevator. Amos thrust his hands into his coat pockets, watching the elevator rise with his head glued to the grate.

Strange, this sudden indifference to everything that was happening around him. It was as if he had lost the ability to take hold of things. There had to be a name for this, when one became the jaded spectator of one's own life. There were some old copies of the *World* lying on the windowsill. He randomly picked one up and leafed through it nervously. How could this rag interest anyone? Fortunately Mukoni wasn't gone long.

They silently headed toward the Boulevard du Montparnasse. It was unusually pleasant out for the time of year. Yebga loosened the scarf knotted around his neck. At the corner of Boulevard du Montparnasse and the Rue de Vaugirard, Mukoni raised the hand he had placed on his friend's shoulder and pointed to the covered terrace of a cafe. Then he started toward it with a dancing gait.

"Do you want to go there? Tell the old *griot* about your life so he can sing about your adventures."

Most of the tables were occupied by students. The two men seated themselves a little out of the way. The waiter arrived instantly.

"An orange juice and a demitasse," Mukoni ordered without consulting Yebga.

The waiter had not yet disappeared when Yebga asked brusquely, almost aggressively, "Do you know someone called Salif Maktar Diop?"

31

Mukoni took out a cigarette and lit it. Yebga couldn't help admiring the flair with which he settled down to work, followed by the hush that falls before a curtain rises.

"Maktar Diop," said Mukoni. "I might. If not, I'll find him. Why?"

Yebga hesitated a second. "I know this may sound stupid. I received a strange call yesterday."

The waiter brought the drinks. They had to pay right away. Mukoni took care of the bill.

"Diop wanted me to meet him over by the Rue du Bac." Yebga started in again. "He seemed completely panicked. He supposedly had some very important news for me. In fact, either he stood me up or someone prevented him from coming. I haven't spoken to Glenn about it for the time being because I don't want to look ridiculous if this doesn't pan out. On the other hand, if the guy really has some serious information, this could be just the ticket to send me on my way."

Mukoni nodded. He was used to these kinds of telephone calls. He had given up long ago wasting his time for the benefit of brothers ready to exaggerate or manipulate for motives unrelated to the Cause.

"You realize that if Diop telephoned *me*," bragged Yebga, "it's because he's read my latest articles. Considering the things that I wrote about, he must've seen that I'm not a coward and that I follow things through to the end, no matter what."

Yebga stopped talking. Even he didn't believe this anymore. He felt illegitimate, lacking any intellectual credibility in his work.

"Don't give yourself an ulcer," counseled Mukoni after a momentary silence. "If this guy has something to tell you, he'll turn up. Otherwise just forget it. The golden rule in this case is "Wait and See." I'd look for him tonight, but I have to get back to the paper. If you want, I'll call you as soon as I know something."

Yebga gestured impatiently. He'd hoped his story would excite Mukoni, but maybe this joker had, like Yebga himself, become really disillusioned, exclusively preoccupied with chasing after African girls who'd just arrived to stay with cousins in the suburbs, or else he was on his guard.

After Mukoni had made his way through the tables, Yebga remained seated, gloomily watching the traffic. Still another boulevard. Still these same demented comings and goings, these horns. . . . The reporter felt he'd spent a lifetime watching cars on avenues. Maybe he could turn out a story on Parisian traffic jams. In Yaoundé that would make the paper sell! Or he could write a novel full of the odor of exhaust fumes, something without social pretensions, the opposite of a story for the *World*. A novel which would serve no purpose but to contain his sorrow, to mark out the boundaries of his imagination, so that for once he might have a place all his own in this foreign city.

Yebga was crouched in front of his answering machine, going over the main characters as one composes the guest list for a dinner party, when he jumped.

Even under torture, he couldn't have told how he'd gotten home. Maktar Diop's nasal voice on the machine hit him like a cold shower, breaking up his reverie.

The Sunny Kingston was a place on the Rue des Petites-ecuries, not far from the Gare de l'Est, where Yebga sometimes went to sample pigs feet in creole sauce. A piece of wood painted with a palm tree served as a signboard. It conveyed the atmosphere inside. This was hardly one of Paris' smart neighborhoods. Just a few blocks away stretched the Boulevard de Strasbourg, with its streetwalkers and porno theaters, its legions of more or less respectable all-night establishments. The restaurant itself comprised a medium sized room where tables overlapped in a subtle mosaic. The regulars who gathered here were connected with the black community of Paris. All of them were friends of the owner, a mulatto with a sympathetic smile. Though an occasional blond or red mane sprouted here, the clientele was essentially black. Amos Yebga pushed open the door and found himself enveloped in a thick cloud of cigarette smoke. There was an empty table near the window, with a view of the street.

This stronghold's secret to success was not exclusively due to the appeal of its spicy cuisine. More likely it was due to the presence of a jazz club, the New Morning, located just across the street. The Sunny Kingston was a kind of temple for blacks who were "conscious" of their cultural heritage. The expression made Yebga laugh. Before the place became an obligatory meeting spot, Yebga had to work hard to find any unifying factor among blacks in Paris that joined the Harlem River to the Congo. Then someone had the idea that a dingy old cafe would make a terrific port of call and transformed an ordinary bar into an Afro tavern. This inspired individual was named Maurice. Maurice felt best when he was kissing laughing girls or slapping palms with friends. His spirit was contagious.

A bronze-skinned waitress walked over to Yebga's table. Her lips were enhanced by a trace of purple lipstick. She was wrapped in a tight skirt, which three large mother-of-pearl buttons could barely hold together. She too, appeared to be a mulatto.

"Tu prends quelque chose?"

Amos did not like to be addressed in the familiar "tu" form by a girl he didn't know. It implied intimacy or at least some progress made in that direction. On the other hand, the "vous" form marked a distance between the external and innermost worlds. It protected him from assaults.

"An orange juice."

As the waitress walked away, Amos pulled a copy of the *World* from his overcoat pocket and distractedly began to leaf through it. When the girl returned with the orange juice, he ventured to ask:

"You haven't seen Maktar Diop lately, have you?"

She straightened up, placing her hands on her shapely hips.

"Salif?"

"Yes, Salif."

"He comes here sometimes but I haven't seen him in quite awhile." She switched to the formal "vous" form. "Does he owe you money?"

"You can go on using "tu" with me. My name is Amos

34

Yebga. I'm a reporter. No, he doesn't owe me money. It's about something else."

"I'm Myriam. Are you looking for some grass?"

"No. No, thanks."

He shook open his paper and tried to keep his cool. Myriam went on to the next table without a thought. Yebga had managed once again to extricate himself with difficulty. He immersed himself in his reading again, trying to decipher the letters which became mixed up with the low-cut neckline of the waitress.

Within an hour, Yebga had consumed an admirable number of glasses of orange juice, whiskey and vodka, and now he felt a little dizzy. Around him forks clattered against plates. He had been relegated to a corner table, priority given to diners. Voices, mostly young, rose in shouts of laughter. He looked at his watch for the thousandth time. He would give Salif Maktar Diop fifteen minutes. After that, let him croak! This remark made him smile. What if the others heard him talk this way?

It was better to count in his head. Fifteen minutes were after all only nine hundred seconds. After that, he would give it up for good. 201, 202, 203 . . .

"He won't be coming now."

Yebga looked blankly up at the waitress. She really was very beautiful with her hair lying flat on her forehead in tight braids. Why had she told him this? So that he would leave, or was it out of kindness, to show she was looking after him?

"What makes you say that?"

"I don't know. A feeling. It looks to me like you don't really know these Africans here."

Yebga didn't reply. He was finished with the trap of endless and aimless conversations. He loathed worthless palaver.

"Are you from Cameroon?"

She was standing over him now. He tried to appreciate the authentic nature of the points which stretched her blouse, but he wasn't in the mood to make new problems for himself. Certainly not for a mulatto waitress.

"Yes."

"I knew it. Everything about you is Cameroonian. Do you mind if I sit down for a minute?"

"If you want to."

"You've been here before, haven't you? Aren't you a friend of Sidi Lamine?"

Yebga sighed. The only thing he hated more than aimless talk were pointless questions.

He thought to himself: And do you give good head?

"The actor? Yes, I know him, but I don't think I've ever been here with him."

Myriam was silent. Yebga sighed. She meditated for a minute, then turned around, resting her elbow on the chair behind her, and surveyed the restaurant, which had emptied out.

"I like it here. The customers are nice, but not much happens here. Maybe it's the location."

Yebga shrugged.

"Aren't you going to eat something?" she continued.

This time the question seemed sincere.

"Can I use the phone?"

"You're out of luck. Our telephone's been out of order since this morning."

"Then I'd better go. But I'll stop by to see you again, soon."

Yebga took the delicate hand she offered him between his fingers. Then letting go immediately, he slalomed between the tables to the bar and paid. When he passed the window, he saw that she was still watching him. She was even smiling. Yebga turned into the Rue du Château-d'Eau. Further up the street, he found a cafe that was still open. There were a dozen Arabs playing dominoes or cards at the bar. The air was thick. He recognized Moroccan music playing in the background. From there he telephoned Faye and then Mukoni. Neither one answered. Yebga's feeling of apathy increased. Since everything was wearing thin anyway, why did he persist in playing the game with such exactness? A job to do and people he respected! To relax his mind, he imagined frolicking on a wrought-iron bed with the waitress from the Sunny Kingston. The stripes of light from the blinds made her look like a stripper from the Crazy Horse. But why a wrought-iron bed, he wondered.

Chapter Six

O ther than the fact that the inhabitants spoke an equally incomprehensible language, which created a certain unity between France and Spain, Ed Smith and Jones Dubois saw nothing in Alicante which could stand comparison to Paris. There were fewer blacks, fewer beautiful women and fewer wide avenues with luxurious window displays; in short, the people here seemed less interesting than in Paris! As they rode in the taxi on the way to their hotel, the two partners were thinking the same thing.

"What ever possessed Himes to come and bury himself in this no-man's-land?" mumbled Ed Smith. His memory of the splendors of the Champs-Élysées rivaled the languors of Pigalle.

They found the hotel very ordinary, as if they'd already decided to judge everything negatively. Then they went out to wander down the long avenue which ran beside the sea. That a guy like Himes, renowned writer, haunted by a restlessness he barely managed to control, had chosen a corner so dismal, so empty, was beyond their comprehension. They had always imagined the writer working in a luxury hotel, pestered by an admiring court, besieged in the deepest corner of his suite. Something baffled them. This was going to complicate their meeting with the man.

"It's like a giant cemetery here," mumbled Dubois.

They walked for a long time. The only positive element being that the sea did not have the typical New York odor of exhaust fumes. You could smell the salt, the sea air. They took off their shoes and strode along the beach. Memories they couldn't possibly have had came back to them. A memory several centuries old, in which an immense sand beach emerges, a light ocean breeze and salt effluvia mix with that of their own sweating bodies . . .

To see them from a distance, hats in hand, big trenchcoats

beating against rolled-up pants, one would have irresistably thought they were characters who had escaped from a burlesque film rather than from a detective novel.

That night they ate paella in a small restaurant by the edge of the sea. The sangria they ordered to accompany their meal rose instantly to their heads, paradoxically sobering them still more. Nevertheless, they were near their goal. Their telegram had arrived at Himes' villa, and a feminine voice agreed, since they insisted, to welcome them the next day, late morning. They would be able to explain themselves at last.

Chapter Seven

When Yebga pushed open the front door and saw that the light in the entrance hall was on, he knew that Faye was already home. He removed his shoes, tiptoeing across the carpet. She was in the living room, sitting in an armchair with the latest edition of the *World* opened to the page of Amos' article, "Lausanne: Elites for the Third World?" He recognized at a glance the row of Africans, "natives of all the countries of French speaking Africa," photographed on the steps of the International Institute of Development and Cooperation. For a long time, Yebga had repeatedly told his companion not to waste her time on "that rag," but she remained the paper's most attentive reader. More so than Glenn himself.

The young woman stood up, smiling.

"My poor darling, you look exhausted."

Yebga vaguely gestured with his hand. He loosened his tie, removed his overcoat. He had a headache.

"Will you fix me a drink?"

"I already have. Your usual whiskey on the rocks."

"Please, no alcohol. Water . . . and aspirin."

"Very well, boss."

Faye disappeared into the kitchen. She was what one would call a beautiful blond. She was really blond with blue eyes and veins running along her transparent skin.

She had smooth legs and was rather tall. Yebga carelessly tossed his clothes onto the couch and collapsed into a chair. For a long time, Faye's blondness had stunned him. As an adolescent he'd been fascinated by Sammy Davis Jr. and his Swedish conquests, but now he found the cliche too obvious, too debasing to merit further reinforcement. Nevertheless he'd let himself go, by thinking of his existence not in relation to the world surrounding him, but in acccordance with his feelings. The day he'd decided to share his life with Faye, he'd broken off from the world of traditions in which he'd been raised, and so from the illusion that they could not be transgressed. He simply decided to live with her. He loved her. He liked to look at her, to make love to her. Who could doubt that a perfect harmony had settled itself between thick lips and thin, straight hair and a woolly fleece, long legs and muscular thighs? Together they had made a liar out of Aristotle: The original being was not divided in half. Or else they had recombined it in black and white. And if Yebga sometimes read surprise in other people's faces, indeed a shameless complicity quick to change into outright hate, he now dealt with the matter. In the eyes of others, their relationship might have the appearance of a cliche, but not in their own.

Faye soon returned with a glass of sparkling water. Yebga drank it. She deposited a kiss on his forehead.

"Well, hello anyway."

"Hello," said Yebga, his mind somewhere else.

"I didn't see the other article in here, the one you told me about."

"I couldn't finish it. It's still not polished. And then there are all these telephone calls. . . ."

"So did you finally meet that guy?"

"No."

Yebga cracked his knuckles one by one. Faye had often scolded him for this at the beginning of their relationship. Since then he had given up this habit. He started to stand up, made a helpless gesture and smiled sadly.

"Would you please play back the messages for me?"

Faye started the machine: the secretary from the *World*, the bank, a friend, a relative and some others who had

39

preferred to hang up. Mukoni hadn't called. Neither had Maktar Diop.

Chapter Eight

In the taxi the next day, the two detective's faces were as gray and immobile as their hats. With no coherent battle plan in mind, each prayed from his corner that the writer would be an understanding man. Someone who might help them, not bowl them over. It would be easy in the beginning. They would bring Chester news from home, from the neighborhood, noises and smells he'd surely not forgotten. They were good at telling stories about Harlem, and after a few slaps on the back, the atmosphere would become friendly. Later it would intensify, when they had to explain everything.

A narrow gravel path which wound through the trees brought them to a large villa. It was built of stones the color of baked earth which reminded them of old photos of Arizona. A haughty looking blond woman waited patiently on the doorstep as they paid the taxi driver. Then she hesitantly stepped forward.

"Hello, gentlemen," she said in a weary voice.

The two ex-cops removed their hats.

"Mrs. Himes?" asked Ed Smith cheerfully.

"Yes."

Then turning her back without a word, she led them through the house to a room lit by large bay windows opening on the sea. It was furnished with low leather armchairs. A cat, disturbed by the noise, ran between their legs, spitting.

"Make yourselves comfortable. I'll be back in a minute."

She disappeared into the next room. Standing at attention near the door, Ed Smith and Jones Dubois looked around, eyes widened in disbelief. In barely three days, they had crossed the Atlantic, France and Spain, but the distance traveled was nothing compared with this unbelievable phenomenon: They were finally going to meet the author who for so many years had served as both their memory and model. He had dictated their sly antics in bars, their conjugal excuses, had chosen their coats and their hats. In short, without Himes their lives would have been the same long descent into hell that bedeviled other unfortunate guys appointed to maintain order where whites had imprisoned blacks: in corruption and chaos.

"It's good to know there are some blacks who do succeed," said Smith.

"Yeah," responded Dubois with a stupefied look, delighted. This exchange didn't mask their apprehension. They had no time to feel melancholy. A portly white woman with brown hair, clad all in black, entered the room.

"Hello, gentlemen," she said in rough English. "The Senora asks me to serve you a drink."

The two partners opted for whiskey. The maid served them and withdrew immediately. Alone again, the detectives looked at one another, dismayed. The formal welcome did not seem propitious.

"Please wait a few more minutes. My husband can't see you right away."

Himes' wife settled into a chair opposite them. Her smile seemed forced and didn't conceal the tension in her features. She removed a cigarette from a case lying on the table and lit it, blowing a stream of smoke up to the ceiling.

"I can't believe you've made this trip all the way from New York merely out of admiration for my husband. I only pretended to believe you on the phone. I needed to talk to some people like you, especially now, but you'll have to explain yourselves a little."

Neither understood what she had meant by "people like you," but they didn't let on. Their chips were on another number.

"Am I mistaken?" continued the hostess in the same soft, monotonous voice.

Although they never would admit it, the presence of a white woman disturbed them and shook their confidence. Dubois sometimes said laughing, "Our asses are still whip marked from the days of slavery!"

41

Smith finally took the plunge without looking over at his companion. He wasn't sure how deep this water was.

"You're not mistaken," he said. "We have come for something else."

"We do admire your husband," cut in Dubois. "But my friend is right. We haven't just come to meet him. We've come to bring him some news from back home. To let him know how blacks are doing back there."

"We thought," continued Smith, "that maybe he'd forgotten Harlem and all its shit, living here like a prince. We came to remind him. He's a great man, but back there, if you're black, you're still only considered half a man."

"Life is so bad back there for blacks that they need something to hang on to," continued Dubois. "If we don't have someone to look up to, we're lost. Especially the kids. We came here to tell him about all this. Malcolm X is dead. Martin Luther King is dead. Jimi Hendrix, even if we didn't really like his music, is dead. Too many people have died."

They hurled the sentences in an uninterrupted string as if their lives depended on their words, as if time was running out. The woman sat smoking, with a lost expression. Finally she laid two big Medusa eyes on them.

"What are you talking about?"

Once again it was Smith who answered.

"Well, what we're trying to say is that Coffin Ed and Gravedigger Jones are important to the blacks back there. They're the last real defenders of the Cause. Guys in the street think they're immortal or something. If they find out that they're dead, I really don't know how they're going to take it."

The author's wife strained to follow the conversation as the two men's accents became more and more pronounced. Finally she gestured impatiently.

"What Coffin Ed and Gravedigger Jones?"

"But . . . Chest . . . your husband's characters!"

She put out her cigarette and stared at the men as though seeing them for the first time. Then she pointed at Dubois' cheek.

"How did you do that to yourself?"

Dubois' face suddenly clouded over. He noticed that a

conservatively dressed man with a long shriveled face had just walked through the door. He was carrying a black physician's bag. Mrs. Himes hurried over to him and they talked softly in a foreign language. Smith and Dubois were suddenly silent. The man left as quietly as he had come. Mrs. Himes, forgetting her last question, motioned with her head for them to follow.

"Please gentlemen, don't stay too long. He's weak. Don't tire him out."

She led them into a room which was vast and light. Before closing the door behind her, she advised once more, "Not too long, please." Dubois and Smith approached the bed. With white hair and moustache and a face worn out by seventy-five years of worry and struggle, undoubtedly the man was Chester Himes. How sick he looked, used up! A small flame seemed to brighten his eyes when he discovered them near his bedside. He acknowledged them by blinking, almost imperceptibly. They drew nearer still, until they reached the bed.

"Mr. Himes," Dubois grew bold, "first, we must apologize for having come to see you like this, after your wife told us you weren't well, but there are some things guys like us can't write about. Writing's never been our bag. It's more up your alley."

"Go on. Out with it, man," breathed Ed in his ear, wetting Dubois' cheek with the sweat pouring from his face.

"You know, we're the inspectors from Harlem you've more than likely heard about," he began again with a voice oddly loud as if speaking from a great distance. Then he began to whisper again. "Well, we're retired now, but, well that's not a problem. We manage O.K. Not like a lot of other guys. Since you left, things have changed a lot."

"Well, there are some things that have changed and others that haven't," cut in Smith.

"Yes, I mean compared to the jobs we pulled off together . . ."

"You and us, and then, the two of us together . . . until you decided that we'd done our time . . ."

"Don't forget, we're really cops, we weren't exactly faking, but now, we got to watch out for ourselves, because back home, the young hoods on the street aren't going to miss us."

"Yeah, and since the whites aren't going to do us any favors either . . ."

"What do *you* think about all this, Mr. Himes?" asked Dubois trying to penetrate the old man's gaze.

Smith put his hand on Dubois' shoulder.

It seemed grotesque and obscene to them that reality could avenge itself to such an extent. Himes, the combatant, the everyday companion, the one who knew all the tangles, all the bad ranks of the neighborhood, Himes who had robbed a bank and done time, whose presence ran throughout Harlem, who scrambled up fire escapes two steps at a time, played with children in courtyards around fire hydrants, never missed one of Father Divine's sermons or a football game, escorted girls with circles under their eyes picked up in the back room of some bar, who never refused to give a hand or a heart, he had become this old man with emaciated features. . . . An ironic smile, an almost mocking grin, clung to his lips. Smith wanted to break the silence again but Dubois shook his head. When Mrs. Himes gently opened the bedroom door, they were still there, side by side, silent, bent over the bed, trying to understand. The great gentleman was asleep.

Chapter Nine

Yebga was still fuming as he climbed the stairs to the *World* four at a time. He only had one thing on his mind: to tell that fake brother, Mukoni, what he thought of him! He had already prepared several piquant sentences designed to strike Mukoni down on the spot. Bitter descants resonated in his head: The only thing these spades were good for was to have a good time; time wasn't the same for them! This "for them" made Yebga smile. He tried to concentrate his anger on his friend. He continued up to the second floor and crossed the telex room, asking everyone he passed if they'd seen Mukoni. Claire, a buxom typist with green eyes and a head thick as cottage cheese, walked over to him. She had been teasing him ever since he started working at the *World.*

"If you're looking for Rodolphe, he left for Chad this morning." She coyly waited a few seconds before continuing. "It seems he left something in Glenn's office for you."

"You might have mentioned it a little sooner! No one ever tells me anything around here. Jesus!"

Tossing greetings and hellos to left and right in a haughty tone, Yebga dashed across the big editing room amid the din of clanging typewriters and burst into Glenn's office. The editor-in-chief looked up calmly.

"Amos, you must get into the habit of knocking. Everyone else here does it. Just follow a few of the rules and everyone will . . ."

"Please, spare me the lecture. Did Rodolphe leave something for me?"

Glenn handed him a manila envelope. It contained a hastily scribbled note:

> Salif was a small-time dealer, half Senegalese, half Malian. He didn't have an address. He had a sister who's a dancer. I don't think it was *the* big scoop, but I see why he said it was urgent. See you later.

With the message, Mukoni had left a press clipping which appeared to have been from the same day.

"Shit!" exclaimed Amos, skimming the article.

"What's wrong?" inquired Glenn who pretended to occupy himself with something else.

"Maktar Diop died last night. Shit."

"Who was Maktar Diop?"

"A black guy, man. He called me. And it just so happens that the police conclude it was an accident."

From the tone of his voice, Glenn knew that Yebga was worked up.

"He warned me," Yebga muttered. "I should have tried to do something."

He dropped the envelope, the note and the clipping onto

Glenn's desk. The editor-in-chief couldn't understand the reporter's reaction.

"There's nothing you could've done, Amos," he ventured.

"These stupid cops who conclude right away it's an accident. You know if Diop had been white . . ."

"Calm down," Glenn interrupted. "That's nonsense."

After Yebga had left the office, Glenn picked up the clipping from the the desk and read: ANONYMOUS DEATH IN THE TENTH ARRONDISSEMENT. So? This wasn't the first. Yebga had the passions of a liberationist from Yaoundé. He was going to have to speak to him about his role at the paper, and fast.

"Rue des Petites-Écuries, the Sunny Kingston!" Yebga told the driver. He felt a strange weight in his heart; the blood rose to his temples. He massaged them for a few minutes and it made him feel better. The taxi left the Boulevard Montparnasse for the Rue de Rennes, then turned onto the Boulevard Saint-Germain and headed toward the Boulevard Saint-Michel. Yebga, eyes fixed, could not stop thinking about Maktar Diop's death. In light of the fact that this "accident" had taken place so fast, and in so "natural" a manner, Diop's telephone messages took on new meaning. Diop had feared for his life. Yebga had hesitated to believe in Diop's anxious stories about threats and disclosures. Now it was his professional duty to get to the bottom of this affair. If he had really been murdered, perhaps he had known something. Why would a dealer bother to telephone a reporter regarding a mundane problem with a supplier or a client? Anyway, quarrels among pimps or addicts were settled with knives or guns, not with cars like in the movie Z. Yebga was certain the man at the wheel had not been black. There had to be more here than met the eye.

It was true that up to this time Yebga hadn't shown great qualities of intuition. However, while changing the way in which he carried out his work, he would change too. He had been a lamb. He would become a wolf! He would investigate by himself, until he was sure of what he had to say. For a moment he imagined the looks on the faces of the old hands, beginning with Glenn. All these fossils would see him with new eyes!

The taxi stopped on the Rue des Petites-Écuries, in front of the painted wooden sign.

The Sunny Kingston was almost empty. It was still rather early for night owls. Myriam was there, busy setting the tables. She set down her tray and walked over to Yebga.

"You're just the person I'm looking for," said the reporter.

She took him by the hand and led him over to a table, the same one as the night before. By day the restaurant looked like any other Paris bistro. Myriam did not leave Yebga the privilege of breaking the silence.

"Have you heard?"

Her face was marked either by sorrow or by a night of bingeing. Yebga bore in mind two things: Myriam had begun using the familiar "tu" form with him again and she was even more beautiful in pants.

"Salif is dead," she continued, "crushed like a dog by a car nobody saw."

"Yes, I know."

"It's disgusting."

Myriam struggled to control a trembling at the corners of her mouth. Yebga felt vaguely shameful. He had felt no sorrow, no real pain upon hearing of Salif's death. He had simply felt indignant, as if this murder had been perpetrated against him.

"Calm down," he said clumsily.

This man must have have been more than a regular in this restaurant, at least to the waitress!

Yebga hated to see a woman cry, and here this seemed likely, judging from Myriam's trembling chin. He mentally reviewed different possible attitudes without finding any that satisfied him. Luckily the sobs soon became less frequent.

"It wasn't an accident," she still moaned. "Everyone knows it. If Diop had been white . . ."

"Don't be ridiculous," Yebga dryly interrupted. Then he heard himself ask in a neutral voice, "Where did he get his money?"

Myriam wiped her eyes, then blew her nose noisily.

"Oh, he managed. Like the rest of us. He sold a little grass from time to time, fenced some hot goods. Nothing really outrageous. He was always getting ripped off. But he was really a nice guy."

"Where did he live?"

"Here and there. Sometimes at a friend's place or at his sister's. He kept his stuff in a little place where he was squatting on the Rue de l'Ouest."

Yebga remembered that Mukoni had mentioned Salif's sister.

"Do you know his sister?"

"Yeah. She came here once or twice with him. But this isn't her kind of place."

Yebga was silent. The owner walked over to them. He gave Yebga a brief nod.

"There are some customers waiting, Myriam. Go take care of them."

"O.K., O.K.," said the girl, sniffing as she glanced around.

The room was almost deserted except for a large man, who looked like a heap of rubber, on a bar stool.

"Would you please bring me an orange juice when you come back," Yebga ordered concilatorily.

She returned with the juice and set it down in front of him.

"What about the other customer?" worried Yebga.

"So what. He can wait for a minute. All he does is drink anyway. It won't hurt him."

The man, leaning on his cane, grew impatient.

"Hey sista! You have to be a reporter around here to get a drink?"

"Shut up!" answered Myriam without turning around.

"I'm going to leave; it's better," interrupted Yebga. "Do you know where I can find Salif's sister?"

"No. She moves around a lot. She travels. But I'll see what I can find out. Paris isn't that big."

"Thanks."

Yebga got up and set a ten-franc piece on the table. He took a card from his pants pocket and handed it to the young woman.

"Here. If you hear anything, don't hesitate to call."

As he pushed open the door, she called out to him, "If you really are a reporter, I hope you won't forget us."

Yebga was silent. He left without turning back. There was always this "we" in Myriam's mouth. Who was "we" anyway? She, him, blacks? And which of "their" preoccupations should he feel concerned about? Their delirium, their problems with women and money? The "community," that hypothetical and abstract family of which they wanted to make him a slave, had to be put and would be put in the background. He was from Cameroon; he lived and worked in France, with whites.

It was two o'clock in the afternoon and Yebga had nothing better to do than to go and knock about near the Rue de l'Ouest. He went down the stairs into the Metro. Unlike his friends, Amos liked the foreign microcosm which prevailed here. There were bums, Asian merchants, girls from the Antilles selling beauty products for blacks, musicians, pickpockets, cops, puppeteers . . . identity checks too, O.K.! But he didn't usually get stopped. He wasn't easily confused with "other" blacks.

The Rue de l'Ouest was the most recent refuge for Paris' small dealers. Transactions took place in the middle of the street, just as they did in places like the Sondaga market in Dakar, between the Medina and the European quarter; the big Bamako market near the Grand Mosque; or in the Nylon quarter in Douala, with everyone looking on. Back in places like Sékou Touré square, amid odors of gas, garbage, spices and smoked fish, dealers sold everything that led one to an artificial paradise, no matter what the path. While Africa contented itself with small euphoria-inducing tablets (except in Senegal where they received grass from Gambia), the clients on the Rue de l'Ouest needed strong sensations. A television report had advertised the fact that there was a free market in this street. It was condemned to be bulldozed, and every sorry junkie was aware of it. Yebga could not refrain from smiling. At the time when this report was aired, showing blacks in the middle of dealing, a sixteen year old kid had accosted him on the Trocadéro esplanade at one o'clock in the afternoon to ask if Yebga had

49

anything for sale! Thus, in the narrow minds of good people, the Rue de l'Ouest was synonymous thereafter with drugs, and drugs with blacks.

As he walked farther down the street, Amos regretted not waiting for nightfall. By day, the Rue de l'Ouest seemed a huge thoroughfare, good for Sunday strolls with the family, but a difficult place for a detective shadowing a suspect.

Chapter Ten

"On days like this, when it was so hot it seemed the heat was going to crush the earth, my mother would draw strange figures in the sand and predict the future from them. It was a trick she'd learned from her father. I remember that these predictions were always morbid. My mother always acted weird on days like today," Ed Smith confided to his friend.

"You had a mother?" joked Dubois. "It's hard to imagine you nursing anything besides your whiskey flask!"

"Go ahead and laugh, man, but my mother was no ordinary woman. I think she really had powers."

The two men chatted over a cerveza as they sat on the terrace of a bar overlooking the promenade and the sea.

"That water is really something else, man," said Dubois to change the subject.

"Yeah. That's the route our grandparents took. A long journey . . ."

Since their interview with Himes, Ed Smith and Jones Dubois had sunk into a deep depression. Now they sat despondently bemoaning their distant roots.

"You know, Africa's just across that water. It sure has taken us a long time to get this close," muttered Smith.

"What are you talking about, Ed? Do you want us to take the boat over there just because you're in the mood? We came here to see Himes."

"Well? Did you like what you saw? Don't you have the

feeling we arrived a little late this time, man? We were too slow on the draw, and now we'll never get our guns back in their holsters."

This was in fact the real question: What could you ask of a guy who was about to die?

Chapter Eleven

Well after nightfall, Yebga returned to the vicinity of the Rue de l'Ouest. As if under an evil spell, the place seemed to have undergone an unsettling metamorphosis. Here and there, the scattered street lamps pierced the darkness with their blue light. Occasional passersby hurried on and the purring of cars grew distant like a dream. A group of six or seven people stood engaged in lively conversation on the corner of the Rue de l'Ouest and the Rue de Niepce. Among them were three tall blacks whose slender bodies led one to believe they were of Mandingo extraction. The others were white. Their manner was a little awkward, and judging from the style, their clothes were old. They were eccentrics from the suburbs. As Yebga approached, they stopped talking. Instead of veering away from them, he drew near.

"Do you know where I can find some hash?" he asked one of the tall black men.

The oldest one looked mean. His face was marked by several scars. They composed a sort of mask, shining in the night. He wore a mauve scarf wrapped around the collar of his white shirt and thrown over the shoulders of what appeared to be a dinner jacket. A bashed-in bowler hat covering his short Rasta mane completed the picture. He looked Yebga over suspiciously. Like a good African, he knew how to spot the imposter in his fellow man. Yebga wanted to look as though he knew what he was doing.

"Don't look like you smoke often," said the black man.

"No, not very often," admitted Yebga.

"How much you want?"

"A hundred grams."

Amos had tossed out the figure by chance. It seemed to suit the dealer.

"Wait a minute."

An order was fired off in Wolof to one of the other blacks who instantly disappeared into a neighboring building. As the third one kept watch, Yebga looked down the Rue de l'Ouest, which extended like a long dark corridor. There wasn't a soul in sight!

The white boys resumed their haggling. They were no longer disturbed by Yebga's presence.

"We only have a thousand francs," one of them said.

"One thousand three hundred or forget it."

"Salif didn't charge that much," protested one kid who looked barely twenty.

The tall black man gestured contemptuously.

"Then go find Salif and stop bugging me. I'm not your mother. Take it or leave it."

They ended up paying and walked off bellyaching, toward the Rue Raymond-Losserand. The second black man returned with an envelope.

"You got the cash?"

Amos only had five hundred francs.

"Do you take checks?" he asked in his most naive manner.

"You must be joking."

"No, really. That's the only way I can pay you."

The tall man said something to him in Wolof. Amos figured he probably wasn't flattering his ancestry. Feeling strangely detached, he wondered if the guy was insulting him for the color of his skin.

"Never mind," Yebga said, turning quickly away from the astonished group.

He ran to catch up with the white boys turning onto the Rue de Plaisance. He slowed down to catch his breath before approaching them nonchalantly.

"Excuse me. Weren't you just in the Rue de Niepce a minute ago?"

The four pairs of eyes which settled on him shone with an unnatural intensity. They were scared.

"Relax! It's just that I didn't want to pay that guy's price. Since I heard you talking about Salif, I thought you might know where I can find him."

The faces relaxed. The kid from the suburbs who looked like a junkie made up his mind and spoke, "We don't really know him. He sold us some stuff once or twice, but that's about it."

"But where did you find him?"

"At some concerts at the Phil'One. He goes there a lot."

Yebga thanked them and crossed the street. The neighborhood was beginning to weigh him down.

"Is that you, Mr. Phantom?" asked a voice coming from nowhere.

"Yes," said Amos loud enough to make himself heard.

In the misty bathroom, Faye was toweling off her back. Amos kissed her on the shoulder. She turned and kissed him passionately on the mouth. Her breasts were wet and a drop of water was heading toward her navel.

"Why don't I ever see you anymore?" she sighed.

While she covered his face with kisses, Yebga had a close-up view of her ass in the mirror facing him. He stroked her hips, then pushed her aside. She laughed.

"Hurry up. Get dressed," he said. "We're going out."

He headed for the kitchen down the hall. It was almost midnight.

Chapter Twelve

The nightclub lay in the heart of La Défense. Blacks from Puteaux and the neighboring Paris suburbs always referred to this district as "Manhattan." Walking through the door, Yebga was pleased to recognize the owner. They had met on several occasions and had even worked together on a broadcast about African music. The tables were arranged cafe style between the stage and the bar. Most of the people who frequented this place were adolescents homesick for Africa; "professional Africans" in search of new sounds;

white journalists interested in a kind of music they still didn't know very well; or prominent Africans passing through Paris, brought here by their white hosts. On the whole, not many blacks came to the Phil'One and those who did lacked spirit. Drug dealers reigned among these interlopers who shared nothing but a common desire to keep bad company, to party and in the process turn their back on Western culture.

Yebga immediately recognized the usual faces and bodies dancing blissfully about. If your sense of smell was keen, you might discern a pungent odor, somewhat sweet. The Zairean Ray Lema and his orchestra were on the bill. Yebga left Faye at the bar and wandered off into the room. He came across Elizabeth, a tired looking blond. Perched on stiletto heels in outlandishly full garments, Elizabeth had the reputation of catering to exotic tastes. They chatted for a while. She had just opened a restaurant in the tenth arrondissement. She talked about having toured Africa and the Africans too, a voyage as deceptive as the continent was vast! She said she had lost nothing by cutting uptight white guys out of her life. They didn't know how to move their hips like Yebga. They no longer dared to dream. Yebga stammered out that everyone was in search of an ideal world. Then, noticing the effect produced by so lofty a statement, he tried to extricate himself, especially when he felt long fingernails taking hold of his ear and others scratching his skin under the neck of his jacket. With a black pilot at the helm, the marooned woman was ready for anything!

When he was free of her, Yebga reflected: This place held nothing interesting for him. At most it might provide a background for the opening of a story. That was always the problem with black material; you could never separate it into parts: dope, nightclubs, music, politics, sex and utopia, it was all inextricably related. Some men died there, like Maktar Diop, whom Amos was beginning to understand now. Others, like himself, just lost convictions.

"Hi, Philippe. How's it going?"

Amos almost had to shout to make himself heard.

"Hey, Amos. A rare privilege to see you."

The owner displayed an enthusiasm which he reserved for VIPs.

"What do you expect," answered Yebga, feigning a distressed tone. "I'm only a poor immigrant worker!"

"Can I get you a drink?"

The two men joined Faye at the bar.

"Good evening, Faye. I knew this old card sharp didn't come out alone. Would you like a drink?"

"No, thanks. I already have one."

The club owner glanced around the room. Everything appeared to be going well. He turned to the reporter.

"Did you come for any particular reason?"

"Yes," answered Yebga. "I'm trying to find out about a guy who died last night."

Philippe lit a cigarette. His face became serious.

"A black man?"

"Yes. A certain Salif Maktar Diop, a small two-bit dealer who sold from here sometimes."

"Poor Salif."

He took a long drag on his cigarette. Faye kissed Yebga's neck. Ray Lema had just broken into a sophisticated reggae.

"I'm going to dance."

Yebga watched his friend disappear into the crowd. Her blondness contrasted strangely with the decor.

"I don't know what kind of shit he stumbled into, that idiot," continued the owner.

"Did you know him well?"

"We had a few arguments because I didn't want him peddling his trash in my place. Otherwise he was a decent enough boy, intelligent. He had lots of interests."

One of the bouncers came over and whispered something in Philippe's ear.

"Excuse me for a minute, Amos. You and your girlfriend can order whatever you want."

The music was bewitching, but Amos didn't have the strength to dance. Besides, all the smoke bothered him. He closed his eyes. Someone placed a hand on his forehead.

"Is it you, darling?" he said, grabbing it.

Myriam didn't answer. She waited for him to open his eyes.

"You!"

"No, the emperor of China. I wouldn't exactly say that was enthusiastic."

"I'm surprised, that's all."

"Aren't you going to offer me a drink?"

Amos motioned to the bartender.

I called you several times today. Did you get my messages?"

"No. I haven't been home yet."

"I have the address you asked for."

Yebga smiled.

"Why are you using the polite form tonight?"

"So we can be on equal footing."

The owner's return interrupted their conversation.

"You really can't be left alone one minute, Yebga," he scoffed. "I am sorry to break up such a handsome couple! You will excuse me, Myriam, but I've got some things I'd like to talk to Amos about."

Suiting the action to the word, he led Amos away from the noise and the crowd.

"Let's step outside and get a breath of air."

In front of the club, they found themselves surrounded by buildings fused in dark masses against the sky.

"You think he was murdered?" asked the owner.

"In any case, he was afraid. He told me."

"Shit . . . That guy never had any luck. He was worth more than that. I told him so a thousand times. What do you plan to do?"

"Find out what's behind this. Before he died he wanted to talk to me. He claimed to have some information. I want to know what this whole thing's about."

"For your paper?"

Amos eluded the question.

"Salif had a sister. I absolutely must find her. Maybe she knows something."

"Malika."

"What? You know her?"

"She danced here once or twice but I haven't kept in touch with her. I can connect you with her agent, Youssouf N'Dyaye. He's a shark, but with a little luck, he'll give you some information . . . or sell it to you. He lives on the Champs-Élysées, number 153."

In the course of their conversation, the two men had strayed from their starting point. They retraced their steps. A light breeze rimmed the night. Yebga lifted his eyes to the sky.

"God, I wish I could read the stars. . . ."

The other smiled. He regarded the reporter as a species of poet on the road to extinction.

"You do a great job, Amos. And you know . . . you guys need all the help you can get."

"Thanks," Yebga ground his teeth.

"Don't hesitate to come back whenever you want."

Taking advantage of a red light, Yebga touched Faye's thigh. She was wearing a skirt. His hand followed a vein whose course he knew by heart.

"You're wearing panties?" he was surprised.

"I always do when I'm on a mission! Serves you right, pervert."

Faye laughed and drove on.

Chapter Thirteen

Himes might have written that, even for a white man, there are days like this to be marked with a black stone. You wake up and smell something unusual in the air, but you can't put your finger on it. Dark days, when the world is upside down, days when you wake up a poor black bastard after having fallen asleep a hero.

Smith and Dubois began to mix up the words in their limited vocabulary. They started sentences in which "hell," "fucking" and "shit" appeared more often than they should have. But these were the words which best expressed their frame of mind on this particular morning. They had seen the tired face with chalky white hair, lying in a semblance of eternal rest, and they had felt the presence of death. Their life had been littered with cadavers far more spectacular, with dying people less peaceful, but none of those were named Chester Himes.

He had slipped like sand through their fingers. It was like waking from a dream in which you were a millionaire, to find yourself as poor as always. Few clients came to the hotel at this time of year; Smith and Dubois were practically alone. The veranda spread out under the chilly November sun, and their strong voices carried far across it. Dubois stood up and collected his jacket from the back of the chair.

"Let's go back there one last time."

The maid recognized them in the doorway. These two huge men wouldn't have gone unnoticed even at a black power demonstration in the heart of Harlem in the sixties! They went into the drawing room. Dubois elbowed his friend in the ribs.

"Take off your hat. We're in the home of proper folks."

Himes' spouse appeared. She was dressed all in black and her eyes were concealed behind large square glasses. The two men leaped up.

"Hello, gentlemen," she said in a flat voice. "If you've come to see Chester, I'm afraid you're a little late. He's already gone."

She had said "he's gone" like that, as if he had gone to buy some books at the neighborhood bookstore. The two large men stood gaping at these words although they had sensed it upon entering the strange smelling house. Ed Smith and Jones Dubois crushed their hats in silence. They felt uncomfortably out of place. Full of awkward condolences, they immediately started back to town on foot. They had nothing left to do in Spain, nothing left to do in Europe. And in New York?

Chapter Fourteen

Number 153 was a handsome sandstone building. On the concierge's door, the name Youssouf N'Dyaye stood out between an import-export company and an office of public relations. Yebga took the old wooden elevator to the fourth floor and stepped straight into a large room. The walls were lined with photographs of black women, all clearly taken in the same studio. They were wearing white draperies, antique-style togas or evening dresses, and were centered in seductive low angles or flattering three-quarter angles. In short, the African woman tailored for Western tastes. Three armchairs were occupied by attractive women, each clutching a large purse on her lap. The receptionist greeted Yebga with a platitudinous smile.

"May I help you?"

She was the only white woman in the room, a faded looking redhead, slightly withered. But judging from her makeup job, she obviously didn't let herself go.

"I'd like to see Mr. Youssouf N'Dyaye, please."

"Do you have an appointment?"

"No. But it's very urgent."

"I'll see if he has time. Who should I say is here?"

"Amos Yebga, reporter from the *World*."

"Yegba?"

"No, Yebga."

Amos noticed that a shudder ran through the room as he stated his profession. Aspiring starlets were always attracted to reporters whether they were food or sports writers; all these starlets thought that journalists held the key to their success. Seeing them subdued this way felt delicious to him. These sluts were ready for anything! The receptionist buzzed her intercom with no result. Yebga's eyes fell onto abundant globes, smooth and shiny on either side of a wrinkled furrow. The skin was very white. He didn't really like skin that was this white, except for Faye's. He looked away, glancing at the photographs on the walls. He tried to avoid the eyes, chests and legs of the women around him. It proved to be an arduous obstacle course.

"Mr. N'Dyaye asks that you be patient for a few minutes. He will be able to see you soon."

Politely as a schoolgirl, a young woman moved over slightly to allow Yebga to sit next to her. He strode across the room and struck a match before laying siege to the wall sofa.

"Have you been waiting long?" he asked his neighbor.

"Yes," she answered, crushing her silver purse. "But it's always like this here. Mr. N'Dyaye helps us so much that there are dozens of us waiting every day. Sometimes he can't see everyone. This is the third day in a row I've been here."

"How old are you?"

"Twenty-one."

She was lying, but Yebga knew that this was the rule among models. They promise you at thirteen, they launch you at fifteen, and they throw you out before you're twenty-five. Yebga mentally drew up a list of the ways age insults women. He was respecting the chronological order of their appearance, when a bell rang in front of the receptionist. She immediately yelped a shrill yes while pressing a button.

"You can go in now, Mr. 'Yegba,'" she said briskly. "It's all the way at the back."

"Good luck!" said the model.

Amos crossed several empty rooms before starting down an endless passageway. He finally reached a padded door which opened with a squeak.

"Hello, Mr. Yebga. Come in. Sit down."

The voice had a distinct Senegalese accent. Yebga entered the room. The atmosphere made him think of a diplomat who at one time had left his son with Yebga for an internship. Bantu, Bambara and Mandingo masks hung above tapestried Louis XV chairs. Thick flocked wallpaper absorbed the daylight, justifying the bright light of a floor lamp. There were photos of black women on the walls. Although the poses were as frozen as the portraits in the waiting room, the necklines were deeper, the skirts slit higher up the muscled thighs. Here and there, a heel sprouted from a gold sandal, a mouth was pressed against a round shoulder.

N'Dyaye was about sixty. He had a stern appearance and sparse silver hair. He held his body erect. His hands were open on a large mahogany desk, not a single paper was out of place. He was wearing glasses and a white *djellaba*. A preacher living in a harem, Champs-Élysées style!

"Hello," said the reporter. "Thank you for giving me a moment of your time."

"It's nothing. If we didn't do little favors for each other . . . Please, sit down."

N'Dyaye pointed to one of two black leather armchairs covered with panther skins. Yebga complied. He didn't like the turn which the Senegalese had given their conversation at the start.

"What can I do for you?" inquired N'Dyaye.

"I would like to know a little about the work you do here and the young people you employ."

"Of course, of course," he complied with a big smile, his gold incisors sparkling. "I've often had the opportunity to talk to reporters from the French press and African magazines. There's even a very nice boy who published an article about me in the States. And who do you work for?"

N'Dyaye took a packet of English cigarettes out of a drawer and lit one with a lighter inlaid with diamonds that marked the positions of the major metropolises on the African continent. Amos noticed he was wearing a gold signet ring on his left hand.

"The *World*. What exactly does your work entail?" Yebga pursued.

N'Dyaye took the time to think about it. He folded his hands on the desk in front of him.

"To find an individual style in those who ask for my assistance," he finally answered in a burst of laughter. "To find them interesting and well paying jobs."

"Why did I only see young Africans in the waiting room?"

"I only work for my people. What do you take me for? I work for *our* girls so that they don't have to peddle themselves to the whites. So that they'll never have to depend on anybody. We must be careful in this country. I've been fortunate enough to succeed. I owe it to myself to be at the service of future generations."

"But why women in particular?"

"Women are vulnerable. They come here to study and instead of going home when they've finished school, they only think about marrying a white man, so they can be comfortable. I'm opposed to that."

N'Dyaye lifted an accusing finger toward the sky.

"God damned Shem and his descendants. We've got to show him that black men can do without his blessing."

He took a puff of his cigarette, then studied Amos to see the effect of his words.

"If I'm not mistaken, Malika Maktar Diop works for you."

N'Dyaye shuddered. A vein stood out on his neck. The savior of young Negresses in peril removed his glasses and wiped his eyes.

"Not anymore now. But I think we're wandering from our subject."

"Do you know where she is?"

"I think she made it big in the States. Things are going well for her," continued N'Dyaye, recovering his good humor.

"You wouldn't have happened to have kept a photograph of her?"

"Sure. I always keep photos of my girls."

N'Dyaye was now completely at ease. He pushed on his intercom.

"Bring me Malika's portfolio," he said and almost instantaneously, footsteps were heard in the hallway.

"Come in."

The redhead entered the office.

"Here," she said, putting the photos on N'Dyaye's desk.

"Thanks. Now go."

He sent her away with a careless wave.

"Look how beautiful she was," he said to Yebga, handing him a snapshot.

She was beautiful indeed. Everything that could be dreamed of an African princess was inscribed on her face. There was the grace and severity which characterizes black women. But Yebga wondered why N'Dyaye had spoken about her in past tense.

"May I keep this?"

"Of course. It's yours."

The reporter stayed in his chair, hesitant.

"Many of my girls are just as beautiful," continued N'Dyaye, "but none of them have her character, her personality. You know my girls are in great demand in Paris and throughout the entire world. You should include that in

62

your article. The work that I do adds value to the image of blacks. Whites are like that. A beautiful Negress drives them crazy. Maybe it's linked with colonialist fantasies, I don't know. In any case, I make my money off of their asinine behavior." He coughed, throwing back his head.

Yebga stood up with a polite smile. He had not listened to N'Dyaye's speech. All that he retained from the conversation was an impression of lies and deception. He was furious for not having the courage to speak his mind. But the Senegalese man intimidated him, and besides, what could he really accuse him of? Yebga held out his hand and the other man took it in his own.

"Where are you from?"

"Cameroon," said Yebga shortly.

"Carry on. The future belongs to us. We must prove to these people that we're not as stupid as they think."

Yebga withdrew his hand and nodded, although he didn't really agree. After his departure, N'Dyaye picked up the telephone.

"Hello? I would like to speak to Mr. Gonzales, please."

He waited a minute.

"Hello? Is this Jorge? Yes. It's me. There's a young reporter who just left my office. He's interested in Malika Maktar Diop. I think we better keep an eye on him. He's a reporter from the *World*, which in itself is annoying. I'm not panicking, but as we say in Africa: The crocodile who eats the most is the one who keeps his mouth open longest. I don't want to find myself with problems at the last minute because of some damn reporter."

N'Dyaye put the receiver back on its cradle and stood up. The window behind his desk looked out on the Champs-Élysées. With a finger to his lips, he observed the stream of traffic flowing on the avenue.

Yebga took the Metro, got off at the Pigalle station and walked the rest of the way to Malika's apartment. Rue Houdon was dotted with local prostitutes of every age and sex. They waited for their clients while smoking and chatting loudly. Yebga recognized the accent of a black transvestite from the Antilles who deployed an entire arsenal of postures for Yebga's benefit. A statuesque woman, tall and sensual as a voodoo priestess, winked at him. Her breasts burst forth from a mini-bra and the contour of her thighs could have made her a champion female body builder. She was wearing dark makeup, brown for the eyes, black for the lips. Yebga guessed she was Ghanian. She addressed him, billing and cooing in the deep voice of a blues *chanteuse*.

"Hey, darling, you coming with me? We'll have a great time. I guarantee the major thrill. It's two hundred francs."

The transvestite from the Antilles turned around to look at Yebga. He was a fat man dressed up as a little girl, who was really repulsive.

"Come on," insisted the Ghanian, with a strong accent which somehow made Yebga think of Petula Clark. "You won't be sorry. I'm the best. Or I can give you the little thrill, it's cheaper."

The reporter laughed.

"The day when I have to pay to get laid, I won't be much good for anything, my dear. Keep your thrills for Treichville, my beauty. I prefer white meat."

"Bastard," spit the whore. Then, losing interest in him, she stood watching him with her hands in her pockets as he walked away.

Amos congratulated himself on his bad joke. His grandfather certainly would have had an attack if he had seen his grandson living with a white woman. Even his parents did not know of Faye's existence. Amos didn't discuss her in their presence. At number 164, the door opened almost immediately after he rang the bell. An African woman of about twenty appeared in the doorway wearing a bathrobe. She stared at Yebga, surprised.

"Yes?"

Her face did not correspond with the one in the photograph. There was still something puerile about it, fuller.

"I'm a friend of Malika. I'd like to see her, please."

"Malika doesn't live here anymore," exclaimed the young woman.

"Do you know her?"

"Yeah, sure. I mean, this place is a . . . Well, we have the same agent if you know what I mean."

"Youssouf N'Dyaye?"

"Yes, why?"

"May I come in?"

The reporter promised it would only take a minute and entered the apartment.

The room was furnished with a brown leather sofa, a low table, two velvet chairs, some shelves filled with detective novels and romances and a painted board on trestles. Photographs of the present occupant enshrined in gold or silver frames lined the wall. Yebga could see from the poses what she would have looked like had she changed from her robe into the lamé g-string she wore before the camera. He didn't dare hang around! He recognized a portrait of Malika on the table, a copy of the one N'Dyaye had given him.

"All right, what's up?"

"Oh, excuse me," said the visitor. "My name is Amos. Amos Yebga."

"Well," said the young woman after a pause. I'm Jeannette. Did Mr. N'Dyaye send you?"

"Yes, you might say that. In any case, don't worry. My visit is of a strictly professional nature. I'm a reporter. Besides, I'm married, happily . . . or unhappily," he chuckled.

Amos was exultant. Finally life was unfolding. This was the first time he had entered a stranger's apartment like this as if by breaking in. The good student had moulted and now made heard the adventurer's booming voice. He drank in every detail of the scene.

The living room was littered with various small objects. Among then Amos recognized a Mexican tray, a miniature porcelain replica of the Sugar Loaf in Brazil, New York's Twin Towers and a statuette from the Andes Mountains. African cloths were hanging on the walls. This gallery was only lacking in souvenirs from China and Japan!

Jeannette smiled without answering and came to sit down across from him.

"You travel a lot, don't you?" he asked in a neutral tone.

"Yes. My job requires it. I've been around the world several times."

She spoke indifferently.

"And you've never gone to Asia?"

"Yes, of course. I brought some Tiger Balm back from To-kyo. It's in my bedroom! But I can't show it just like that!"

"I would love to go to Asia. Japan must be extraordinary."

"Oh, it's the same shit everywhere. The same people. I divide the world and men into two categories: on one side, those who are stupid; on the other, those who aren't. I found that there were a lot of jerks in Japan."

"Which category do you put me in?"

"I let you come in, didn't I? Aren't you here on behalf of a friend? I must confess, I always want to make love to people I don't find stupid. They're so rare."

Yebga looked away. This was just the sort of line that, under different circumstances, he would love to have told Faye about for a laugh. But what he imagined under the spongy material made his temples burn.

"I'm surprised that Malika never told me about you."

"Why? Did she tell you everything?"

"I thought so. We were inseparable. We went everywhere together. She taught me a lot of things. But like they say, you think you know someone and sooner or later, you realize you were completely wrong about them. But how can I be mad at her? She was my big sister, my best friend, and then she split without even telling me where she was going. She didn't even leave a note or send a postcard."

"She didn't really leave without telling you anything, did she? She must have hinted at it. Maybe you just didn't realize it."

Jeannette swallowed her vodka, shaking her head.

"Never. The day she split, she pretended she had a date. That's funny, isn't it? Especially since she wasn't the sort of girl to get shipped out."

"I'm sure she'll send you news as soon as she's settled."

"In two months? You think she still hasn't had the time to get settled?"

The young woman swept the air with her hand.

"Let's change the subject, O.K.? Malika isn't here and I'm the one who let you in. Let's talk about us. I know how to size men up, you know. Do you like me?"

This is normal, Yebga told himself, I'm in a movie. And to think that for years, I lived in this city, I did my little white nigger job, I boasted about my studies, I showed my press card at all the conferences and all the cocktail parties. My life lost its flavor. It wasn't fun anymore! I lost the thread.

He was aroused by an incredible energy. His eyes dropped to her breasts, eloquent, offered.

"You're pretty, baby!"

"I don't need a man to tell me I'm pretty, lover! Malika taught me that. That's not what men are for. When you're sure of your beauty, you can make them do whatever you want. Of course I'm pretty, and I didn't ask you to tell me either."

"I like you," Yebga sadly confessed.

Jeannette laughed, lolling back in her chair. With an affected gesture, she dropped her empty glass onto the carpet, without taking her eyes off of Yebga.

"It's because men like me that this old idiot N'Dyaye took me on. It's not enough to be pretty, Amos. You have to sell yourself. My body is my tool. I have to make these idiots come when I parade in their fancy dresses. I feel their eyes burn with desire. A little longer and I could see their pants swell."

Yebga stood up. He was suffocating.

"With you, I would do it with my heart," she said in a childlike voice. "Because you're like my brother."

"I've disturbed you long enough," he heard himself say, holding out his hand. "I wanted to see Malika. It was nice of you to let me in."

Jeannette winced. "Don't talk about that slut anymore. She's gone. I'm free. I don't want to hear any more about her. She screwed me. She had everything I wanted. You would have slept with her, but you turn your nose up at me. Screw you! Get lost. Go tell N'Dyaye what I said."

She raged about, then stood still for a moment before collapsing onto the sofa. She pressed her long fingers onto her eyelids.

Yebga stood for a moment without moving, helpless, then he went over and took her in his arms.

"Calm down. Don't worry about N'Dyaye. It doesn't matter."

There was a salty taste under her tongue. She had a flat, athlete's stomach, and strong thighs that tenderly wrapped around his own.

Chapter Fifteen

Smith and Dubois returned to the Hôtel du Vieux-Colombier the way men return home after a long journey. But their trip had only lasted two days and the hotel was not home. They felt displaced, removed from the real world, and yet they delayed the moment when they would have to cross the ocean. They were getting even with life, which they intended to savor to the maximum. In the United States, their sergeant's pension would never have allowed them this sort of lifestyle, favored as they were by the exchange rate.

Although they could not reclaim their original rooms, those they were offered were still adjoining.

"Paris, my man. Let's go hit the town again!" said Dubois as they were settling in at the bar, pretending to be more cheerful than he was. "Let's go have some fun! I think you really need it."

"Yeah," agreed Smith without conviction.

The concierge walked over and handed them a map.

"Here is the map of Paris, you did ask me, sirs," he said obsequiously.

"Thanks," grumbled Dubois.

"All the places interesting to visit are colored in red."

Smith made a vague gesture as if to say, "O.K. Buzz off," and the man withdrew.

"We've got to forget we're going home the day after tomorrow."

"We already went up the Eiffel Tower. What a scrap heap. What else do you want to do?"

"There's still plenty of other stuff to see. This city's loaded with old things. Back when we were still slaves, these folks were already making statues after all their battles. And since we came and freed them from the Nazis, they're still here, my man. You see?"

"Besides, they don't have bricks here. It's all in stone."

"Maybe they just can't afford anything else."

Smith explained to his companion that as far as he was concerned, the United States would do well to buy one or two of France's monuments. He thought this might give them a historic patina which he felt maybe they lacked. To this Dubois replied that the clean-up crews back home would never venture out onto things like that.

"Your famous French ancestors were really just humble peasants. They copied a lot of our stuff, but they didn't have enough money to make this one as big as ours.

Smith, pointing out the obelisk, was talking about the original model for the Statue of Liberty.

Chapter Sixteen

Yebga dropped by the newspaper to see Glenn. He wanted his editor-in-chief to know that he hadn't lost interest in the paper or in his livelihood, even if an important matter was keeping him away temporarily. A newspaper was, after all, made up of subjects, ideas and investigations as well as the guys who went in search of all this, and their energy shouldn't be drained by mundane tasks. Either Glenn agreed with him or he was too overloaded with his own work to discuss the matter. As he was leaving, Yebga found a package in his mailbox. His first inclination was to dash back to Glenn's office, but he chose another course instead. He concealed the precious booty under his jacket and rushed off to the cafe where he'd been only recently with Mukoni, although now it seemed as if that was centuries ago. Yebga waited until he was comfortably settled in with an orange juice, then examined the contents of his package. It contained an ordinary school notebook; displayed on the cover was a splendid rocket, all engines switched on. In the center of the first page, Salif

Maktar Diop had written his name in the same tight and forceful writing which filled a good part of the notebook. Yebga read:

> September. What's wrong with me? For once, I have some cash and I'm still fucked anyway. I can't get in touch with little sister. Dread Pol rants and raves when I tell him about my problems, but he does think about things and he does give a damn about Malika. Not like Massa Soya who bores us with his talk about a screen play. But I'm still alone, like a black fly in his shit. A face you've never seen before appears out of nowhere and proposes an incredible scheme. You jump into it, hands tied, and fall flat on your nigger-nigger face. I'm going to check it out anyway.

> September 27 I'm like a dog in heat. DEAR GOD, WHERE IS LITTLE SISTER? Jeannette told me Malika was traveling. So? Where? Maybe she went to the country again to get herself worked over by one of her bastards. These sisters make me sick. At least Jeannette has a sense of humor. She says she leads them on, but she doesn't go all the way (Hmm!) She leaves the guy with his pants down around his ankles if he's not an African. I wouldn't appreciate that. Whereas Malika, if she felt like it, she'd fall for a member of the K.K.K. . . . .

What can you do when the clouds cover the sky
And from an upper story
A glance falls upon a naked body disappearing.
World, my world. Africa, mother of every
   civilization
Someday to the south, north, east and west
I'll build a gold pavilion on your shores.
My body will be tortured
But I will never stop protecting you.

Other poems followed in the same vein, then sentences written in a language he didn't understand. Malika reappeared several pages later.

October 5   I make the solemn vow in this official journal, to build Malika a house on Gorée as soon as I can find her and raise the money. And the family will never find out how she's been peddling her ass. When I think about this house, my eyes fill with a bitter liquid, because the rest of us are scattered about the world. Our families are always cold in foreign countries.

October 11   It wrenches my heart when I take Malika's passport to the consulate. At least her papers will be in order when we leave. The crocodiles, the caymans and the savage birds will rage at us. But the boat will hold out against the cross-currents and we will reach the beaches of truth. Too many vile people who pester us with their threatening words whetted like sharp spears.

October 14   I went to ask old N'Dyaye to look for little sister too. He scares me, that man, with his evil slander, when he tells me that Malika split with a white dude and that he's not interested anymore. When I'm in his office, I'm speechless. I told him I had cash but he treats me like a bum anyway. I'm going to thrash that old hypocrite one of these days. He walks around like an automaton. When I give him a dirty look, he warns me to beware and to go back to Gorée. I'm going to stop by Fnac and buy myself a Toots and the Maytals record. I really dig their music. YEAH! JAH LOVE!

October 27   6:30 p.m. I ring the doorbell. Jeannette is there. She is dressed like a space cadet. Her magnificent ass strains her zipper. I took

her to a party Lam was giving for Alésia. Everybody took me for a star with my prize. But my
heart sank when Jeannette told me that some
guys came to her house looking for Malika's
clothes and all her things and that the only
things they left behind were some Ghanian
statuettes. But then we were separated by the
crowd and I wasn't able to find out any more.
Afterwards with what D.F. gave me, my head
was raging and I didn't think about it again.
Later, like a slender gazelle, Jeannette pursued
my love and offered me her body.

October 29 I'm going to stop by N'Dyaye's
place one more time and if his white woman
tries to keep me out, I won't let her get away
with it. I'll piss in her face. I know enough
about N'Dyaye to hassle him and Dread Pol
connected me with a great reporter at the *World*.
I'm going to make an appointment with him
and tell him everything. I think Maz is pissed at
me. He warned me as I was leaving the Sound
System in Malakoff: COOL MAN. COOL.

The pages that followed were empty save for a few exotic
sketches. Yebga sighed and rubbed his eyes. He wondered
how he was going to find Dread Pol.
   Despite the fact that everyone traveled in different circles,
with different white friends and different co-workers, there
were certain meeting places for Africans in Paris. This was
where you heard news from home or ate African food. The
one good thing about exile was that it strengthened bonds
which might not have existed back in Africa. The simple
fact of being black and African created affinities which gave
an illusion of strength to these poor devils abandoned in
the turbulence of Paris. You were not alone. You recreated
family structures modeled on those you had left behind.
Paradoxically, it was only away from home that Africans
formed a real nation. In Paris, Congolese, Ivorians, Camer-
oonians and Senegalese considered themselves brothers

from the same country. African unity could only exist out-side the frontier, in reaction to the surrounding hostilities.

Yebga mulled all this over. He was struck by the blinding revelation that he was going to have to bring his address book up to date again, give up the Scandinavian dishes in favor of the African ones. After all, he was one of them!

Chapter Seventeen

At the usual hour, Youssouf N'Dyaye pushed open the door to his agency. The waiting room was packed.

Moist eyes lined with kohl turned in perfect unison to-ward the master of the house.

"Hello, girls," he said paternally.

A chorus answered him. He was wearing a blue cash-mere coat and had abandoned the *djellaba* for a black gabar-dine three-piece suit. He leaned over to the receptionist, placing a wide hand on her shoulder.

"I'll be waiting for you in my office in two minutes."

Then he rapidly crossed the string of empty rooms, closed the door of his lair behind him and placed his ma-roon leather attaché case on the desk.

He closed his eyes and concentrated on the day ahead of him.

Three knocks sounded at the door.

"Come in!"

The redhead complied, trailing behind her a wake of soap, toilet water and what N'Dyaye was resigned to ac-cept as the "famous odor of redheads." He separated the double curtains and peered down at the avenue.

"Sit down," he ordered. "I have some letters to dictate."

The woman flourished a writing pad to show she was ready.

N'Dyaye stood by the window a few minutes longer, rubbing his chin. Down in the street he noticed Yebga's sil-houette. He was waiting for the green light at the cross-walk. N'Dyaye clenched his fist.

"Leave me alone for five minutes. I'll buzz you."

Without the slightest objection, the woman set her pad on the desk, stood up and left the room.

Later, when she showed Yebga into the office, N'Dyaye was still standing in the same place.

"I saw you in the street, young man," he said without turning around. "Sit down."

Yebga did not budge. He waited for N'Dyaye to continue.

"What gives me the honor of seeing you again so soon, my dear friend?"

Yebga felt a little ill at ease. He heard himself say, "I've already done a good bit of work, but I'm still missing one detail. I'm sorry to disturb you again. What's become of Malika Diop?"

"It seems to me I've already told you."

"Are you really sure about that?"

N'Dyaye turned around briskly and looked Yebga up and down.

"What else do you want?" he hissed

"That depends on you."

N'Dyaye smiled scornfully. He emitted some odd little sounds, light clickings of his tongue against his gums. It was the sort of noise that women in line at the dispensary use to comment on their progress, while carrying a child with a licorice stick in its mouth on their back.

N'Dyaye took out a cigarette and lit it deliberately. Then he settled into an armchair.

"Do you know who you're talking to?" he asked, raising his eyes to the reporter.

Yebga didn't answer. He remained standing, his face distorted by anger, like a sulking child.

"A few years ago, this insult would have been settled between your father and me. I would have called him and said to him, "Your son is young. He doesn't know anything about life yet. He came to my place and insulted me." Your father would have apologized for you and we would have decided on your punishment. Unfortunately those days are over! We live in times of trouble and disorder. The West has ruined your minds. You think you're men as soon as a little hair starts to appear on your chin. You want to remake the world."

74

N'Dyaye pushed his cigarette case toward Yebga.

"Help yourself. You insult me, but I don't forget that I could be your father."

The journalist felt a rush of hatred overwhelm him. He had put up with being addressed in the familiar "tu" form and with the sermons. But the reference to his father was more than he could bear.

"You don't even know what you're talking about."

He had wanted to find other words, more cutting, more decisive, more distinct. He regretted his feeble sentence as soon as he had uttered it. "Get yourself out of this. Get yourself out of this fast. . . . ," he thought to himself. N'Dyaye was confident.

"You're doing your job and I respect you for it," he continued. "Your generation is reaching a level of success that we never would have dared to hope for. But don't be blinded. No matter what you do, I am, like you, an African. Like you, I am a black man. We have the same skin. You should trust me instead of trying to shoot me in the leg, me or anyone else. Don't mistake your enemy! Malika Diop crossed me and walked out. Now I don't know anything about her. I don't want to know. Let her get by on her own. You must believe me."

"Why didn't you tell me that to begin with?" Now Yebga was almost apologetic.

"I didn't think it would be that important to you."

"It wasn't that important to me . . . until I found out that her brother was dead."

N'Dyaye crushed his unsmoked cigarette into an aluminum ashtray and played with the lighter in his other hand. Yebga silently watched him, then turned the doorknob. Before leaving he found the strength for a last warning.

"I hope that you've told me everything. Because whatever the color of your skin, I won't overlook you if you're involved."

The door slammed shut. Left alone, N'Dyaye hesitated a few seconds, his hand poised above the telephone. When he had regained his composure, he picked up the telephone.

"Hello, Mr. Gonzales?"

His voice had taken on a slightly sugary accent.

He listened for a moment.

"Yes. He's just leaving the office. He knows that little Diop's brother is dead."

He listened again. Then his face turned grey.

"But we agreed that . . ."

Gonzales prevented N'Dyaye from finishing his sentence. There was nothing N'Dyaye could do but agree as his forehead beaded with big drops of sweat.

He dropped the receiver in its cradle as if it were burning his fingers and mopped his face with a white silk scarf. Then he removed his rosary from a desk drawer and distractedly began to tell the beads.

Yebga sat daydreaming on the carpet in Faye's apartment. As a child he had imagined that Europe lay suspended somewhere in the sky and that airplanes had to soar up into the atmosphere to reach it. In this way, France was perceived as a terrestial paradise in the clouds. It was time immemorial that N'Dyaye had called to Yebga's mind. This time of childhood, this time of Africa and the benevolent promiscuity which made you the son of all your uncles and permanently filled the house in Yaoundé with aunts or grandmothers. It was the evocation of this time that had paralyzed him while the old Senegalese man spoke. It had seemed as distant as a dream. N'Dyaye's voice had the familiar intonations of friends from home. Although these voices were lost in the dust of time, under hundreds of feet of occidental snow, they had not really vanished.

Brazilian music resounded in the room, not a samba but one of those sad and melancholy airs that are often heard in the slums. Yebga saw the vast beaches, the sun, the wealth and the opulence; then further on, not more than six or seven hundred feet away, lay the misery of shanty towns. This was Brazil and Africa too. There were the same contradictions, the same corruption, the same shit. Whatever the color of the guilty man's skin, it was fair that he pay. For the first time, Yebga was thinking about the investigation in other terms than those of cold reason and personal self-interest, and he didn't quite know what to make of it. The ringing telephone interrupted his reflections.

"Hello, Amos Yebga?"

It was a woman's voice.

"Yes. This is he. Who's this?"

"Jeannette. I remembered that you promised to call me if you heard anything about Malika. But we both forgot one detail: You don't have my telephone number."

Jeannette had recovered the clear bright laughter of care-free youth.

"That's right," he lied, straining to take on the same tone. But we'll take care of that."

He pretended to go look for a pen and came back, smiling.

"O.K. I'm ready."

"It's 254-1418."

"That's easy to remember, just think of the war."

"No. It's 254-1418. Well, I have to go. They're calling me for some new fittings. So anyway, how's it going?"

"As well as can be expected. You didn't tell me you'd kept some of Malika's souvenirs."

"They're nothing really."

"I'd like to see them anyway."

"Come by the house tonight. Let's say around ten o'clock?"

"O.K. Ten o'clock is good."

It was as if Amos felt Jeannette's breasts through his shirt. He exchanged a few banalities with the young woman in a neutral voice before hanging up, but the impression remained while he labored over an article for the monthly edition of the *World*; it was a vague commentary about a constitutional change in a central African country. He typed in his study, under the glaring beam of an architectural lamp, while vaguely listening to a Curtis Mayfield record. He heard a key in the lock and pushed the machine far away in front of him, relieved. Faye's return announced the end of his moral suffering. He went to greet her. He was wearing a turquoise bathrobe.

"Oh, you're here!" said his friend, kissing him on the cheek. "I'm on my knees. I'm fed up with this job."

He liked her light Boston accent.

"You always say that, my dear. Change your tune."

He wanted to tease her. She played the game while taking off her shoes.

"Don't laugh. The clients really drive me crazy sometimes. They always think they know more than I do. It's as if years of studies didn't count for anything. If they want a door in the middle of the kitchen and it's technically impossible, they treat me like a shit. They threaten to take their business somewhere else. They're really stupid!"

She dragged her purse and her shopping basket into the living room and tossed them onto a chair.

"The worst part," she continued, "is when they tell you that an engineer would have been able to do the thing . . . because they're not entirely wrong."

"You just have to keep those clients in their place and let them know from the beginning who's really in charge."

With her legs drawn up in front of her and her chin on her knees, Faye glanced at Yebga half teasingly. He went over to her stealthily and took her in arms. She struggled, murmuring insults and reproaches. He undressed her while he held her down. She cried no, stop, you're crazy, I'm dirty, but she helped him slide his jeans down. When she finally freed herself and leaped up, it was to unhook her bra.

"Go on, pervert. Do it. If you dare!" she said, throwing back her shoulders.

He took her fast. A few minutes later, she deposited a kiss on his bare chest.

"I like it the way you don't have hair there," she whispered.

Suddenly changing tone, she said, "Did you know that Chester Himes died yesterday?"

Yebga was in the middle of pouring bubble bath into the steaming tub. He adjusted the temperature and returned to the living room. Faye finished the drink he had fixed for himself.

"What were you saying?"

"Chester Himes died."

"What?"

"Yes."

Yebga was standing naked in the middle of the room. He collapsed into a chair. He no longer saw Faye, stretched out nude in front of him. There were people whose death had the power to change the course of time. There had been Ruben Um Nyobe, Sartre, Lumumba, Boris Vian, Kennedy, Martin Luther King, Louis Armstrong . . . and among those still living, Stevie Wonder, Robert Badinter, Sidney Poitier, Gregory Peck and Chester Himes . . . and then all the relatives, the close family, friends, all the faces on which you could put a name. Yebga was always surprised by death, flabbergasted each time, with renewed force. His love of certain men made them immortal in his eyes.

"When did it happen?"

"Yesterday. I'll never understand how you can be a reporter and not be up on things like this. I know that the *World* is not a literary review, but there are still several reasons why Himes should interest your little pals, aren't there?"

"I've had a lot of work lately, you know? I never imagined . . ."

Yebga was exasperated. Faye looked at him with the same eyes as that first time, on the deserted beach at Penguen, in Brittany. He seemed like a lost child, always lost, always too fragile to bear life's weight. A black seagull, as she said! That's what had seduced him. The certainty that she knew how to protect him. She left her place and came over to him.

"Hold me tight. I'm alive. I'm here. I'm not a dream."

"I'm not a dream," Yebga repeated to himself. Then what am I? Who was Himes? It was awful. What was the point of living if it was to die? To leave a testimony, maybe, like Himes. Living was for speaking. To tell about life as one lived it, candidly, without deceptive subdued light. To live was to struggle against others, wasn't it? Against oneself. For a writer, for a journalist, it was a little bit the same. N'Dyaye had said the same in veiled words. The alternatives were few: He either had to keep quiet or betray, and Yebga was already ready to betray. There was no other way out.

Chapter Eighteen

Go up there, you'll see Montmartre. Rather let's say let's go up on Montmartre, you'll see Paris. Ed Smith and Jones Dubois were far from metaphysical reflections. They took some fresh air on the butte, trying to chase away the blues which undermined them. On the threshold of Sacré-Coeur, Ed bought several combs and a fake ivory elephant from a Senegalese merchant. The merchant scribbled the figures on a piece of worn-out carton, and Smith systematically countered them.

"He takes me for an idiot," he told his companion. But we'll see who's really the sucker."

He laughed. The merchant shook his bracelets and his knick-knacks, glancing nervously around. His friends, three other peddlers who were strolling about the threshold, had more or less the same nervous attitude. Finally, after acquiring his goods at triple their value, Smith flashed a triumphant smile at Dubois. Suddenly, as if bitten by invisible flies, the four merchants packed up their stuff and ran off toward the stairs. They had barely disappeared when a police car pulled up to the sidewalk.

"Those bastards split again," cursed one of the cops. "What's this?" he said, looking incredulously at Smith and Dubois. Their smiling hardened his anger.

Smith and Dubois bought a return ticket for the tram, then had their portraits sketched by a Chinese caricaturist. Next they chose a seafood restaurant where they spent a good part of the meal making fun of one another with their sketches laid flat on the table. They tried to pretend they were on vacation, but the specter of returning to Harlem, tails between their legs, tormented them. On this particular night, Ed Smith and W. Jones Dubois, who'd forgotten whether they believed in God or not, made several attempts to evoke that distant day when, as children (because they had once been children), they sang canticles to His eternal Glory.

Just as they were beginning dessert, Smith and Dubois forced themselves to address two German tourists who had been making eyes at them all through dinner, though their hearts weren't really in it.

Yebga kissed Faye.

"Are you sure you don't want to take my car?" she asked.

"Positive. I'll try to hurry."

On his way down the stairs, he swore he would devote the next weekend to his friend. Maybe they would go to the country or just stay in bed for two days. He never tired of the spectacle Paris offered by night. He walked to the Ternes Metro station. The shallow faces of the other passengers seemed like ghostly figures from an ambiguous universe, a kind of modern Court of Miracles. He dropped a five-franc piece into a bum's hat. The light streaming from the ceiling tinted the faces strangely and made them look unreal.

Pigalle was an essential point of passage for Yebga as he headed toward Jeannette and her opulent tenderness. The silence on the platform calmed his nerves. On the street above, lights shone on a spectrum of peep-shows, game rooms, porno theatres and stalls of merchants selling french fries and sandwiches. The street was bustling. In the Rue Houdon, Yebga's Ghanian whore approached without recognizing him until he had replied with a familiar "Hello, sister." This aroused her suspicion. This time she was barely dressed in a Davy Crockett style outfit for adults: fringed boots and strategically placed suede scraps and fur. Yebga didn't notice that a car was following him from one waiting spot to the next, adjusting its speed to his.

Dubois and Smith were walking down Rue Lepic singing the German songs from the Belle Epoque they had just been taught. For the price they had paid to learn these songs, even though the drinks had been included, singing lessons somewhere else might have launched a number of musicians' careers. Their heads were spinning, but it helped them forget their troubles. They were still walking more or less in a straight line.

"Now that we know their neighbors, let's go see if French

81

chicks are worth all the fuss people make about them," Smith said, laughing. "That'll put the local socket diggers in their place when we tell them about it back home."

Instead of heading toward the Place Blanche by the Rue Lepic, the two partners continued on toward the Rue des Abbesses. They were practically alone in the street save for a few old people taking their dogs out for a late night walk. Since they were used to driving with their headlights off in Harlem as they made their rounds, Smith immediately noticed a car tailing a man along the sidewalk, across the street. It stopped, then continued on again following the rhythm of the man's gait. Smith elbowed Dubois.

"Check out that car over there, behind the black guy."

At that precise moment, the car sped up, then abruptly braked. The doors opened. From where they stood, neither Dubois nor Smith could distinguish exactly what was happening. They hastened their steps and finished off at an easy trot, making a racket similar to that of a company of mounted police. They soon discovered that a black man was being worked over in the shadow of a carriage entrance.

"Those bastards are beating the shit out of him," Smith cried.

Jones Dubois was too breathless to answer. Their arrival out of nowhere and the forceful way they used their fists quickly drove the henchmen off. After all, this was a public place. Smith had just enough time to trip one man as he ran by and the Mercedes took off, leaving the unlucky attacker lying flat out in the gutter with Smith's big shoe across his throat. The victim lay whimpering on the ground near Dubois like a sick child. The two winded ex-cops carried him into the light, revealing a swollen eye, a split lip and several bruises. He wasn't injured seriously. Dubois and Smith looked at one another in silence, scoffing. Paris was beginning to look like New York City; blood, wounded people sprawled out in the street, it was a real Harlem sidewalk! And in Harlem that was not the worst of it. Slapping each other on the back, the two men shared one thought.

Dubois looked after the wounded man while Smith knelt over his victim. Then he lifted him from the ground with soothing words, "I wouldn't get too comfortable on my back if I were you, sweetheart." Smith didn't have time to see the car or to hear Jones' warnings. The shots cracked, dry like a whip, and he felt the body of the man he was holding up against him, after a long shudder, slide between his arms, limp. The old cop also felt blood flooding his hands. He could not repress a "shit," which rang like a sigh. He held up the inert body, placing his hands under the armpits.

"Ed?"

"I'm O.K. They got the white guy. He's finished."

"We've got to look after this one, he's a brother. I bet he wouldn't be too happy to wake up at the police station after an incident like this."

Dubois dragged his load into the lobby of a building, immediately followed by Smith wrestling with the cadaver. They set the two bodies side by side on the cold ground and looked at each other. In the darkness, they could only distinguish two vague forms.

Smith took a lighter out of his pocket and lit up the human shield which had just been turned into a strainer. He was a young man of about thirty, with very short blond hair, a long thin body and pale lips, a woman's lips. Blood spotted his chin. Smith bent over him, closing his eyelids, and in the same movement began searching him. After decades of this, dead people no longer affected him. He had seen too many of them. With the routine gestures of an indifferent man, he methodically explored the clothes, burying everything he found in the pockets of his own trenchcoat: keys, lotto receipts, a red leather wallet, a photograph of a small girl in sweat clothes, a pack of gum, mint candies and an automatic with a second clip. In his pants pockets were pieces of a rumpled notebook.

While Jones held his hand plastered against Yebga's mouth, Smith quickly dragged the corpse over to the stairwell, propping it up against the bottom steps. In the street, they guided the wounded man like a friend who had been put off course by abundant libations. Yebga, who continued to moan in Dubois' arms, began moving his legs in all directions like a child learning to walk. In the deserted square, they hesitated a short moment before starting off toward the lights of Pigalle.

They wanted more than anything to put some distance between the corpse and themselves. Some cops watched them pass by with their limp companion and didn't even blink: two black men carrying a third!

While Dubois kept Yebga in a standing position, holding him by the shoulders like a jacket on a hanger, Smith went through the regulation search. They discovered a document covered with stamps. Attached to it was a photo of the wounded stranger. In the photograph he looked younger and fresher. They shoved the green card under a taxi driver's nose. As if it were an everyday occurrence to see two guys built like huge armoires transporting an inert body, the taxi headed off toward 36 Boulevard Voltaire. When the vehicle stopped, Yebga, who had remained silent during the ride, surprised his nurses with an agonizing groan.

"I know what it's like," grunted the driver. "I've been smashed a few times myself. Especially since I've been working nights."

"No, thanks," answered Dubois, who thought the old man was offering to go get a doctor. "It'll be O.K. now."

Then one dug into his bills, the other into his change. The only thing left for the the three of them to do was discreetly make their way past the concierge's door and then execute an almost normal entry into the apartment, thanks to Yebga's keys and the panel by the mailboxes where his name was listed. Smith and Dubois stretched Yebga out on the sofa, then found mercurochrome and bandages in the medicine cabinet. After a summary examination, they cleaned the wounds on Yebga's face and put out the light. He was in shock, nothing more. They figured he was a bourgeois who was not used to taking a full round in the gut. After a beating like his, New York dealers were still capable of climbing an entire fire escape faster than the entire Harlem squad! In the living room where they fixed themselves a drink, Smith and Dubois noticed the tri-color card which Yebga had left near the typewriter.

"Shit, Gravedigger, you think 'Presse' is like 'Press'?"

"In any case, this photo's of our little patient."

"How about that! We've always had reporter's on our tail and now we've got one at our feet. This almost makes it worth crossing the pond."

They settled into armchairs, pushed their hats back on their heads and left a night light burning.

The ringing of the telephone woke them up.

"Allo?"

Smith had taken pains to pronounce the word French style. A woman's voice was already apologizing.

"I'm sorry. I must have dialed the wrong number."

"No!" barked Smith in English. "Don't hang up, please. I don't speak French well. Speak slowly."

"But who are you?" asked the voice in English. "I would like to speak to Amos. Amos Yebga. This is his girlfriend."

Smith recognized the voice of a white woman, possibly East coast judging from the accent, anyway a snob.

"Thank God we understand each other. I'm here with my friend because we've just brought your man home. You see, he got himself a little worked over down in the street. Me and my buddy here, we thought he'd prefer to wake up in his own crib rather than at the police station or the hospital. Don't you agree?"

"What's happened to him? Is he hurt?"

"He's still in shock, but he's asleep right now."

"Did they break anything? What kind of cuts does he have? Has he lost much blood? Has he seen a doctor? Why won't you let me talk to him?"

"Listen, little lady. We're not doctors, but we've taken care of everything. The brother is sleeping, and tomorrow when he wakes up, he'll have a little headache, that's all. Nobody ever died from a couple of bruises."

"Don't move; I'll be right over."

Smith stood stupefied for a moment in front of the telephone before hanging up.

"Who was it?" inquired Dubois, without opening his eyes.

"The guy's old lady. Sounds like he's got himself a white chick, an American. If you want my opinion, he must have been a lot more dashing when he picked her up than he was tonight."

Smith returned to his chair bursting with laughter and pulled his hat down over his eyes. From time to time, one or the other went to see how Yebga was doing. Although he had trouble breathing through his swollen nose, he was hardly moaning now. Smith and Dubois were just about to drift off to sleep when they heard the key turning in the lock. Smith jumped to the lamp and turned it off while Jones rolled behind the sofa. A bright light flooded the apartment and they saw a young blond woman dash across the living room and hurry into the bedroom where they had put Yebga to bed. They sighed. False alarm. The young woman reappeared after a short instant. She made a slight backward movement upon discovering the two big men standing in the middle of the room.

"Was it you then on the phone? Are you the ones who helped Amos?" she said, taking hold of herself.

"We couldn't leave a brother sprawled out in the street," grumbled Dubois.

Faye was silent for several seconds. For once, Amos had been lucky to be Cameroonian. Who knows what these two would have done to him if he had been white? The two men sized up the young woman with their customary insolence and mistrust.

"Are you from New York City?" she asked.

"Harlem."

She would have bet on it. That accent peculiar to blacks from over there, that way of carrying themselves, of saying "brother" when speaking about another black man, that way of looking at her like a piece of luxury merchandise, with a mixture of lust and disgust. The memory of the three weeks she had spent near Lennox Avenue came back to her. It was a very bad memory.

"How did this happen?"

Smith recounted the trip to Montmartre, the walk down Rue Lepic, the Mercedes with its lights off, the four guys, the fight, the taxi. He built up the high points, dramatizing them, and didn't breathe a word of the dead henchman who was probably still propped up against the staircase.

"Thank God you kept your cool," sighed Faye.

"You know," Dubois said modestly, "we've seen this kind

of thing before. Like old Himes said, 'If hard punches were money, both of us would've been millionaires a long time ago.' Isn't that right, Ed?"

Faye smiled. She made some coffee, changed Yebga's bandages and returned to the living room to keep the two men company.

"His wounds are superficial," she announced with a practiced air. "They'll heal fast enough. You did just the right thing."

She was answered with snickerings of "Thank you, Professor," "Thank you, Colonel," and "Do you think he'll still be useful?" "Have you checked the mechanism and the rear axle?"

Neither Ed Smith nor Jones Dubois were in the habit of chatting with a white woman in a decent living room. They improvised the technique while hiding their seriousness.

"We're experts in this kind of thing," said Dubois. "Harlem is a rough school. Isn't that right, Ed?"

"Yeah. And if we told you about a quarter of what we've done back there, you'd think we were just pouring on the sauce. Besides, since your old man's a reporter, he must know us."

Faye answered yes, surely, with a smile, and that anyway she would prefer not to know everything. Then she went to check on Yebga again. She returned five minutes later.

"Well, I think he's really asleep now. I closed the door so our voices won't disturb him."

Dubois scratched his head, hesitated, then said, "Don't you have any idea who could've done this to him?"

Faye looked at the two men in turn and decided to trust them. After all, they had earned that much.

"Amos is investigating the death of a young Senegalese man. The police have concluded it was an accident, but Amos doesn't believe it. You might imagine certain people might feel threatened by Amos' investigation."

"We thought maybe it was one of those mix-ups over a piece of ass," Smith joked, leaving it at that.

"A man might do anything for a beautiful woman like you."

But only Dubois' laughter echoed Smith's. Jones stood up and buckled the belt of his trenchcoat.

"Are you sure you can't wait a little longer? I know Amos would like to thank you personally."

Faye's eyes were red from lack of sleep.

"No, baby. Sorry, but we got a plane to catch."

The woman insisted that they take Yebga's phone number and address just in case. Then she escorted them to the elevator, a wan smile on her face. In the hall, Dubois bantered.

"You know, as soon as you do these white folks a favor, they'll forgive you for anything. They're all the same."

They took a taxi back to the Rue du Vieux-Colombier. As they were pulling up in front of the hotel, they saw a familiar silhouette climbing into a big light sedan. They ran over to it, eyes wide, then looked at each other, dumbfounded. How could they forget the face of this handsome black man of indeterminate age whose temples had just begun to turn gray? Smith even had a photograph of him in his bathroom! The car was already driving away.

"Do you realize that we had to come all the way to Paris to see him? It's like we're in the middle of New York. Americans are everywhere."

"It's a small world, my man," said Smith philosphically.

The American car disappeared into the Rue de Rennes, carrying off in the rapidity of its eight cylinders the legendary figure of Don Knight.

Chapter Nineteen

Jeannette waited for Yebga until midnight, then she went to bed. She still wondered the next morning why Youssouf N'Dyaye had insisted that she invite the reporter to her place. Did he suspect what had happened between them? Perversity was not his usual cup of tea. What did he expect to get out of it? She packed her bags, wondering why the Cameroonian had stood her up, yet this had not displeased her.

He was cute and very much her type. She looked at her watch. There were still four hours before her plane left. Even if he did show up now, for her it was too late. Even a sentimentalist cannot take pleasure in furtive kisses when it isn't clear what they are about. Heart or work? After showering, Jeannette collected all of Malika's souvenirs and made up a package. These objects reminded her too much of what her life had been before, her life with Malika. And since this idiot reporter (perhaps an obstinate lover?) seemed more interested in that whore than in herself, it seemed better not to be there anymore, serving as an intermediary.

She walked to the post office on the Place des Abbesses. On her way home, Jeannette marvelled at the transparency of the late autumn daybreak. She took in the old stones around her, the paved road, the small bakery squeezed between the butcher shop and the hardware store, then closed her eyes. She saturated herself with this landscape, relishing the fact that in a few short hours she would be in New York modeling a new collection, adding dollars to her bank account.

Finding a cousin you hadn't seen in ten years was not really a problem for an African in Paris. The only inconvenience those people posed was that, for the most part, they were always wallowing in trouble. For some, it was a matter of unpaid rent, of landladies who had run out of patience, or late school registrations; for others it was that the telephone had been turned off, or the burden of housing distant relations who planned to visit the capital one day. Others were free from domestic worries. Legimate addresses were offered them by friends, brothers, women or cousins. They simply showed up on the appointed doorsteps wearily dragging their odd, scant bits of luggage. The African population of Paris was divided into several distinct groups which nevertheless communicated with each other. There were secret and invisible ties between the lawyer and the Rasta, the musician and the poet, the businessman and the reporter. There was a sense of solidarity among them, a feeling that there were others they could count on, men who didn't try to back out on their exacting trust. In this fantastic world, the whites played their part too—at least the wives and daughters paid their share to "tropical decadence," for the pleasure of seeing a black in uniform smooth out their bedsheets.

Yebga, in the hollow of Faye's arms, could not stop thinking about the taboo subject. Dread Pol didn't fit into any category either. Sometime seducer, sometime businessman, sometime steady lover, sometime squatter and always musician, he knocked about from one "vocation" to the next with a facility which rendered him elusive.

Faye made up her mind to care for Yebga, and found in the confidences they shared on pillows scented with a pharmaceutical odor fair return for the eight days' vacation time she had arranged with difficulty. She forbade him to go out for at least forty-eight hours, and despite his protests, took full charge of his telephone calls, preparing meals and dictating the hour at which they put out the lights. She had her revenge and intended to savor it. She had Yebga to herself and it was he who had put himself in this situation.

Chapter Twenty

Dubois and Smith had two hours of restless sleep. Images of the dead man haunted them. Smith woke up first and knocked on his friend's door. He looked as if he'd gotten up on the wrong side of the bed. Dubois, still in his T-shirt, let Smith in and closed the door behind him.

"Are you O.K., Ed?"

Smith walked over to the window. He could see the traffic and the passersby in the Rue du Vieux-Colombier. He sighed and walked stiffly over to sit on the bed.

"I can't go home like this, Gravedigger. Not like this. . . ."

Dubois was leaning against the desk that stood in a corner by the bathroom. He deposited a look heavy with bitterness on his friend.

"We haven't even visited any French brothels yet," continued Smith in a tired voice.

Dubois switched on the bathroom light with a swift karate kick and finished dressing. Then he went over to sit by his friend.

"What do you want us to do, man? I know things didn't work out, but what do you expect us to do about it now? We should've been more careful and found some clever way to get out of this back home. That's that. What do we have to risk at this point, that someone's going to laugh at us? People will forget, you know."

"People never forget and you know it. Big John and that other idiot, Teddy, will carry it all the way to the grave."

There was a moment of heavy silence. The two men didn't dare look at each other. Cries, horns, wild shouts and other sounds of life reached them from the street below.

"We got to have something to tell them. We have to take something back, it's our only chance," said Dubois.

Smith stepped away from his companion and methodically began to empty his pockets. When Dubois noticed the forty-five, he got up and locked the door, then returned to the bed.

"These are that stiff's things," sighed Smith. "I know what we've got to do about this whole thing too. Well, no one could have seen us back there, so I think we're O.K."

He spread out the package of candy, the dirty handkerchief, the photograph of the little girl, the driver's license, the crumpled papers, an entire life against a single piece of metal, and the metal won. There was also a Belgian passport from which they learned the guy had been twenty-nine years old.

"It's awful," sighed Dubois.

"Maybe, but better him than me," said Smith philosophically.

He cautiously refolded the papers while his friend searched the wallet. He froze in front of a page torn from a small address book and tapped on Dubois' shoulder. A name and address were written on the paper: Alan

Coetzee, Room 311, Hôtel du Vieux-Colombier, Paris VIe.

"My God, that's our hotel," whistled Smith.

"This hotel? Where?" Dubois started in again.

Then everything happened very fast. The gun disappeared into Smith's pocket, the dead man's papers into the toilet bowl, and the two partners charged out into the hallway.

The young clerk at the desk committed the error of letting a few seconds pass before lifting his nose.

"Yes, gentlemen, what can I do for you?"

"We'd like to know if there's a Mr. Coetzee staying in this hotel," Smith carefully articulated. The veins in his neck were already standing out.

"I'll have to check the registration file," said the clerk in an affable voice, "but I don't have time right now."

"You're going to make time," insisted Dubois quietly.

The clerk glanced nervously from one man to the next. "But . . ."

The two hefty men's ironically benevolent attitude convinced him not to take a stupid risk for matters of principle. He began to consult his file cards. He thumbed through them once, then checked again. His nervousness contrasted more and more with the absolute immobility of Smith and Dubois. Just when everything seemed about to explode, he found it.

"Coetzee. Ah, here it is! Alan Coetzee. Room 311."

"Let's see his picture."

The little green eyes opened wide.

"Don't you have a piece of identification for this gentleman?" Dubois' scar began to turn dangerously red.

"No, no, I don't. Since the new regulations came into effect, the registration forms have changed. We don't keep the guest's identification."

"Look, man, we're not asking for your girlfriend's address or for a crash course in law, so don't be stupid. We're in a hurry!"

The clerk understood at once that it was better not to compromise the good relations painfully established by his first search through the file. He did not like the demented gleam of these four dark eyes. He searched in some other drawers and took out a passport which he handed to Dubois. The ex-cop took the object between his fingers. It was a South African passport, from which they learned that Coetzee was a bearded redhead who wore large glasses in tortoise-shell frames. The passport stated that he was forty-two years old, five feet, ten inches tall and a businessman by profession. Big business, if anything!

"Traveling salesman," muttered Dubois returning the passport. "Yeah, sure, right."

"Will that be all?" the clerk stammered out, trying to be curt.

"No, pal. One more thing. We want to surprise our friend. So it would be silly if he knew we'd asked about him. Get it?"

The man nodded. Dubois and Smith left the hotel. Smith posed the question which had been burning on his lips.

"What are we going to do?"

They walked toward the Rue de Rennes.

"We're going to buy our presents, and this afternoon we'll be on the plane for the States."

"But, we can't go home like this! It won't be long before those guys back home find out Himes kicked the bucket. And sooner or later the book's going to show up too! We'll be cooked, man. Do you realize that?"

"Think for a second, Ed. We don't know anybody in this damn country. We go out to chase the whores, and we find ourselves with a stiff on our hands and a forty-five in our pocket. It's not our beat, man. This thing's none of our business. We're going to send word to the kid we saved and tell him what we know. After that, he can deal with it. It's none of our business."

Dubois was almost shouting, as if to convince himself. Smith said, "Whatever you want," and they killed their morning buying knick-knacks.

Around noon they headed back to the hotel. They asked the desk clerk to total up their bill and to call them a taxi for Roissy in an hour. They clambered up to their rooms, arms loaded with packages. Pushing open their respective doors, each let out an "Ah!" of stupor at the same instant: the suitcases scrupulously buckled had been turned over on the floor, clothes were lying everywhere, the mattresses were ripped open, the drawers emptied. They were overcome by a sudden uncontrollable, cold, deaf anger. Nothing had been spared, not even their family photos. Smith gathered the scattered pieces, one by one, of the only portrait he had of his wife, Edna. Dubois left him alone and began to put his own belongings in order. When they met up again in the lobby, half an hour later, they had on their Sunday best.

They ate lunch glancing inquisitively all around. They did honor to the succeeding courses without paying any mind to the blatant curiosity of the other guests. They gulped down their steaming coffee and stood up. Their baggage was waiting in the lobby. Dubois spotted the little desk clerk and walked toward him with a slow and steady gait. The clerk blushed like a peony from his chin to the roots of his hair. The ex-cop did not utter a word. He motioned to the man with his finger as if he were going to whisper a secret into his ear. The clerk stood docilely on tiptoe, behind the counter. A resonating slap sent him colliding into the metal filing cabinet. Then he remained kneeling, head between hands, silent. No one had noticed a thing. Ed Smith and Jones Dubois loaded up their bags and got into the waiting taxi, parked along the sidewalk.

"Roissy?" asked the driver.

"No, we just want to get to another hotel."

"Comment?"

"Hotel. Another."

The driver soon understood what they were talking about, but he took them for a ride to add some time onto his meter before dropping them in front of a newly redone Greek style facade. It was like most of the neighborhood hotels one saw in Paris, not an establishment of any great standing. Dubois and Smith found it suitable enough. There were neither cockroaches nor bedbugs; the price of the room was a bargain. They booked two adjacent rooms. Dubois called his wife to say that he missed her and that the Eiffel Tower was only a scrap heap. Then he added that the chow was good, the streets were small and he would be home later than expected. He was glad to hear that the people back home were asking after them.

Settled in before a cup of coffee, in the small lobby of the Hôtel Delavigne, the two men decided to let a day go by before starting out on Coetzee's tail.

"We'll need some wheels," said Smith.

"We don't have time to rent a car, man. Besides, we have to start economizing."

"But I know someone who can fix it up for us.

"Allo?"

It was Faye's voice.

"Good evening. This is Ed Smith. The guy who helped your husband."

"Ah! Hello. You haven't left?"

"Something came up at the last minute. We're going to stay in Paris for a few days. We need some wheels. We were sort of hoping to borrow yours."

Faye put a hand over the phone and looked at Yebga.

"It's the two guys who helped you. They want to borrow my car. This is really crazy, you know."

"So what?"

"I can't lend them my car just like that. We don't even know them. We don't know who they are or what they're going to do with it."

"Are you afraid they're the murderers?"

"Of course not, but . . ."

"So? What's the problem? Are you more afraid for your shitty Austin than for me? If they wreck it, I'll pay for the repairs. My poor darling."

Faye turned her back to Yebga.

"Are you still there?"

"Still," laughed Smith.

"Sorry, I had something on the stove. When would you need it?"

"First thing tomorrow morning."

"How should we do this? Do you want to drop by and pick it up?"

"It would be better if you came here. Do you have something to write with?"

Smith gave the Hôtel Delavigne's address to a furious Faye.

"Be there at eight o'clock sharp. Thanks, baby."

Faye said yes, she would be there. She hung up the telephone and was angry with herself for having been pushed into this. They had a lot of nerve, those brutes! She turned her indignation against Yebga, who had taken their side.

The next day, precisely at eight o'clock, a red Mini parked in front of the Hôtel Delavigne and Faye stepped out of it. Her features were distorted with restrained anger. The two ex-cops were seated in the lobby, waiting for her.

"Is that your machine?" asked Dubois, with a touch of surprise, after they had all gone outside.

"Yes. Sorry I didn't have time to trade it in for something better." Faye gritted her teeth and stalked off, snapping her purse shut.

With empty stomachs and stiff to the bone, they waited all morning, curled up on the seat, immobile, in front of the Hôtel du Vieux-Colombier, only looking up when a taxi or car drove up to the entrance. This was not their first stake-out. They were terribly relieved when the nth taxi pulled up and the man from the photograph stepped into it. It was just past noon. There was no doubt. His beard was glaring like the hindquarters of a she-monkey in heat, and his thick glasses were in attendance too.

Smith quietly started the engine. Shadowing was their speciality, but they didn't feel at home in the twisting and congested Paris streets. The taxi turned into the Rue de Rennes, heading toward the quay that it followed along the Seine.

Just before the salmon-pink tower of the Hôtel Nikko, the taxi signaled. Smith was still on its tail. When the taxi stopped in front of the hotel entrance, the Mini continued on several feet before stopping in the parking lot. In his rear-view mirror, Smith watched Coetzee study the surroundings before going into the hotel. As soon as Coetzee had disappeared, Dubois rushed in after him, in time to see him sit down at the bar. He was framed by two men. Smith tried to engrave their faces in his memory. One was a very elegant black man, undoubtedly an African. He had short hair and wore glasses with fine gold frames and a black suit. The other man was white. He was as much a brunet as Coetzee was a redhead. Jones eyed them hastily, not wanting to risk being seen. Then he rejoined Smith, who was hanging around the car looking like a lost dog.

"Well?"

"There are two of them. One looked Puerto Rican and the other like a black diplomat."

Jones took a whiskey flask out of his inside jacket pocket and offered it to Smith.

"Here. Let's get some use out of this thing. It'll warm you up."

Standing still and waiting had chilled them to the bone. At the end of a long half-hour, Coetzee and the dark-haired man left the hotel.

"You see those sharpies? That's them," said Jones.

Smith switched on the engine and posted himself near the parking lot exit. As soon as the BMW had slid out onto the Quai de Grenelle, Smith put the car into gear and followed it.

Muttering insults, Dubois happened to notice that the numbers on the green plate preceded the letters *CD*, for *Corps Diplomatique*. Apparently suspecting nothing, the diplomats crossed the Seine in the direction of the radio station. Soon they picked up a young black girl who had been posted on the sidewalk. From there, they returned to Saint-Germaine-des-Prés, where they made several short stops. Dubois carefully jotted down the street names and the times. Jammed in the tiny Mini, it was all he could do. Finally the BMW dropped the young girl off in front of 7 Rue du Cherche-Midi.

"Pretty girl," grumbled Smith, "but what are we going to do now?"

"You keep following them, I'll stay here and try to get something out of the chick. We'll meet back at the hotel."

With his ungainly walk, Dubois entered the building. A glass door opened on to a courtyard planted with trees. He walked through it. There was a marble plaque nailed onto the wall. Dubois was trying to figure out what "Ateliers de

Confection Marco Paladio" might mean, when a shrill voice interrupted his thoughts.

"The public is not permitted to visit the workshops, sir."

"I don't speak French," Jones retorted, turning around so briskly that the other started.

"Do you have an appointment?" replied the other in an English derived from the coast around Lagos.

"There's a young woman who just came in here. I have to talk to her. I have something important to tell her."

With a mocking smile, the Cerberus quickly changed his tone.

"There are a bloody lot of chicks who come in here, big boy. You'd need a lot of patience to find yours. Anyway, they're all about the same, don't you think, handsome stranger?"

Dubois placed his hand on the man's shoulder and squeezed, pushing his fingers behind the clavicle.

"I'm not here to joke around, man. Don't keep me hanging around, or else . . ."

"Don't get mad, papa," the other apologized with a forced smile. "It was just a joke. I'll go find her for you. Let go of me, I'm going."

Dubois was looking around the courtyard with his hands in his pockets, when the door opened again. The young woman was there, warily sizing him up.

"You wanted to see me?"

Her eyes shone with curiosity on seeing the infinite sartorial resources of the detective. She spoke a very pure, fluent English which was slightly affected. Dubois gave the young man a menacing look and then led the model down the courtyard.

"It'll be better to talk here," he began. "Aren't you cold, beautiful?"

The young woman shook her head.

"Don't be afraid. I won't hurt you. What's your name?"

"Sidonie."

He jotted in his notebook.

"Well, Sidonie, I won't beat around the bush. I'm a cop from Interpol. I'm currently working on a case, and the man who drove you here seems to be involved in it. So I want you to be straight with me."

Dubois held his old plastic badge case open in his palm, but Sidonie seemed not to notice.

"Jorge?"

"If he's the guy who drove you here in a gray BMW, then that's the one. Now, I would really like to know who he is, what he's doing in France and what he does with his free time."

Chapter Twenty-One

Yebga waited for some time before sending Faye out to the Sunny Kingston for some news. The more that time passed, the more essential it became to find Dread Pol.

To those practiced sweet-talkers who frequented the Sunny Kingston, a white woman, alone and pretty too, throwing herself into the wolf's jaws, was a godsend. Yebga had recommended that Faye rely on Myriam, the waitress. Faye did not have to wait long. The mulatto was already making her way over between the chairs. She was wearing a long, fluffy, turquoise pullover.

"Good evening. What'll it be?"

Myriam managed to make it known when she was not in an amiable mood.

"Aren't you Myriam? Don't you remember me from the other night?"

"Yeah. So what?"

The bursts of voices, the laughter, the noises of chairs being pulled and tables pushed muffled their conversation.

"What are you doing out without your man?"

"He was attacked on the street two days ago. Didn't you know? He must've told you."

"And how is he?" asked Myriam dryly.

"Not too well," Faye lied. "That's why he sent me here. He wants to find this man named Dread Pol. He's really counting on your help."

Myriam appeared to be thinking for an instant. At

neighboring tables, customers were calling out her name, clamoring for drinks. She glanced once more at the blond hair, the light eyes, the long and angular face and the pale mouth without lipstick.

"Wait," she said. "I'll be right back."

Faye smiled. Myriam had been troubled too. Faye admired the ease with which the waitress slid her supple body between the tables, picking up the empty glasses, the way she put the customers back in their places and was indifferent to their compliments. Myriam flaunted her African figure, offered and at the same time out of reach, with an ease which fascinated the American. In a flash, she thought of Yebga and of herself. She had an inexplicable sensation, barely perceptible. It was pleasant and disturbing, like a caress deep in her chest. She was afraid and didn't even want to know why.

Myriam lingered beside a customer wearing a cap and dark glasses. He seemed to be a regular. Faye saw them talking in low voices, then turned away as they looked in her direction.

"This is Massa Soya," said a voice. It was Myriam.

Faye jumped. An oily skinned man with a false smile bordered with a slight mustache was leaning toward her. She gave him her hand with a restrained pout. Myriam savored this moment, thinking: This one didn't know that when you take one black, you take them all.

"So," said Massa Soya in a slightly husky voice. "I hear you're looking for Dread Pol."

Between his teeth, reddened by chewing too much cola nut, a matchstick bobbed with each syllable.

"Yes," answered Faye with conviction.

Massa Soya burst out in laughter and drew up a chair.

"What could you possibly want from that lunatic? He's crazy, you know. If you're looking to score, ask me. You can trust me."

"Cut the crap," Myriam broke in. "You're going to make her puke. She's Yebga's girlfriend."

The other went on calmly, "Dread Pol should be here later. But if it's something urgent, I know where to find him."

"She'll wait here," Myriam cut in again. "You said he was coming, didn't you?"

Faye sat turned toward the door rather than meet the gaze of Massa Soya. To begin with, she couldn't stand his smoked glasses. And then that mouth, a mouth full of . . .

"Dread Pol just pulled in," somebody cried.

Myriam and Massa Soya turned their heads at the same time while Faye's eyes grew wide.

She had not seen the small man with a jovial face come in. He was clothed in a slovenly manner with abundant layers of fabric. He had an unkempt beard and was wearing a shoulder bag. Thin braids of black hair poked out from under a green, yellow and red cap and the incessant movements of his head made them wriggle like serpents.

Dread Pol greeted the onlookers like a boxer after a victory. A visionary's smile flitted across his lips. Massa Soya pointed him out.

"That maniac, he's still loaded up on ganja. If you're looking to score, I think you'll have to come back later."

"Come over here, Dread," shouted Myriam, and the Rasta instantly plunged toward their table.

"Hi, sister. May Jah protect you," he said, flopping into a chair.

"Hello, Dread Pol. This is Faye."

"Babylon is everywhere around us. These people spend their life lying to us. To us, the chosen ones. But soon we will be through with all this shit. The prophet said, 'We don't need no more trouble.'"

"She wants to talk to you about Salif."

A gleam of intelligence flashed in Dread Pol's tired eyes. He looked at Faye.

"Babylon kills. Babylon always kills. But these times will soon be over. The prophet said, 'How long shall they kill our prophets while we stand aside and look?' I say, no more ever. I swore on my brother's grave. A new day is dawning. The soldiers of the revolution are on the march."

"You're more full of shit every day, Dread," scoffed Massa Soya. "You should give up this trash and take the cure."

"Listen to me, Dread," begged Myriam. Faye is here to

101

help us find Salif's murderer. You've got to tell her everything you know."

"They are lying to us. They always lie to us. How long are
you going to let yourself be fooled, sister? I speak for you because I love you. It is time to sweep away the old days. You
mustn't trust their word any more. Their word is a lie. Look
what their racist politicians are doing today. They're all the
same. They've always lied to us. They've always betrayed
our trust. They've made slaves of us, sister."

Faye spoke. Paradoxically, Dread Pol's presence relieved
her.

"Perhaps I am from Babylon, as you say, but I was sent
here by one of your brothers. You trusted him once. And
Salif trusted him too. He couldn't come himself because he
was attacked last night by one of your common enemies."

Dread Pol looked at her distrustfully.

"You're Yebga's woman?"

"Well . . . yes."

"Pay for my drink and lead me to your man's place. I
can't bear serious discussions with a woman unless she's
black and old enough to be my mother!"

He snapped his fingers, keeping time to a music which
only he could hear.

"Come on. Let's go. You pay for the taxi."

A half-hour later they were in front of Yebga, who was
still lying on the sofa with a wet towel on his forehead.
Dread Pol, who had only opened his lips to hum an endless
Bob Marley song, stepped cautiously into the apartment.

"This place is big," he whistled.

Yebga stood up. He kissed Faye, shook Dread Pol's
hand. Except for a few wounds on his face and several
bruises, his condition had clearly improved. His lips appeared normal again and his back was hardly hurting him
anymore.

"Thanks for coming."

"Why don't you hug me, man? We are brothers. We all
come from the same cradle. The cradle of the world."

Yebga looked at Faye out of the corner of his eye. She
shrugged her shoulders, smiling, then disappeared into the
bedroom.

"Sorry," said the reporter to the Rasta.

"Don't apologize. It doesn't mean anything. You're not guilty. Get me something to drink instead."

"Sure. I have black tea, herb tea, fruit juices . . ."

"Do you think my mama's still nursing me?"

"No, but Rastas, the pure ones, don't drink alcohol. . . ."

"Who told you that crap? Alcohol is the blood of Jah. It's the fluid of life."

Yebga went over to the bar and filled two glasses. Dread Pol dropped into an armchair and laboriously began to roll an enormous joint. The journalist watched him and sipped his whiskey. When the operation was finished, Dread Pol blew smoke up toward the ceiling with relish.

"What do you want to know, man?" he said in a thick voice. "Are they the ones who beat you up like this? It was a warning. If you don't watch your ass, you'll end up like Salif. That's the way they work. That was just a taste of what they can do. They bumped off Salif without giving him a chance. Not the slightest chance, man."

"Who's they?"

"The money men, man. The devil's envoys. Babylon's thugs. They don't like to be crossed. Salif knew about their scheme. Their judgment day will come. I wouldn't give a penny for their white asses."

"Did he tell you what they were up to?"

"No, he didn't really know anything. But he knew they were up to something. See, that guy told me everything. He was my bro. Him and me, we were like fingers on a hand."

"Why do you think they killed him?"

"Because of Malika. He claimed that N'Dyaye had her snuffed out. He even went to accuse him one day. A few days later, there was this accident. Now our own brothers shoot us in the back. You see the shitty world we're living in? You see what Babylon has done to us?"

Dread began puffing on his joint, his eyes closed. Yebga was silent for a minute.

"So do you think N'Dyaye's the one who organized the accident?"

Dread Pol kept his eyes closed.

"No. He's too stupid. Those blacks who act like white

guys are too stupid. He was probably happy to sell Salif, like Judas, for some bread."

A long silence settled in, broken now and then by Dread Pol drumming his fingers on the armrest. Yebga mentally recapitulated all of the variables. Suddenly he remembered Jeannette. He had been on the way to her place when he was attacked. The reporter had a sudden hunch. He jumped up and grabbed the telephone. By this time Dread Pol had launched into an endless monologue.

"What must be created is a republic without money. A republic ruled by love and respect. I'll even give you a cabinet post if you want one, on the condition that you let your hair grow. . . ."

Yebga picked up the receiver and dialed Malika's number. He got an answering machine. Jeannette had left on a trip for several weeks. Faye came into the room and noticed her companion's worried look.

"What's wrong?"

"I'm worried about Jeannette, the girl who lived with Salif's sister. I hope nothing's happened to her."

Dread Pol carried on, surrounded by a thick cloud of smoke.

"No cars. No dishwashers. No pants for women. If Jah created women, it was to wear native cloths, to show her legs, to be man's greatest pleasure."

"Your pal's starting to get on my nerves," muttered Faye.

"He's a chosen one," said Yebga. "He's untouchable."

Faye suddenly wondered if he was kidding.

Chapter Twenty-Two

Dubois looked at his watch. He had been sitting for an hour on the terrace of a cafe in the Place Saint-Sulpice, staring at the church and drinking beers.

The hips of passing women finally made him seasick. Sometimes he imagined himself at Himes' white house in Spain, sometimes beyond the ocean, in Harlem. He tried comparing Paris to New York, the people there with the people here. All these white men and women kissing black men and women caused him great discomfort. One day Malcolm X had said, "When you put a drop of milk in your coffee, the coffee becomes weaker." These Paris blacks reminded him of bad coffee. They were blind people who didn't realize that they were losers trying to screw the whites with their fast talk. They collected a few smiles, no doubt managed to pick up one or two of those girls who were hanging on their arm, but afterward they were left to drown in their shit.

In Harlem this old sly fox had learned to distrust anything that was white, like an unripe peach. The pastors, the politicians, the women . . . even the cops. He knew where everything belonged and this was good. In France there were too many white things offered to blacks. There were too many handshakes, kisses and shams. This whole damn scene appeared suspicious and disgusting to Dubois, who knew the truth. All these black people who roared with laughter, who fucked as often as they could . . . Dubois paid for his beers and stood up. Despite what had been drilled into him in Harlem about the bounty of French spirit, this all looked like troubled waters to him. He decided he would discuss this with his partner when the occasion presented itself. In the Rue Delavigne, the ex-cop smiled when he noticed the red Mini double-parked in the street. His friend had returned. Dubois found Smith in his room, stretched out on the bed.

"Hey, man, where'd you go?" asked Smith, without even moving his head.

"I was sipping a little beer in the square."

"That's a relief," said Smith, opening his mouth as if he were swallowing the world. For a moment I thought the chick wanted to make it with you."

They burst out laughing.

Smith's room was in every way identical to his companions. Except for the color of the upholstery and the bedspread, you wouldn't know whose room you were really in. Dubois pulled up a chair and sat down, resting his arms over the back. The bathroom door was ajar, and from where he sat, he noticed the mirror above the sink.

"Well? What'd you find out?"

"The guy's name is Jorge Gonzales. He's a commercial attaché to the Argentine embassy."

Dubois was silent.

"Is that it?" Smith was astonished. "It took you two hours for that? Damn, what'd you do, tell the sister your life story?"

"Well, what did you expect? Shit!"

There was a silence. Jones stared at the beige carpet, Ed at the ceiling.

"You know," Ed began, "I think even if these bastards hadn't come around to make trouble, we would've stayed here awhile anyway."

"What are you talking about?"

"I don't know. Something's bothering me. Sometimes I wonder if I wouldn't be better off just staying over here."

"But this is our only chance, Ed, and you know it."

"Yeah, I know," said Smith. Suddenly he stood up. "We'd better take the kid's car back."

Dubois rose and followed in his steps. Smith took out the forty-five, which he wore stuck behind him in his belt. He checked the clip. His companion shot him a questioning glance.

"You never know," said the ex-cop laconically, putting the weapon back in its place.

In the car, Jones recounted in detail his interrogation of Sidonie, the Marco Paladio model.

"There are some incredibly well shaped sisters in this sector, buddy. But I don't like them looking at me like I was their father. The kid didn't know much. The only interesting thing she came up with was that she had a date tonight with our man in a nightclub called the Day and Night."

"And how do you expect us to find the place?"

"The kid they beat up must know."

It took them close to an hour to reach the Boulevard Voltaire.

Faye's face lit up when she saw them on the doormat.

"Hello. Well, come in."

They removed their hats in unison.

"We're here with the limousine," Jones said.

Faye smiled, relieved. In the living room, Yebga was still engaged in his discussion with Dread Pol. When he saw the men, he stood.

"Let me introduce your saviors," said Faye with a little twist.

"I'm happy to be able to thank you," said the reporter, shaking the two men's hands. "Please sit down."

Smith and Jones settled in, barely hiding their embarassment. They looked around the room again. They were counting on Yebga to begin the conversation.

"Then you didn't leave for the United States?" he asked.

"No," answered Jones in his low voice. "We still have a few things to see. It looks like they're after us too."

Yebga pursed his lips. Suddenly Dread Pol grabbed him by the sleeve.

"Why are you talking to them in English?" he stammered.

"They're Americans."

Dread Pol exploded.

"You don't understand anything, man. You talk like Babylon. Have you forgotten who you are? Don't let them throw powder in your eyes or you'll end up like our fathers' fathers!"

He jumped from one leg to the other as if to punctuate the words leaving his mouth.

"Old pirates, yes, they robbed I, sold I to the merchant ship, minute after they took I from the bottomless pit," sang the Rasta. "There are no black Americans," he continued in his strange sounding English. "We blacks only have one land, one nationality. We are Africans. I, you, us, every fucking nigger on the earth!"

Touching a switch, Faye suddenly lit up the room. Yebga smiled, made as though to open his mouth. Smith rose with a contorted face and turned to Dread Pol. He had not put his glass down.

"We are Americans, pal. Whether you like it or not, and there's a good chance that our fathers' fathers were sold into slavery centuries ago by your fathers' fathers. Since then we've fought every damn God-given day to attain the rank of human being. Now we're almost at the end of the tunnel. We have mayors in big cities. We pay our taxes, but we've never kissed the white man's ass, little brother. We've earned the right to be bent on war like any other jerk, and we like it that way. Africa let us down, brother. Don't ever forget that. Ever."

Dread Pol stared at him with round eyes like somebody who had just been told that, if you look closely, God exists. Not the God of Rastas, the God of everyman. Ed Smith was suffocating. The words had left his mouth in a furious torrent, uprooting everything as it passed, words of melted metal, words of concrete, words in the shape of old rusted-out cars and filthy scum, words whose meaning only the old inhabitants of "the bottom of the coal barrel," in Harlem, would have grasped. Dread Pol broke away from his drugged lethargy and let himself be carried off by the flood. The important thing was not to grasp the words, it was to be in the flow of it. The Rasta forgot his forced Cambridge English.

The old cop slammed his hand into his fist, which had its desired effect.

"Don't get mad, man," said the Rasta, suddenly mollified. "We're all brothers. That's what I was trying to say. Because there are some guys in this damn country who still don't get that. Calm down, man. Don't get angry."

He walked over to Smith and fell into his arms, crying.

"You're a little tall to be Bantu, but I'm sure your great-great-grandparents were."

Dubois scratched his head without a word. He observed with bright eyes this strange exchange between the men. He took his glass from the low table and emptied it in a single gulp.

"Do you know where the Day and Night is?"

"The nightclub?"

"Yes. I think that's it."

Yebga wondered what Jones could possibly have to do there. The nightclub's reputation could not have crossed the ocean, and the big cop didn't exactly have the "grotto" look.

"Do you want to go there?"

"Yes."

"I'll go with you. First let's eat something. I just received a package from my mother back home. I'm going to show you what Africa is really like."

With these words, Yebga disappeared into the kitchen, followed by Faye. While he was bustling about the refrigerator, she leaned against a cupboard with her arms crossed.

"You're not going to go out already?" she asked, in a voice so soft it was hardly audible.

"Why not?" he said without turning around. "I feel great. Do you want to come with us?"

"No. I have some work to catch up on. Besides, I don't really feel like it. I'll set the table."

When Faye entered the living room with a stack of plates, she found the three guests side by side holding each other by the arm, raising their right legs in the air.

"Can you believe they didn't even know who Bob Marley was!" laughed Dread Pol. "You want me to tell you what I think? These guys know the ropes but their education needs work."

The meal was lively. The ex-cops appreciated the French wine, and Yebga's cooking reminded them of Mama Dodge's, although less heavy.

At a quarter to midnight. Yebga suggested they leave for the Day and Night. Dread Pol decided to go along with them, to cast a spell, he said, referring to the club as a Satan's den. Faye didn't change her mind. The four men rushed down the steps of the apartment singing Zulu songs that Dread Pol had taught them during the meal. A little later the small troop rushed down the Rue des Lombards before lining up in front of the nightclub's iron door. A suspicious looking mulatto opened it.

"My brothers and I are here to have some fun," said Dread Pol, who had already started dancing as they approached the Satan's lair.

"Do you have a membership card?" asked the bouncer.

"A what card? No. Are you kidding? Since when do you have to have a card to get into this rat hole?"

The mulatto worked hard at keeping his cool. If Dread Pol had been alone, he would have hit him hard enough to make him spin full circle inside his baggy trousers, but the build of these two Malabars who were with him incited calm and good sense.

"Anyway, you're not dressed right. This is a high-class club."

"You call yourself classy?" Dread Pol fumed. "You're just a flunky, you know that? Do you think I don't know you? Do you think you'd be here if you weren't the boss's brother-in-law? We haven't lived in slavery for centuries and centuries to let some half-breed give us shit! Understand?"

Dread Pol drew up his small frame and looked the bouncer straight in the eye. He stood on his toes, shouted and raised his fist. Some rubberneckers slowed down, enticed by the propitious prospect of a black brawl in the middle of the street.

"What's going on?"

Yebga, who had gone back to the car to lock the doors, arrived out of breath. Smith and Dubois, deprived of their interpreter, had been prudently looking on.

"What's happening is that there are some guys who don't know their place."

The bouncer instantly recognized Yebga and appeared relieved.

"Ah, Mr. Yebga. Are these people with you?"

"Look how he's acting now, the jerk."

The bouncer made a threatening gesture in Dread Pol's direction, but a hand clasped his arm.

"Watch those hands, you bastard." Smith had stepped forward.

"Come on in," said the other, visibly reluctant.

Yebga went ahead of the little group. Since Smith and Dubois were so large, it was preferable to proceed single file to the stairway leading to the checkroom. The music was crashing in their ears.

The pale-complected woman from the Antilles who worked the coat-check reserved a somewhat cool welcome for them. Although the heat was stifling, Jones and Smith refused to part with their trenchcoats. The evening was already well underway. Young women with muscular bodies and appetizing hips were executing their number on the dance floor in front of mirrors. They were encouraged by a double circle of spectators of both sexes. For those seeking a little solitude, there were chairs over to the right, by the bar. As for the men, they all had "big bucks," meaning they were bankers, businessmen, diplomats or all of the above. There were practicing presidents among the owner's clientele, and the presence of this high society made him one of the best informed men on African affairs in the country. He was also the most discreet. As for the women, they were for the most part either high-class hookers, who added value to their benefactors, or candidates for this eminently privileged position. They weren't usually required to sleep with these men more than once a week because the men were so preoccupied with business.

Dubois and Smith made a tour of the club. Jorge Gonzales and Sidonie hadn't arrived yet. A waiter walked toward them smiling professionally, although he stared coldly at Dread Pol.

"Follow me, I'll show you to a table."

As he began leading them away from the exit, Smith stopped him. He wanted both to check the people entering and to reserve an easy access in case of a row. An emergency exit was located behind the bar. Smith pointed out a table in that direction.

"It's reserved, sir."

Yebga stepped forward.

"I don't think Samba would be too upset, Ismaël."

Just as Yebga spoke, Samba materialized at their sides, as if he had been summoned. He had stepped through the door of his office, which was probably fitted with a false mirror.

"Is something the matter?"

He raised his eyes to the reporter.

"Yebga! My boy! What are you doing here? It's been ages since I've seen you!"

He embraced the young man. The waiters came and went in the shadows, striped by multicolored beams. The soul music was replaced by salsa.

"I came with some American friends who are visiting Paris," said Yebga.

He introduced Jones, Smith and then Dread Pol.

"These are just the kind of bouncers I need," guffawed Samba. "They're welcome here!"

Samba called a waiter over and soon he returned with an ice-bucket and champagne glasses. Samba uncorked the bottle, filled the glasses and instantly stood up. A man had just walked past their table.

"Drink to my health and excuse me. I have to make time for everyone."

Smith and Jones recognized the man Samba was now holding by the arm. It was the man they had seen with Coetzee, the man they had followed and whom they wanted to interrogate: Jorge Gonzales. He was alone. Smith walked over to Yebga.

"You seem to know the boss well."

"Yes. A few years ago I found him a lawyer who got him out of a racketeering charge he had nothing to do with."

"And the man he went into the corner with?"

"No. But all I have to do is ask Samba when he comes back."

They quietly began to drink their champagne. Yebga took out a pack of Davidoffs and offered them around. Jones stood up.

"I'm going out on the dance floor to stretch my legs."

Through the speakers, James Brown yelled like a lunatic about his black pride. Dubois made his way over to the small dance floor, which was already occupied by all the queens-for-a-night. He turned his back to the big mirror, which gave an illusion of space, and gazed into the darkness of the room. After a few seconds, he distinctly made out Jorge Gonzales and Samba, who were talking earnestly. Jones forced himself to watch the two men, despite the diversion offered by the regular passing of black bottoms, firm and full as papayas, which he couldn't help reaching out to pat, provoking an even more exaggerated swaying as they escaped his clutches.

For their part, Yebga, Dread Pol and Smith lapped up the champagne. Each time a bottle was emptied, another appeared as if by magic.

"He's lost his touch, that old wreck," said Smith, standing up just as his friend was extending his hand toward a forbidden fruit.

Dread Pol had wandered onto the dance floor, shaking his hand in all directions. On his knees, then raising his half-closed eyes, he began singing the song of the prophet, "Exodus," by Rasta Bob Marley.

Yebga, staying alone with Smith, noticed things, schemes which Smith missed. He spotted a young man with a shaved head, wearing a long blue *boubou,* an emerald stuck in his ear.

"Hey, big chief, how's the painting?"

"And you, big reporter, how's the writing?"

Yebga only replied by pulling on the hand in his and whispering into the dandy's ear:

"Tell me. You're a regular here. You know everybody. Who's the guy talking to Samba? The white guy, over there, across the room?"

The other swelled up at this flattery.

"That's Jorge Gonzales. He's a commercial attaché to the Argentine embassy, but everybody knows he's got his hands in all kinds of traffic."

"Be specific, man. What kind of traffic?"

"Precious objects, weapons, bullfights, castanets and mantillas. He doesn't touch a thing himself. He's in the middle."

"What do you think he's up to with Samba?"

"You know Samba's in cahoots with all the important guys who hang around Paris. They're the only assholes willing to be had in these kinds of rackets."

The painter waited for another compliment.

"You should drop by the *World* with some photos of your latest paintings," said Yebga. "We might be able to use some of them."

"Sure, my man, great. I even have some on me."

With the wave of a hand, Yebga signaled him to be quiet. Two men had just appeared in the doorway, posting themselves on either side of the door, hands behind them. They were big, with short hair and dressed in poorly cut suits. Their unpleasant air, a necessity in this line of work, was accentuated by their uneasiness at being assigned a job in a place like this.

113

Bambaras, Yebga thought to himself, surprised. They shoved aside a waiter who stopped in front of them as N'Dyaye made his appearance draped in white, a long cigarette holder between his fingers. He extended the long sleeves of his *djellaba* to greet a man who climbed the stairs toward him. N'Dyaye looked as if he were welcoming a friend on the steps of his own home. Then he walked across the room to greet Samba who had doubtless been alerted by the doorman. The owner of the Day and Night was flanked by Jorge Gonzales. The three men exchanged a few words, then, still preceded by their gorillas, turned around and went back toward the exit.

The music stopped long enough to let the men on the dance floor empty their glasses and the ladies to mop the sweat which streamed from their armpits or flowed between their breasts, with Hermès scarves knotted to the straps of their crocodile purses. Dread Pol leaned against Dubois' shoulders the way a person leans against the back of a chair.

"Who's the guy who left with his holster boys and the Argentine?" asked Jones.

Yebga was in a daze. He mechanically answered:

"Youssouf N'Dyaye."

"N'Dyaye?"

Dread Pol jumped up.

"That bastard's here. Where is that son of a bitch?"

"He just left," mused Yebga in a loud voice.

At these words, Dread Pol hurried toward the stairs like a lunatic, not leaving anyone time to react.

"What's wrong with him?" worried Smith. "Is he crazy or something?"

Yebga did not answer. He was staring at the spot left empty by the Rasta. Then he stood up.

"We'd better go see what's happening upstairs. I feel a little nervous." They rushed to the stairs together. A few seconds later, after they had emerged into the open air, two gunshots rang out up the street toward the Boulevard Sébastopol.

A few strides later, they were standing over the body. Dread Pol's eyes were half-closed. Blood stained his layers of multicolored clothing. They were now useless shreds in the middle of his chest.

"Go call a doctor," Yebga said in French, turning around to Dubois who stood behind, bewildered.

He held the Rasta by the neck, cradling his head.

"They got me in the heart. . . . They've turned us against ourselves and they don't even know it. . . . I'm going . . . This had to happen. I'm going to return to the promised land. . . . They'll have to pay. They'll have to pay for all their mistakes. . . . You hear . . . N'Dyaye . . . He was afraid . . . Take the passport . . . and Malika . . ."

The little man felt his chest nervously with the last of his strength. The blood reddened his thin fingers. He raised his hand to his mouth and avidly licked it.

"The passport is here," he said again. Then his body stiffened one last time and was still.

Yebga shook like a leaf, incapable of standing up again. He didn't know what to do with the convulsed face in the hollow of his arm. Dread Pol had died before his eyes. They had killed Salif. They had killed Dread Pol. They had killed their brothers. Then rage overtook him. It supplied him with the energy to cautiously set the dead man's head down on the handkerchief that Smith had spread out on the sidewalk. Dubois pushed them both away, took Dread Pol's childlike body in his arms, and guided by Samba, descended the steps of the Day and Night into the paneled office. The tiny room included a small round oak table, several chairs and a single bed, bordered by a large shelf that occupied one wall. Jones put Dread Pol on the bed, and there was a moment of silence while each one meditated in front of the dead man. Samba stared as if prey to hallucinations.

"How did this happen?" he finally asked.

"I don't know," answered Yebga, depressed. "But I swear to you that the guy who fired the shot wasn't planning on sending him to paradise."

Smith and Jones slipped out of the office and returned to the open air. They spotted the bouncer amid a small group, stationed at the door of the establishment.

"Hey, mister," called Smith, motioning him over with his finger.

The bouncer left the gawking circle. In the confusion and excitement of the first rumors, no one saw the two American's trenchcoats open up or heard the thud of their first blows. The bouncer sagged in a whimper, but before his legs were doubled up under him, Smith and Jones had seized him by the armpits. They pushed him down the stairs, and with a last shove, threw him face down into Samba's carpeted office.

Everyone stepped back.

"What's going on?" cried Yebga.

"Nothing. To make them open their mouth, first you have to shut their trap," Smith grimaced, speaking to his partner.

"He never would've talked," he added to Yebga in an apologetic tone. "We know these kind of punks. Now he's ripe."

The reporter sighed. All this was turning into a nightmare, a bad film noir. Besides, not since leaving Yaoundé for journalism school on the Rue du Louvre had he ever felt the sensation of being locked in a ghetto like this. Ah, the embroilments of these blacks! And now it was the sound and the fury, crimes and violence! He felt sure he was going to go crazy.

"Ask him what he saw," Dubois resumed. "If he lies, we'll know."

They put the man in a swivel chair. Yebga walked slowly over to him. In the Americans' eyes a strange light shone, nourished by anger and satisfaction, as if they were finally in their element.

"I swear I didn't see a thing," stammered the bouncer. "Tell these two nuts your pal left running and yelling at Monsieur N'Dyaye and Monsieur Gonzales. He ran past me like a lunatic."

"Who fired?"

"I told you. I didn't see anything."

Before Yebga could intervene, Samba slapped his employee's face so hard it turned around. Then he slapped him vigorously again.

"You're going to tell us what you know, bastard," he

hissed with anger. Someone's been murdered. I don't want things like this happening at my place."

The bouncer began to tremble like a lagoon shivering under a breeze. He yelped.

"I don't know, I swear. I don't know a thing!"

Smith and Dubois took no further interest in the interrogation. They obviously intended to have Yebga translate it later for them. They methodically began searching the dead man. Because of his strange outfit, this was not so simple. A few minutes later, Smith drew a packet soaked with blood from the inside pocket of the Rasta's loose jacket. He handed it to Yebga but Samba grabbed it first.

"It may incriminate his family."

Samba always thought first about the family. For the twenty years or so he had scoured Paris, this notion remained deeply anchored in him. The family! He was sure Dread Pol carried drugs and that his family would not be happy to find out about it. Samba didn't have time to open the packet. Someone knocked.

"Open up! Police!"

Samba immediately let the packet slip into Yebga's hands. There was hardly time for Yebga to hide it in his jacket before the cops began to invade the room. There were three of them plus a photographer, who made an incalculable number of exposures. Lost in their notes, they asked several routine questions about the victim's name, age and address. The biggest of them was a blond man whose cheeks were reddened from drinking too much *pastis*. He was bundled up in his blue uniform and said that it was stupid to die like this. Another, a tall mustachioed brunet with short hair, asked Samba if the place was opened to whites, or strictly reserved for blacks.

"Because I really like your music, only I never know where to go. . . ."

Samba, amiable without excess, invited him to come there whenever he might like. He would be welcome.

"Gentlemen, if you don't mind," the chief cut in, "as witnesses, I want you at the station. Let's go," he said, herding everybody into the stairwell.

117

On the sidewalk of the Boulevard de Sébastopol, a group of curious bystanders were forming a mob around the pool of blood. With their tired looking faces and darkly circled eyes, these blacks were enough to worry the coolest night owl. At the police station in Halles, the witnesses' depositions were taken down in the police officer's report. Yebga interpreted for Smith and Dubois.

The daylight was already staining the Place des Innocents when they were released. They all felt a little sick, like the day after a drinking bout. In silence they returned to the Rue des Lombards, where Samba was waiting for them. The club was now deserted. The light, white and dense, lit up the smallest nooks of the smoky cellar. The waiters, sleeves rolled up and collars opened, were armed with napkins and trays. They were going from table to table, cleaning up the puddles of alcohol, collecting glasses, emptying ashtrays.

"That's enough for this morning," Samba quietly told them. "Go home. You'll finish up later."

Then turning to Yebga, "Did he have family here?"

"I don't think so," said Yebga hoarsely. "I don't know."

"This can't happen here," sighed Samba. "You'll never make me swallow this kind of killing."

Smith and Jones felt out of place in the empty club with men they didn't understand. They had no control over this affair. They were not the sort of men who would be content to follow behind the action especially when it involved a murder. Smith decided to take charge. He elbowed Yebga.

"Do you know where the guy Dread was following lives?"

The reporter turned and gave him a blank look. A picture of the treatment they had inflicted on the doorman came back to him. If N'Dyaye had to be pounced on, he wouldn't be the last one, Yebga thought. He translated the question for Samba. The latter appeared confused. He stopped pacing for a moment and leaned against the bar.

"You think N'Dyaye's the one who did it?"

"If not, he has some explaining to do."

Samba stared at the two big men seated next to Yebga.

118

"Number 102, Rue de Charenton, tower B, sixth floor, apartment 613. But . . . be careful!"

Chapter Twenty-Three

The car sped through the deserted streets, where the garbage collectors had begun their duty. A truck forced Yebga to slow down. The garbage men were all blacks except the driver. Yebga remembered a conversation once at the home of a friend in Paris. The man's twelve-year-old son had brought home a bad report card. "If you keep this up, you'll end up a garbage man," the father had threatened, watching for Yebga's agreement, as if the reporter were an expert on the topic. And Yebga, poor sucker, had agreed with his "white friend," not wanting to risk his own skin. The men in front of him were probably from Mali or Senegal. Back home, people thought they were rich, leading the good life in the luxury of the capital, but they hung around here, in the Hôtel de Barbès and the Montreuil hostels, in the same pants they'd bought at Tati's, which they'd been wearing for months. For months, they wore the same rubber shoes, in summer and winter, the wool cap, which served more as a symbol than real protection. For years, their existence unfolded to the rhythm of money orders, packages sent back home or entrusted to visiting cousins. And then, one day, they would be regrouped in a reserved corner of the airport. They landed dressed in large *boubous* and the new wrinkles at the corners of their lips dimmed their laughter, in the arms of parents who had become blind and brothers and sisters whom they had not known as children. They discovered a single pleasure: In Dakar and Bamako, being black was everybody's lot.

It took Yebga a long time to pass the big green garbage truck. His eyes fluttering with fatigue, he followed the predictable movements with which the garbage cans were lifted, emptied and put back down on the ground again.

Smith and Dubois pressed their noses to the windows; the sights of peripheral city life didn't impress them. Here, there were no rutted roads, no old cars left to rust in the corners of intersections, no forbidden zones under the viaducts, no double grills in front of the occasional stores. This was not Central Park, but it wasn't Harlem either. The car stopped in front of a big gray, dirty cluster of apartment buildings. Yebga checked the address, parked the Alfa Romeo at the curb and opened the car door silently, scrutinizing the surroundings. Papa N'Dyaye never failed to surprise him. Was this where he sported his cigarette holders and recruited his prostitutes? He hesitated to let his two passengers know of his astonishment. How could they possibly understand a thing like this? And why did they insist on coming with him, these two depressed looking men? Was it just because Dread Pol was black and they had shared the same dance floor? That was too much to believe. There had to be more to it. Something had brought them to the Day and Night and had fired their interest in Jorge Gonzales. Yes. There had to be something else. He would think about it another time.

The intercom at the doorway wasn't working. They had to wait half an hour before someone left in order to enter the building. The elevator in which they rode to the sixth floor was overrun with a strong stench of urine and sweat and the musty smell of cheap cologne. As they stepped out of the elevator, Smith couldn't repress the question which had been haunting him since the moment they arrived at the front door.

"Is this the black neighborhood?"

Yebga smiled. Smith and Jones preferred things plain and simple, clear explanations which were cleanly cut like keys to the vast works of the world. It was easy to conclude, from having seen this gray building with its stinking elevator, that blacks were cooped up here.

"No," answered the reporter. "It's a normal . . . neighborhood. A few blocks from here there are beautiful apartment houses where wealthy people, whites, live. There are whites in this building too."

"You mean to say that no one has his own neighborhood in your city."

Yebga refrained from pointing out that he felt no more

at home here than any other black. He decided this was not the time for an ethnographic study of the Parisian pavement.

"Yes. People have their own neighborhoods. But they're not divided up by color. For instance, there's a neighborhood more to the liking of artists, writers and painters, and another one for businessmen."

The reporter shook his head. All this was damned complex. "It's like this," he finally said, as if he had just found the right answer, "In Paris, people are housed according to their incomes. The rich on one side, the less rich on another, the poor, somewhere else."

Smith nodded, but the question had visibly ceased to interest him.

Apartment 613. Yebga rang the bell, then rang again a minute later. Nothing seemed to have stirred in the apartment. Looking at his watch, he saw it was only six a.m. N'Dyaye's family was probably still asleep.

Finally there was the sound of a key in the lock and the door opened halfway. A gray-haired woman hid herself behind the panel of wood.

"Hello," said Yebga to reassure her. We're friends of Monsieur N'Dyaye. He told us to drop by to see him."

"At six o'clock in the morning?"

She looked from one man to another.

"Is it that early? We were just with him, a couple of hours ago, at the Day and Night.

Smith turned his back on the scene, trailing his finger along the graffiti in the corridor. Yebga remembered seeing this face before. Where? In N'Dyaye's office, on the Champs Élysées! The receptionist without her red wig! With one hand she held her robe closed around her heavy figure, while with the other she gripped the door.

"My husband isn't here," she finally blurted out in a shrill voice, slightly hysterical.

"He hasn't come home yet?" Yebga was astonished.

"Yes," hesitated the woman, "with another gentleman, but he left again almost immediately. He only collected a few papers. It was business."

"Did he tell you where they were going?"

A shadow fell across the woman's face. Her lips trembled.

Yebga explained these details to his friends, who were beginning to lose patience. Dubois pouted skeptically, then he roughly stepped into the doorway.

"I think you're lying. Women are the best fucking liars in the world. You're taking us for assholes!"

Smith turned around slowly. He fixed the woman's wide eyes with his own.

"We're coming in," he said quite slowly.

He pushed her with his shoulder and sent her waltzing. The others followed him into the room. Dubois was careful to close the door behind them.

"You have no right. I'm going to call the police. Poliiiice!"

"We're going to do it for you," retorted Yebga in a harsh voice. "Especially if your husband is here. We're not murderers. So calm down!"

Just behind the front door, some steps descended to a room hung with panther skins. It was a veritable jungle. There were plants; African musical instruments, amulets and masks were hanging on the walls. Leather armchairs gave the impression of a living room. Through the door, they saw a room of equal size, furnished with stainless steel chairs and a glass table. The same luxuriance of plants and objects reigned everywhere. N'Dyaye had been bent on reconstituting in his world the Africa he carried within himself. It was a chaotic Africa, full of contradictions and lies. Two fake crystal chandeliers hung above the tables, mythic stamps of occidental grandeur. The reporter smiled. On the ground, thick goatskin rugs created a feeling of walking on cotton. Smith and Dubois whistled in admiration.

"Jesus Christ!"

Before Yebga could catch his breath, the two Americans had disappeared into the apartment. He heard doors slam and even thought he discerned a few shouts. Dubois returned, shrugging his shoulders, his hands open.

"I told you he wasn't here," yelped the woman, who still stood planted in the middle of the living room, clutching her robe.

Dubois gave her a slap which sent her waltzing past the masks and the amulets on the wall.

"I couldn't help it," the ex-cop apologized.

Yebga broke in.

"If you know where he went, lady, you'd better tell us!"

Crouching on a fur rug, all modesty forgotten, the hostess opened her bloodshot eyes. Under her open robe she was naked from her wrinkled neck down to her toes, save for the marks left by her underwear. She huddled instinctively against the table as she saw the reporter coming near her.

"Go ahead, rape me, dirty nigger. . . . You too . . . since I told you I don't know anything. For twenty-five years I haven't known a thing! He never tells me anything. I'm like his whore. He spends his life outside, with people I don't like. He never listens to me. He's the man of the house. That's what he always says. But he's never here. You can hit. You know how to hit women, especially the big bastard over there with the hat! You're all exactly alike. You're hypocrites. You should have seen how gentle he was in the beginning. I was warned. You're all the same. Savages. I hate you with your stink and your woolly hair that sticks out everywhere, your prayers to Mecca! I'll be damned for Youssouf. We used to spend our lives in bed. But now he's never here. And you come to me with your questions? But you're the same as he is, so shouldn't you know him better than I do? I hope he drops dead with all his bullshit. I hope he did something to send him to prison forever. . . . I . . ."

She began to sob, worn out, exhausted. She moaned obscenely. A beautiful mulatto with a slightly pale face, a slender body and long, fine hair entered the room. She was wearing silk shorts and a colorful top.

In silence, with a self-assurance and a precision to her gestures, which gave the impression she had practiced them a hundred times, she took her mother in her arms and rocked her. She must have been about fifteen years old. The three men stood petrified.

"What did you do to her? What are you doing here?"

The young girl fixed her hard adolescent gaze on Yebga.

"Are you cops? They send black cops to take care of black stuff now? I hope you're not too ashamed! I guess this must cause some problems for you, doing other people's dirty work, like slaves."

Smith didn't understand one treacherous word, but he stepped toward the girl with an ashen face. Yebga stopped him.

"She's getting on my nerves," the ex-cop said.

The reporter pushed him toward the door.

"Let's go. He's not here."

Soon they were in the hall jostling one another. Outside the day was breaking. Yebga explained to Jones that he knew where N'Dyaye's office was and that they ought to drop by there rather than linger over this meaningless episode in the investigation. They lifted their eyes in disbelief toward the building, remembering the strange decor of stuffed animals, amulets, panther skins, spears, with poisoned tips, of course.

"Cute kid!" said Smith, but he lacked spirit.

In the streets the traffic still was moving smoothly, and Yebga pushed the accelerator pedal to the floor. Fortunately, on the Champs-Élysées, the building's side entrance was already open. They climbed the staircase to the third floor and found themselves in front of N'Dyaye's office. Yebga rang the bell without response, no one appeared.

Smith, with a tense look, silently pushed the reporter aside. He flung back the tails of his trenchcoat, opened his jacket and produced the forty-five he'd taken off the corpse on the Rue des Abbesses. Yebga watched the scene, fascinated, absent. He felt panic at the thought of the noise the automatic was going to make and that this shot would have irremediable results, but he dared say nothing. So it had come to this. Playing with guns in a story which was being written with him but not by him. The ex-cop raised his arm and aimed the automatic at the lock. With his thumb he pushed the safety off the pistol. His index finger was tightening on the trigger when the noise of the elevator rising toward them made him stop. Yebga thanked a God in whom he had never really believed. The elevator stopped at their floor. Amid the rattling of elaborate grillwork, they saw a bucket with a broom inside it, crowned by a canvas apron, pushed onto the landing. Clad in a checkered scarf, the old woman who appeared seemed to have stepped straight out of a publicity brochure advertising vacations to the islands. Dubois took the bucket, Yebga took the broom. An Antillean, he thought.

"Thank you," the old woman said. "At my age, it's not so easy. But you have to make a living," she added without a trace of bitterness. A simple investigation, she searched the pocket of her apron, extracting a bunch of keys. With a hesitating step, she walked toward N'Dyaye's door and opened it, thanking them again, not surprised to see these gracious men hurry off toward N'Dyaye's office. She figured they were friends of the African who ran the agency. Yebga ran directly to N'Dyaye's office without lingering in the waiting room. He turned on the lights. The drawers and the cabinet had been emptied, and the floor was flooded with printed matter, letters, papers, photographs, a real ransack. Dubois gathered up some typed papers and handed them to Yebga.

"What do these say?

"N'Dyaye must have stopped by here before us and cleaned house. He's eliminated everything that could have put us on his trail."

Jones removed his hat and began to crush it in his hands.

"There must be a way to find this puppet."

"I suggest we get a little sleep," said Smith. "After that we'll be able to think a little more clearly."

Yebga agreed. If Smith hadn't proposed it, he wouldn't have gone to bed himself. Besides, he hadn't telephoned Faye since they'd left her. In fact he felt so little in control now, his life seemed too absurd to be his own, more like a parenthesis, a fiction, a window open at night to a storm across the peaceful sky of his existence, that he would have willingly believed that people were not meant to eat or sleep.

They worked their way toward the exit, nodding good-bye to the cleaning lady polishing the furniture, the floor, the windowpanes, pretending to ignore their presence.

First Yebga stopped by Rue Casimir-Delavigne to drop off the two ex-cops, then he decided to stop in at the *World* on the Rue de Vaugirard. He still felt haunted by his last image of Dread Pol. It was the first time he had seen a corpse. It was the first time he had ever seen a final glance close on the world. Tears welled up in his eyes. From now on this investigation would be a settling of accounts too, a personal affair. Only God knew how far it would lead him!

Arriving at the office of the *World*, Yebga felt on firmer ground again, despite his fatigue and the doubtful looks of his colleagues, who made a lot out of the way he looked. He called Faye to say he sent her his love, that everything was fine, that he would call back later. Then, remembering to knock first, he pushed open the door to Glenn's office.

"Hello, Amos. What's the matter? Aren't you awake yet?"

The editor-in-chief did not so much as raise his head. Yebga found a chair and sat down. Glenn pushed away the papers he was reading and stared at him.

"They even messed you up, eh? Who did this to you? You shouldn't make a play for your buddy's wife!"

The reporter was not really listening. Random images paraded through his head. Jeannette, Myriam, those men bursting out of the shadows who had beat him up, N'Dyaye, Malika's photo . . . then the two cops, N'Dyaye's daughter. And he had complained to Faye of "not meeting anyone."

"Hey, are you listening to me?"

It was Glenn's voice. Yebga realized that he had almost fallen asleep the moment he'd returned to his own turf.

"Yes. I'm listening to you."

Resting on his elbows, Glenn sighed.

"Are you getting anywhere with this?"

Yebga felt like a child. To tell the story would prove him innocent, wash away the night's stains. He almost wanted to hug Glenn, but a reflection behind the steel-rimmed glasses dissuaded him.

"There was a new murder," he finally let drop, in a hollow voice. "Dread Pol, the musician. Absurd, no reason for it."

"He was Diop's best friend, wasn't he?"

"Yes, but that doesn't explain anything. They could have killed him in a thousand different ways. I don't think it was premeditated."

Yebga fell silent. Glenn looked blankly at him.

"Come on, pal, calm down. Let's take it from the beginning because I don't really get this story of yours. I don't spend my days traipsing around with you, let alone my nights. I only have to make sure you earn your salary. Yours and seventy-five others'! So, I'd like you to throw a little light on this."

"I always lose the thread. I slip and fall again. I don't know any more now than last week."

"Don't say that. You know that N'Dyaye is involved up to his turban! Look, Amos, it's your job. Dig around in every direction. Search Paris' African community. Meet girls who knew Malika. People who worked for N'Dyaye, friends of Diop. There has to be a hole in this net some place. If they killed so stupidly, it's because they panicked. They think you know a lot about it. They're beginning to get frantic. So dig in. Take a stab at everything that moves. We'll cover you. If you put your finger in some shit, we'll be behind you."

Glenn delivered his last sentence in a stern voice. It struck Yebga like a cold shower.

"This is the first dead man I've ever seen, Robert."

The words caught in his throat. He stood up, staggering a little. Glenn's voice, detached again, accompanied him to the door.

"A cop dropped by earlier. He wanted to talk to you about the murder. He's an inspector from the station at Halles. Morand or Moreau . . ."

In his mind's eye, the double silhouette which had escorted him all night came back to him. He did not understand why the image of these two Americans was his only comfort. He felt worn out and useless. The scoop he had been waiting for for years seemed to be slipping through his fingers. Then what? He took the stairs to the editing room. He found a package in his mailbox there. He grabbed it, fled into the morning, his mind a blank, incapable of taking his bearings or of thinking. What good was it? What was the use of running around in circles all your life? To earn money? Maybe a black man really was just a beast of burden, a stupid animal, or else Yebga was delirious. On the cassette player inside his car, the saxophone of John Coltrane flooded his brain like a beneficial drug. The whites came to our homeland to do a good turn. To show us the good life and bring us industry. Because we were lazy good-for-nothings, they treated us like dirt. Coltrane makes music for the shiftless. They'll never understand us. Coltrane is dead. White men are ants. They only think about eating and bringing in the goods. And they think we're idiots because we don't want to be part of their system.

The Alfa skirted the quay. Opposite the Pont des Arts, Yebga parked along the sidewalk. He looked for a bench on the bridge where he could sit. He needed air. Right near him, a bum was having a basic breakfast, essentially red wine. He addressed Yebga with a smile exposing black gaps between his few remaining teeth. He raised his bottle.

"Come on, comrade! If you're thirsty, there's enough for two. You and me, we'll crap on the bourgeoisie."

Yebga had a headache but he returned the bum's smile anyway. He was a man of indeterminate age whose skin was covered with a thick layer of dirt. The bum held out his bottle of cheap wine to the reporter, who took a large swallow.

"You don't look so hot," remarked the man. "How'd you get lost in this desert anyway? Go back to your savannah lands. You and your friends should never come to graze in this shit pile. This country's not the place for you."

He patted Yebga on the back, offering him a piece of sausage. The reporter thanked him and stood up. Some barges glided past on the Seine. The blood pounded in his temples like a drum beating an inaudible, mystic incantation. Really, what am I doing here, he muttered to himself. What am I doing in this damned country complaining about my fate? What's the use of struggling like this? He felt he was about to pass out. Tears flowed down his cheeks despite himself. Men don't cry, shit! Not a warrior. Not Yebga. But to evoke the spirit of that long lost ancestor who had downed a lion with his bare hands was useless here. An irrepressible flood of tears overwhelmed him. He was sick of being black, sick of being here, helpless, on the Pont des Arts, in Paris, sick of this country that looked so much like a mirage. A mirage of course peopled with friendly faces, full of happiness and smiles. But where were they today? He found the package on the car seat, opened it hastily. His tears dropped onto the white paper as he unfolded it. "Something promised, something due. Here are Malika's mementos. Take care of them until I get back. Love."

It was signed Jeannette.

The package contained nothing but African objects of no apparent value—miniature ivory masks, old bobbins of synthetic thread, statuettes, Bouakian cloths folded into little squares—objects which today in the inverted flow of commerce took the place of those shoddy goods the first colonialists used to buy off tribes.

Yebga turned the objects over and over again in his hands. A strange anxiety overtook him. It was as if he were handling relics filched from a cadaver, a cadaver which could only be Malika. He still felt a little ridiculous calling the morgue where a brief investigation failed to turn up any record of the young woman's body. His dull uneasiness began to change into a vague conviction as he made his way toward the police station at Halles. Moreau immediately received him. He noticed the change which had taken place in the reporter's face in so few hours: the hollow features, the unshaven stubble covering his cheeks and chin. The man looked like he'd aged ten years.

Moreau offered him a cup of coffee. Yebga wanted a quick finish to this affair. Irritated, he waved his hands, this man who usually was so reserved. Like a leitmotiv, the question constantly came back, "Why hasn't N'Dyaye been brought in for questioning, and why has no warrant been issued for his arrest?"

"You do your job and we'll take care of ours," Moreau finally replied, slightly irritated.

Yebga exploded, "If you had done your job in the first place, we wouldn't be sitting here now. You called it an accidental death when Salif Maktar Diop was murdered. You're responsible for the death of poor Dread Pol too—yes, I know . . . Paul Dadié. Is this what you call doing your job? I pay taxes in this country too. You make me laugh with your big words! France, the land of refuge!

Dread Pol really was right. You lie to us. You've always lied to us. Look at the sort of life you offer these poor jerks you brought here when you lost the colonies!"

Moreau stiffened. He had remained polite and accepted this as a conversation between reasonable men, but he was not about to swallow the abuses of this raving maniac. Undoubtedly, reporter or not, these blacks were really all, all the same!

"Listen, man. If it's so much better in Cameroon, go back! Maybe the police are more efficient down there! I don't think anyone's forcing you to live in France. You're not a worker, you're not in political exile. So, if you're not happy . . ."

Yebga leaped up, unable to control his fury. He pointed an accusing finger at the policeman.

"Find N'Dyaye. Find him! If you don't . . . If you don't, we won't let up on you. Your name will be everywhere. And you'll have to come up with some answers!"

Moreau grabbed him by the arm. Yebga was still yelling when the door slammed shut behind him. A disheveled cop stared at him, holding his kepi in his hand. Yebga shoved his fists into his pockets and strode off down the hall.

Chapter Twenty-Four

Dubois sat down on his bed and stretched out without taking off his clothes. Later he walked over to the window in his stocking feet. Curiously, he did not feel too out of his element despite the newness of the landscape. In the long run, stones and bricks are all the same. The big difference is the people, and here for the most part they were very likable, for instance, this young reporter with his white woman. Well, he still seemed very natural, and as for the woman, after all, she had let them use her car. Jones remembered the photos he had seen of the liberation of Paris. There were black GIs kissing curly blond girls right on the mouths as they clambered onto the hood of their jeeps. Even now, forty years later, an air of old dance tunes and accordion music still floated through the streets. To be a cop here didn't seem too difficult; it was easy enough to spot a rodent on the carpet. Not like in Harlem, where the entire city was a sewer, a perfect place for traps and hustlers, where the gangrene had spread so far it wasn't possible to distinguish between the diseased limb and the healthy body. Here the abscess had a name and he was going to lance it. He picked up the telephone and dialed the switchboard.

"Call me a cab," he said. "Room 107."

He waited, irritated, on the edge of the bed, hands folded. He sensed violence in the air. He scented waves of it in the distance, the way animals in the forest shiver when fire sets the first twigs crackling. He didn't feel either tired or anxious. Violence was a way of life for him. Maybe Himes' Gravedigger was dead, but Dubois was going to show them that he hadn't lost his touch.

He slipped on his jacket and surged into the stairwell with his trenchcoat folded on his arm. He rocketed past the reception desk. Outside, in front of the hotel, a beige Mercedes taxi was waiting.

Dubois threw himself into the back seat.

"Hôtel du Vieux-Colombier," he said in his horrible French.

The cabbie glanced back, a bit bewildered.

"Just drive!" barked Jones, as he finished dressing.

The cabbie shrugged and the car took off.

When they arrived in the Rue du Vieux-Colombier, Jones told the driver to continue on a little way, pull up to the curb opposite the hotel and stop the engine. Every fifteen minutes he gave the driver another bill to keep him dozing there behind the wheel. Before he'd gone through the first wad of bills, Coetzee came out of the hotel, talking with a short fat guy, another white man. They paced the sidewalk as they chatted. Jones figured they must be waiting for someone. When Jorge Gonzales' BMW pulled up beside the men a few minutes later, Jones said simply "Go," pointing to the car with an authoritative gesture, brandishing a a bright new one-hundred-franc note. The cab took off.

The ex-cop wasn't thinking anymore, his brain was now on automatic pilot. He leaned forward toward the grumbling driver, ready for anything. He marked down their route on a map of Paris opened on his lap. What a labyrinth this city was! Fortunately he recognized some landmarks along the way.

Traffic light after traffic light, the two cars crossed the boulevard encircling the city and entered Neuilly. The people in the BMW were unaware of the taxi following them. By now they were driving deep into Neuilly, with its mansions and lanes lined with wealthy villas. As the BMW slowed down, its right turn signal began flashing. "Go on around them," said Jones excitedly. In the rear-view mirror, he saw that the car had turned into a cul-de-sac.

Jones carefully noted the names on the blue street signs, and then told the driver, who was more and more out of sorts despite the tips, to drive him back to Rue Casimir-Delavigne.

Smith was in a state of great excitement. Dubois had just handed out a lot of cab fare, but he was exultant.

"You should have woken me up, Gravedigger," whined Ed reproachfully. "This isn't our territory. What would I do if you got into deep shit here?"

"I didn't have time, man. I had to go. I couldn't wait. And anyway, I didn't know what I was going to turn up. I was too uptight to wait around."

Their voices resonated in the room. Gradually they calmed down.

"What do you think he was doing there?"

"If we knew that, pal, we'd be in good shape."

Smith was silent for a moment, then snapped his fingers. "We need a car."

"Yeah," Jones soberly agreed.

Chapter Twenty-Five

Despite his headache, Yebga ordered another drink. He didn't wait for it to come before he cried to the owner of the Sunny Kingston, "Give me Myriam's address!"

"She's off today. Besides, I can't give out an employee's address just like that."

"What's that supposed to mean?"

Yebga rose and lunged uncertainly toward the man behind the bar. Massa Soya burst out laughing.

"Rearrange his face, Amos. He's been kicking us in the balls for too long now!"

The others echoed their agreement. Yebga continued toward the bar. His face was spotted with bruises, and the lumps he had picked up in his previous run-in gave him the look of a veteran tough guy. He grabbed a bottle from a table.

"Are you going to give me her address, you little asshole?"

The owner of the Sunny Kingston had stopped smiling. There was nothing worse than these hysterics who couldn't control themselves. Even if this one was a good mixer once he'd sobered up.

"Listen Amos. Look at it from my side. I . . ."

The bottle was inches from his nose. He had no choice. He grabbed a card and quickly scribbled down an address. A sigh rose from the tables.

Yebga staggered out of the restaurant. He waited until he'd reached the Boulevard de Strasbourg to hail a taxi. His head ached and the scenes his eyes reflected appeared a little blurry to him. He handed the card to the driver, heard him vaguely decipher Rue de la Colonie and figured it must have been Myriam's address.

The young mulatto was still asleep when Yebga rang her doorbell. Once the shock of seeing him there had passed, she touched his face and felt his breath. A strange rush of desire overtook her. This time she had him to herself. He was drunk. He had come to give himself up, mumbling, disarmed. Beyond the point of feeling ashamed, he exhibited his wounded body, stripped of the armor of words, ideas and principles. She felt herself naked and warm as she stood in the living room, saw herself fall with him onto a pile of crumpled copies of the *World*.

She pushed Yebga into the only armchair in the room, this time without fear of touching him, letting her fingers run along his shoulders, his chest. Cushions covered with

African cloth were scattered here and there for furniture, a bed in a corner, more cushions and some shelves filled with books. The young woman stretched out on the floor in front of Yebga, caressing his ankles, his outstretched legs, his waist, with her gaze.

"I'm happy you're here, Amos."

Her muffled voice reached the reporter as if through a series of padded doors.

"You always have to prove you're men. What use is that? Look at yourself, my poor dear."

She set her elbows on his knees.

"Dread Pol is dead."

Myriam shuddered. One phrase too many, threatening to spoil everything. It was a simple sentence: subject, verb, object. But behind the words, there was something else. Dread Pol. And the bad luck these two shared.

"My God," she said, breathless. "It can't be true!"

Yebga recounted what had happened at the Day and Night in a flat voice, the way someone retells a nightmare in which all the creatures shrink away and everything disappears except the horror. She handed him a cup of steaming tea on a tray and sat down on a cushion facing him. Yebga gulped the tea. He felt the liquid burn his throat, then his stomach.

"Do you have anything to eat?" he asked.

Myriam disappeared into the kitchen. Voices rose from the street, engine noises. Yebga closed his eyes and almost fell asleep. Myriam served him what was left of her last meal, veal and some cereal pounded into a paste which, back in Cameroon, they called *foufou*. While he ate, she plugged in the radiocassette and the voice of Michel Jonasz enveloped them.

"So, was it N'Dyaye?"

"N'Dyaye or someone else, Gonzales."

Yebga took a gulp of water.

"I've got to find N'Dyaye and make him talk."

He ate, then drank some more water. His neck muscles gradually relaxed.

"A little while ago, I had a drink with a bum on the Pont des Arts!"

He smiled to fight off the wave of despair which pricked his nostrils.

"I almost rearranged your boss's face too . . . that half-breed is an asshole."

"Why?"

"He didn't want to give me your address."

"But that's normal, Amos. He doesn't have the right to give it to just anybody."

She spoke to him in a low voice which was very soft, leaning over him, her legs crossed on the armrest of his chair.

"So I'm just anybody?"

"That's not what I said. . . . I don't know. . . ."

"He's an asshole. And I would've whipped his ass."

Myriam put a finger to his lips, plucked a morsel of meat stuck to the corner and put it in his mouth.

"You're drunk, Amos. I might have been with someone else here. What would you have done?"

"I would have kicked his ass. But you're alone."

The young mulatto smiled. Her arm stretched across the back of the chair began to tremble from her shoulder to her wrist. She couldn't speak or breathe. After what seemed like a century, Yebga set his plate on the floor, wiped his mouth and looked at her.

"The truth is, I'm completely lost," he confessed in a broken voice. "I'm marking time, I'm going around in circles, I wouldn't know an apple from an orange. They're all waiting for me. They're waiting for me to take a stand to show just how worthless I really am. And maybe they're right. Maybe I should forget everything, my car, the paper, my white woman, give up everything and go back home. Maybe after all, I never really understood the rules they play by. . . . I'm lost, Myriam. I need someone to help me. . . . Help me."

Leaning forward, he pulled her toward him, pressing his nose, his forehead, his lips, against the young woman's smooth belly. He caressed her hips, her breasts, under her gray sweatshirt. He would have liked to disappear inside her, immersing himself in her perfume, like a shipwrecked sailor giving up, incapable of swimming any farther, ready to roll to the bottom of the sea.

Myriam followed his movements, returning his caresses. But now that she felt sure she had him, she didn't want to rush things. She relaxed.

"Me too, I could've been one of N'Dyaye's girls if I'd wanted to. Don't you think I'm as pretty as any of those tarts?"

She pecked Yebga's forehead, his throat, his ears. She brushed his eyelids, his beard, the surface of his skin.

"A little longer and I would've fallen for his line because it would've been a good arrangement. I'd have known for sure I wasn't by myself, that somebody was taking charge of my life. It's nice, you know, to have a father, an adult strong enough to protect you from life. Being an African and seductive was enough to make it work. He could've lined up jobs that would've taken me around the world and earned me a lot of money. Only the first time I saw him, I immediately knew that he wasn't the man I needed, the adoptive father I was looking for."

"Did he ask you to sleep with him?"

"No. That's not his style. Well, at least not with me."

"And you turned down the travel and the dough for a bullshit job? Do you like your restaurant better?"

"Don't act meaner than you really are, Amos! You know there's more to life than money and travel. Sure I like money, everyone does. But I don't put it before everything else. I have other priorities of a . . . how should I say this, of a moral order," she had pronounced the word very softly, as if afraid of being laughed at.

"I'm here to study, Amos. And when I finish, I'll go back to my country. My life here is only a parenthesis."

"You do have some white blood, don't you?"

"What good is that? Back home is where I'm needed. Not here."

Yebga shook his head.

"That's crazy."

"What? You mean you've never wanted to go home? Just because everything's going well for you, do you imagine all the problems are resolved? Sooner or later, your turn will come, Amos. And you'll understand that everyone returns to the point from which they departed."

Myriam stood up again. She gazed around the room, taking care not to look too long at Yebga in order to spare them both embarrassment.

"Do you know any of his girls?" he asked.

"Yes, of course. I can find out where they're hanging out these days, if they're in Paris."

Yebga stood up, still uncertain.

"Are you leaving already?"

"Yes. I'm glad we talked. I feel better."

Their faces were almost touching. She felt Yebga's breath. She kissed him furtively on the mouth, then quickly ran into the kitchen.

"Well, then go. . . ."

She pronounced the words almost gayly. He could leave, then he would come back. He hadn't possessed her, but she already belonged to him. And even on an empty stomach, she was not afraid to touch him anymore.

Chapter Twenty-Six

Yebga stirred slightly on the sofa. Was it dawn? No, it was nightfall. How long had he been sleeping? That disagreeable vibration spiraling up his head was the telephone. He groped for the receiver and picked it up, on the verge of nausea.

"Hello! Faye? What's up?"

"Amos? This is the third time I've called! Where were you? Everybody's looking for you: a detective, inspector Moreau, someone named Samba, and the two Americans are here too. What were you doing? Tell me, Amos. Don't leave me in the dark like this. Not me, Amos, please, because I won't put up with it. . . ."

It took Yebga a few seconds to put his thoughts in order, to connect faces to these names, even to recognize his own apartment.

"What time is it? I was sleeping," he answered. "Tell them I'm on my way. And you calm down. I'll explain things to you later."

He hung up, disgusted, irritated. If she was going to start in too . . . After taking a shower and changing his clothes, he found himself in the Metro during rush hour, jostled by the crowds pouring out of office buildings. His mind a blank, he traipsed along the passageways, the transfer points, followed the yellow neon lights, passed the flower sellers, the beggars, without flinching. Arriving at the Avenue de la Grande-Armée, he climbed heavily up the stairs and rang Faye's bell. She opened almost immediately.

"Amos, it's about time."

She fell into his arms and began to sob hysterically.

Yebga, who had almost recovered and had completely forgotten his own earlier emotion, was surprised by her reaction. He had always considered self-control one of Faye's foremost qualities, and they had long discussions with Glenn about what might have caused it: the settlers of the old American South, the ups and downs of exile in Europe, even life with a black man sometimes demanded a certain self-control!

"What's the matter with you! You're acting like I've just come back from the front. Come on, Faye, get a hold of yourself!"

Yebga was stiffer than usual, his voice cold.

"I want you to drop all this, Amos."

Yebga stared hard at her, then pushed her away, cocking an ear; he thought he heard some movement in the living room. A look that way reassured him: it was Smith and Jones, looking serious and quiet. The enthusiasm with which they greeted him surprised him.

"We didn't want to bother you again," said Smith in his most polished English, "but we're going to need the car."

Yebga rubbed his eyes. So this was what Faye's scene was all about? It seemed unlikely.

"You're not bothering me at all."

He heard Faye calling him.

"Make yourselves at home," he told the two men. "I'll be right back."

She was still in the entryway, huddled on a bench against the wall. She had never looked more like a beaten dog. She trembled, her eyes red with tears which wouldn't flow.

Yebga sat down next to her. The hallway was immersed in a sort of golden chiaroscuro. He took the young woman in his arms, but with restraint. He felt her tenseness, hostility, but acted as if there was nothing wrong.

"Something's breaking," she uttered in French, in order not to be understood by the detectives. "You're not the same anymore. I feel like I've been pushed into the background. It's because of this stupid accident. Why have you changed? We were getting along so well. The two of us, just you and me. Why are you letting the world come between us?"

She clutched at him like a child.

"That's exactly it. We were wrong to think we could avoid the world, my dear. Now it hurts. Even more so because we stopped our ears and closed our eyes."

"It's not too late. Drop everything. Let's get away from here. We need a rest, just the two of us."

Yebga kissed her quickly on the forehead and stood up.

"Come on." He held out his hand to her, pretending to be cheerful. "We're ignoring our guests."

In the living room, Smith and Dubois were talking in low voices.

"Here's what I think we ought to do," Yebga announced. "I left my car at Halles. I think it will suit you better than Faye's car. I'll drive you over there. I'll keep the Mini."

The two Americans stood up. Faye handed Yebga the keys to her Austin. A gleam of reproach shone in her eyes. She watched him leave without the slightest movement.

"Samba is waiting for you at the Day and Night," she blurted out, rather than "I love you. Come back soon."

From the lower landing, Yebga answered, raising his fingers in a V of victory. Gravedigger and Coffin were farther down the stairs. Once inside the Mini, Jones put his huge hand around the reporter's neck.

"That kid up there's got a crush on you, Jack. You're a lucky bastard."

"Yeah . . ." said Yebga shortly.

He shifted into first gear and the car rumbled off toward Étoile. The three men began to talk. This was their first real conversation.

"Have you lived here for a long time?" began Dubois.

"It's been awhile," Yebga said. "I was still a kid when I got off the boat."

"Why didn't you stay home?"

"The universities there didn't offer what I wanted. The best profs aren't sent down there, and my parents wanted me to have the best so I'd have an equal footing with the whites. Anyway, life's hard down there.

In his mind's eye, Yebga saw the savannah again; the barefooted children in their beige school uniforms; the legless cripples pushing themselves along on soap crates; the laterite roads running past compounds reddened by the dust; the procession of women so beautiful, so erect in draped cloths, who looked as though they were carrying the entire village to market on their heads: chickens, vegetables, pots, bed frames . . . He told Smith and Jones about all this. They thought he was exaggerating in order to impress them, that Africa was no longer like that. They remembered photographs they'd seen of the last Panafrican concert in Lagos—the laughing crowds, the drums and the blood-red dawns on mountains in the background. It all came back to them like a millenial blast from the dark continent. Every time they spoke about Africa, they said "the motherland," the way Christians in Jesus' temple believe that paradise was established in the sky, behind the clouds. They didn't want to give up this ultimate dream.

Yebga saw the mud-brick houses, the tin roofs, the games they played in the rain, the outdoor cinemas where shouts from the audience marked the blows received by bad guys on the screen, the bars, the refuges where, with the help of beer, you staved off hunger, a landscape enclosed in columns of figures, words and statistics, crushed by analysis that took up an entire page in the newspaper. These memories made Yebga aware that Africa had become his prey, his pasture, his theme, in short, his livelihood, but that it had not been his vital element for years. He paid his way by stockpiling diagnostics on the patient, then proposing treatments to bring it back to health. But did he really still love this continent whose convulsive ailments he had fled? He was just a lecturer, and they were nostalgic lookers-on. He fell silent, struck by the absurdity of his speech here in this car, while down there, at this very moment, they were struggling and dying. Myriam knew the truth. He suddenly desired her, reproached himself for having left her. Her mixed blood was blacker than his own.

"We'll take a trip there," bellowed Smith, with a brilliant smile. "Now that we've become great travelers, we won't hesitate to take a jaunt down there one of these days. Right, Gravedigger?"

The other man nodded.

"You're doing fine here," Smith continued, watching Paris flying by. "You know the ropes. Blacks where we come from have a hard life, but they're hard too, boy."

Of course there was room here for discussion. The exiled Africans often envied the fortune of the black American community, which brought forth senators and mayors in their new land, and which was quickly being integrated into the modern world. Someone else's grass is always greener. But Yebga wasn't in a mood to continue the debate. He had argued over this for years, engaged in jousts in which, every time, his point of view prevailed due to his education, the rhetoric he'd learned as a student at good schools. He was ashamed of the pride he'd so often derived from it. "Whiter than the whites," was what he had become.

"What do you plan to do with your girlfriend?"

Jones casually let the question drop as if asking "What time is it?" or "Got a light?" A skein of random images unraveled in Yebga's mind. A beach in Brittany, a bar somewhere on the Côte d'Azur, the threshold of the Dome in Milan. And like a doorstop, Faye's bland face smiling the tranquil smile of a self-assured woman.

"I don't know," he heard himself answer. "I don't know anymore."

The Mini turned onto the Boulevard de Sébastopol.

The Alfa sat quietly parked in the rue des Lombards. Yebga could hardly believe his eyes: It seemed like an eternity since he had been inside the Day and Night. . . . He automatically drew his car keys from his pocket and handed them to Smith. He realized he had never seriously intended to marry Faye. Even so, the thought was unbearable.

"By the way," he said, trying to sound pleasant, "I forgot to ask what kind of work you used to do."

"Used to do, you're right to put it that way," answered Smith with bitterness. "We were the best in Harlem."

"In all New York," Dubois raised the bid.

"Yeah. In all New York, man!"

"The best what?"

"Cops."

Already by this time of day, Halles was crowded with its usual jungle of famished faces sprouting green, yellow, red and pink hair.

"Who are these guys, *zazous*?" inquired Smith, remembering the French word.

"There are no more *zazous*. There are only punks, 'New Wavers' people call them."

The two friends looked perplexed, then thanked Yebga again for his generosity and promised to return the favor when he came to Harlem. Then the car headed off down the boulevard. The reporter watched them drive away, afraid he might have just made a mistake. He stood facing the dark wall of the Day and Night. He rang the bell. Samba himself came to the door. The nightclub was bathed in silence, like a church deserted after the service. Descending toward the altar, Yebga saw that Dread Pol's body had been removed.

"Do you want something to drink," the Senegalese offered.

"No, thanks."

Yebga sat down in the same chair he had occupied the previous night. Samba served himself a soda and sat down beside him. The two men sat locked inside their silence. Samba had changed into a dark flannel suit.

"You're not opening tonight, are you?" asked Yebga.

"No, tonight we mourn."

They fell silent again, as if to talk were too tiresome. Samba took little sips from his glass and stared into the distance. He rubbed his eyes. It was one of Samba's habits the reporter had picked up.

"Everything's beginning to look rotten," he sighed. "People don't respect life anymore. There's no place for me in a world like this." He rubbed his eyelids. "Things escape me. I'm getting old."

He began to pace his club like a lost soul.

"It's a dishonor to our race, a terrible shame. I'm worn out, Amos. I have struggled my whole life to be a good man, a respectable man. But take a look around. Everything's falling apart. Kids don't respect their fathers anymore; they braid their hair like women. What can anybody do?"

He came back and sat down again next to Yebga.

"Why did they kill that poor kid?"

"I don't know. I'm trying to find out. But everything is so absurd, so mixed up."

Samba had a little head with close-cropped hair, which he shook back and forth like a captive animal behind iron bars.

"I thought I knew Youssouf. We grew up in Ziguinchor together. And now look. How could a man change so much?"

"We've got to find him, Samba. Before he goes too far. He's been blinded by the money."

The owner of the Day and Night continued to shake his head.

"The money . . . maybe, kid. I don't know.

Chapter Twenty-Seven

Dubois and Smith had no trouble getting back to Neuilly, where they found the hideout just as Smith had left it. Then they planned to take turns walking a beat around the mansion walls. Meanwhile they said nothing, knowing from experience that a conversation, no matter how banal, might alert a guard, in which case things would happen very fast.

It was about eleven o'clock at night when finally a car turned into the dead-end street. Dubois advanced toward it. From his new observation post, he saw the front gates of the mansion. A man he didn't recognize stepped out from the right side of the car and rang the bell. The American heard the man's voice rising in the night and regretted not knowing French. Then the man returned to the car. It was the sort of car you didn't easily forget, and the ex-cop distinctly saw it again in his mind's eye, driving away in the Rue des Abbesses the night of the attack, a large black Mercedes limousine. The gates opened up before the car. Dubois looked on, amazed. A sumptuously lit driveway led up to the house, detached in the darkness like a fairy-tale castle. The mansion was bathed in a silver halo created by floodlights fixed into the ground. Jones was struck with wonder. No previous investigation had brought him to a place like this. He suddenly spotted men coming and going under the trees behind the mansion wall; they didn't look like gardeners, with gray overcoats and running shoes. Someone stood waiting on the steps. The guard was posted in such a way that Dubois couldn't clearly make out his features. But he was white, and Dubois would have have bet an arm and leg that he had seen this man before at the Hôtel Nikko, with Coetzee. The limousine stopped at the foot of the steps and three men got out. Among them, a guy with an impressive build and a shirt so white it appeared phosphorescent. The ex-cop would have recognized him from miles away! His name was Don Knight.

Chapter Twenty-Eight

Yebga parted company with Samba late that night and returned to Avenue de la Grande-Armée. He found Faye bent over her drawing board. Her complexion was fresh and her cheeks were slightly rosy. Her face was freshly made up and she smelled pleasantly of bath salts. She made no mention of their last encounter. It was clear then that the pact still held: Respect the freedom of the other. The philosophy of California in short! They kissed each other quickly.

"Did you eat?"

"I'm not hungry."

She could see by his discouraged face that his efforts these past few days had turned up nothing—only immeasurable fatigue. Yebga announced in a neutral tone that he was going to bed. He showed neither animosity nor rancor, just his "factual" side, as he would say. A transparent film shielded his skin. In the intimacy of their bed, Faye crept closer to her friend, whispering, seeking a response.

"Coffin Ed and Gravedigger didn't come back with you?"

"What are you talking about?"

About your two attendants. Didn't you notice how much they look like Himes' characters?"

"You're crazy. The two Americans? You're really crazy. Please, Faye, it's already hard enough. Don't make it worse with your literary fantasies. I know all blacks are supposed to look alike, but . . ."

"It doesn't matter," she continued, trying to sound gay. "To me, they'll always be Coffin Ed and Gravedigger Jones. And whenever I open up a book by Himes, I'll see their faces."

She detailed in the same low conspiratorial voice the two men's mannerisms, their clothes, the scar one carried on his face, to no avail. Yebga was already asleep.

Yebga rose early the next day and passed a good part of his morning on the phone. The rest of the time he spent writing the beginning of an article which he intended to entitle, "Harlem on the Seine: A Strange Affair." The article opened with an old blues rhythm balanced by some phrases in a pure detective novel style.

Around noon Yebga set out for the Sunny Kingston. He was a little apprehensive about seeing Myriam again, but she was perfect. First he made his apologies to the owner, then approached her feeling happy and relieved. He could see in her face that not one ounce of earlier tenderness was lost. Still, her actual expression betrayed nothing, and Yebga admired her for being as strong as she was beautiful. He almost lost his head and kissed her on the lips. He restrained himself at the last possible moment and jotted down a singer's name on the corner of a newspaper. One of N'Dyaye's girls whom Myriam had located, which was purportedly the motive for his visit to the Sunny.

Shortly after making a phone call, he arrived at the Hôtel Méridien.

Yebga had arranged to meet the black singer in a small corner fitted out as a cozy living room. It was embellished with a miniature waterfall, which further cooled the air-conditioned room. Her eyes were slightly almond shaped, and she had high cheekbones, a flat nose and thick, red pearl lips. Her skirt was slit so high her inner thighs were showing. Yebga took a sip of tea and faced her squarely. The young woman called herself Sarah M'Bamina. She was originally from the Congo.

"Are you happy to be singing in Paris?"

She crossed her legs, which raised the skirt still higher and began to reveal to Yebga the more intimate aspects of her personality.

"Oh, sure! It's great. It's kind of like back home here."

"It's going well for you then? Lots of friends have told me good things about you."

"It's O.K. I don't have anything to complain about," simpered the girl.

"Youssouf N'Dyaye got you your first job, didn't he?"

Yebga conducted the conversation like an interview, and Sarah M'Bamina, conscientious, attentive, tried to provide him a presentation that would please him.

"Yes. That was a few months ago. I auditioned for him and he hired me on the spot."

"Monsieur N'Dyaye heads up an agency of international dimensions which has produced several African stars—and you're one of them. Do the two of you keep in touch? Are you friends?"

"You know, we really don't have much time to get together. Still, we try to chat from time to time."

"Malika Diop began working for N'Dyaye's company about the same time you did, didn't she?"

"Malika . . . Yes. We were even good friends for a while. But we lost touch. I think she gave everything up to marry an American."

"Did she ever discuss this plan with you?"

"We'd lost touch with each other as I just said. Monsieur N'Dyaye told me she'd left."

The hotel's constant sterile murmur made the reporter uncomfortable. Disco music oozed from speakers behind a velvet partition. Before long he perceived a certain irritation in the woman's voice. He gave up on Malika and lead the singer to another subject.

"What kind of service does N'Dyaye provide you? Does he take care of your contracts?"

"Yes. Monsieur N'Dyaye has contacts all over the world. Those of us he chooses don't have to worry about getting contracts anymore, or payment either. He takes care of everything. Without him, we wouldn't even be working!"

"Have you seen him recently?"

The girl hesitated for a moment.

"No. I was supposed to see him before I left for New York, but he was called away on business suddenly."

Her face froze and took on a dead set expression. Yebga could see he wasn't going to get more out of her and that was fine; all these "Monsieur N'Dyayes" were beginning to get on his nerves. He had lowered himself enough, faking an interest in the singer's career. Now it was time to throw his mask away. Coldly looking her in the eye, he said, "He's on the run. He killed a man."

Sarah M'Bamina did not react at once. It was as if she hadn't heard him, as though the sentence wasn't meant for her. Then she looked startled.

"Killed a man? Do you mean to say Monsieur N'Dyaye is on the run? What are you talking about?"

Her voice was an octave higher.

Yebga nodded. He gauged the effect of his words. If she knew something, it was time to press for more.

"The police are after him," he continued. "Anyone who can help to bring him in will be of use now. Anyone who conceals his whereabouts will be considered an accomplice and risk going to jail."

Sarah took her head in her hands. Yebga calmly turned around to watch the constant coming and going of businessmen out on a spree. Their pleasures must be costing them a fortune; they could afford it. And black girls were in demand these days. Had N'Dyaye simply found a way to profit from this fact and then his scheme had been

147

discovered? Yebga looked back to Sarah. Victim or perverse accomplice? You could tell by the way she was dressed that she liked money; by the way she sat that her morality was lax. A visible gulf separated her from Myriam! What was Malika like? An innocent who had backed out on her contract or too greedy a partner? Anything was possible. Some African women even refused to sleep with blacks because for them it represented a higher rung on the social ladder. You don't mix up dust rags with table linen.

"Well?"

There was neither warmth nor condescension in his voice anymore. The singer sensed this. She took hold of herself, regaining her composure.

"I haven't seen Monsieur N'Dyaye for several weeks. If you intend to question me about him anymore, I have nothing more to say to you."

"Really?" said Yebga. He grabbed her by the wrist.

Sarah M'Bamina's eyes flashed with contempt. Yebga's grip tightened on her arm.

"Let me go," the woman cried. "Let go or I'll call the police! Leave me alone."

The reporter could not hold back his sudden flood of anger. With his other hand, he slapped her in the face. An earring went flying onto the carpet. This was the first time in his life that he had ever hit a woman and he felt a genuine thrill. At the same time, the ease of it astonished him.

"Help me," Sarah howled. "He's crazy!" He's going to kill me!"

The clients cautiously looked on, satisfied to watch the spectacle; only a barman intervened.

Yebga raised his fist.

"I don't advise you to come closer, you little prick. Mind your business. You can fuck our women, but you can't stop us from disciplining them!"

The man stopped dead in his tracks. Bit by bit, excitement spread through the lounge. Cries of "Someone stop him. Do something!" burst forth from feminine throats. Sarah sobbed, barely struggling.

"I hate to be lied to." Yebga continued to shake her violently. "A slut like you can't get away with this. I know you

148

saw N'Dyaye. I also know you were hired to replace Malika. So, are you going to cut the crap and tell me the truth now?"

Fury distorted his features. He hated this slut, all these suckers, these tragic fools.

"I don't know anything about it," cried the singer.

Yebga hit her again, violently enough this time to knock the girl off balance. Her hairdo lost its perfect order, and the tears gushing from her eyes plowed rainbow furrows down her cheeks. Yebga began to thrash her, and his face took on the color of eggplant with all the anger he had restrained these past few days. It was all too much. The ones who had held back at the beginning of this fight could no longer stay out of it at this point without losing face, even if it was between blacks. Now they stepped in. In any case, Yebga was not so physically impressive. In the twinkling of an eye, two men had jumped him and held him down while the singer ran over to the hatcheck girl, drowning her with sobs. Pinned to the floor, crushed under what looked to him like a sack of white meat, Yebga paradoxically regained his spirits and a frank desire to laugh! When the forest opened up, the weight disappeared from his chest and he saw the sky becoming peopled with kepis. A little out of breath, he warned, "I'm a reporter. Watch out. Don't mess up, gentlemen, or it'll cost you. Then he followed the cops with a supple gait, like a tired athlete escorted back to the dressing room after a lost match, still victorious.

Guided by his honor guard, he crossed the hotel lobby while indignant clients and hotel porters looked on. Outside it was raining. He was pushed into the paddy wagon. From where he sat, Yebga could see slices of the Boulevard Gouvion-Saint-Cyr through the barred windows.

The paddy wagon turned onto the Avenue des Ternes, turned right into the Avenue MacMahon, went up the Rue de l'Étoile and finally stopped in front of a police station. The policeman who sat on the bench across from Yebga didn't pay him the slightest bit of interest.

At the station, Yebga felt he'd been in places like this all his life. In the days when he was still assigned to news items, he'd been asked to scan the small neighborhood police stations in search of spicy news items concerning the black community. Of course, this time his situation was a little different. These gentlemen hadn't been introduced to him! Yebga, who felt no affinity for the peanut gallery, especially when he was in an inferior position, and the ticket holders around him were white, took on the haughty attitude of an important man. He looked coldly at the officer before whom he was brought.

"What is it?"

Yebga felt all the muscles in his body stiffen, as if the "it" meant him.

"We're bringing this one in. He raised a ruckus at the Méridien."

The cop stared at Yebga.

"He doesn't look too mean," he concluded.

"You'll have to ask his old lady. He made mincemeat out of her."

"Why didn't you bring her too?" the officer asked, laughing. "We could've done a thorough examination, to check out the bruises."

Then turning to Yebga, "What color are bruises on you people? Green or yellow?"

"Pink with stripes, I can vouch for it!"

This friendly bit of information emanated from a creature Yebga hadn't noticed until now among the other blue uniforms. But the mounds beneath her shirt weren't pockets which bulged from being stuffed with paper, and the white hair which framed her powdered face fell in curls over silver tinted eyelids.

The lady cop addressed Yebga with a friendly pout.

"Who do these guys think they are? Eh?"

But from across the counter, the other policemen were already railing. "Well, are you going to stand there all day? Anyway, you won't have time to write your article."

Yebga was escorted toward the cell.

"What were you doing at the Méridien? You people always bite off more than you can chew. I've seen a lot of your friends parade past here. You could call this the arrival platform."

Yebga tightened his jaw. His fists were clenched. It had taken fifteen years for him to come to this experience, and

150

finally here it was, and at first hand. At the paper, he'd specialized in ironic comments on the "paranoia" of blacks. Now he was getting his just deserts.

"I want to make a phone call," he managed to get out, although it cost him quite an effort.

"I'm not authorized to let you do that," replied his guard, looking away.

Yebga insisted.

Finally the guard shrugged his shoulders.

"O.K. Go on, go ahead. But put it in your rag that Marcel let you use the telephone. Go on, go on."

He opened the cell door and Yebga nonchalantly strolled toward the phone. He dialed the number of the Sunny Kingston, not even asking himself why Myriam was the first person he thought to tell. Once he had her on the line, he quickly explained the situation, asking her to call Inspector Moreau at the police stationt at Halles, and Glenn at the *World*. What he had done upset her more than finding out he was at the station, and he had to assure her that nothing serious had happened, that he was simply very tense, that he had stupidly lost control, that everything was fine now. Hanging up, he felt invulnerable, exultant: He'd been picked up by the cops, he'd called a great girl . . . and she had a crush on him!

Was he going to call Faye too? He thought about it for a moment, but recoiled at the prospect of being snubbed if he should ask a second favor. Head held high, he went back to his cell. No one even bothered to lock the bars behind him.

Sitting on his wooden bench, Yebga folded his hands and raised them to his eyes. As a child, like any other pickaninny, he used to run barefoot in the rain. The promised land that Dread Pol spoke about was nothing more than those childhood years when one raced through life like a wild dog. The first doubts and questions marked the gates of hell. This woman, Sarah, was a slut to whom N'Dyaye had promised the moon. Or else she was a lost woman frightened by his threats. On the whole, Yebga preferred to place the singer in the first category. That sort was less dangerous than the others who knew nothing.

The drone of voices in the station was like a lullabye

accompanied by the beating rain. Yebga began to dream he was in a classroom, which opened onto a courtyard planted with mango trees, on a wet winter day. The teacher was reading something, a passage from *Les Miserables* maybe, and he was gently falling asleep, eyes open.

"Inspector Moreau, from the Halles station," a voice announced.

Yebga jumped up. Moreau stepped forward with a measured pace. Behind him, with disheveled hair and a raincoat too large for her, stood Myriam. A wave of surprise swept through the police station.

"Who is this man?" said the inspector, designating Yebga, "and what is the motive for his detention? Why is the cell unlocked?"

"He . . . He raised a lot of Cain at the Méridien," stammered a low-ranking officer, shuffling a file.

"May I see the officer's report for his arrest?"

"I . . . we . . . It's not . . . It's not made out yet, sir."

Moreau made no comment and disappeared with the sergeant into a nearby office. Myriam sat on the edge of a chair, hidden by a counter from Yebga's view. Several minutes later, the two men reappeared. The sergeant, brandishing his useless key, made Yebga leave the cell and led him to the station door, where Moreau stood waiting with Myriam.

"Let's go!" said the inspector simply.

"The last time we saw each other it didn't go very well," Moreau began, on the sidewalk. "I asked you to be frank with me, and now I realize you weren't involved. At this point it's my duty to inform you that this matter concerns the French police. The fact that a black man was killed doesn't give you carte blanche to do anything you want. It doesn't give you any special jurisdiction. This case will not be solved by beating up women in hotel lounges, Monsieur Yebga."

Moreau enjoyed having the upper hand now. He continued.

"Why didn't you tell me about this singer in the first place?"

"Because I didn't know about her then! Until just recently, no one had told me about this Sarah M'Bamina, who knew Malika Diop and works for N'Dyaye!"

Yebga fell silent. Moreau played with his lighter. He finally lit a mild cigarette.

"Why don't you tell him everything?" Myriam suddenly asked, looking sad. She was standing near him now and quite naturally had slipped her arm through his. To the inspector, they must have looked like an old couple.

"Damn it! Don't be a jerk," blurted out Moreau, sending his cigarette smoke toward the clouds. "Especially if you really want to find N'Dyaye! Gonzales flew back to the jungle. He went home to Argentina. Anyway, he had diplomatic immunity. He has a concrete alibi. Youssouf N'Dyaye is our only lead, our only chance. He's probably hiding somewhere in France, and we need him before he leaves the country too! I know I can't write your article for you. But I can be of some use to you. I can guarantee you exclusive access to this case. Anyway, it seems to be your sole preoccupation!"

The shot struck home. Yebga relaxed.

"Good. Do you think we could go somewhere for a drink?"

They went into a cafe on the Place des Ternes. The night fell softly, much too fast.

When they were seated, the reporter began, "The way I see it, Malika's at the bottom of this whole thing. Her brother thought she'd been killed because she'd found out about something compromising to her boss. N'Dyaye made a feeble try, pretending she'd left because she was in love with an American. But his story didn't hold water.

"Why not?"

"Malika Diop would need a passport to leave France."

"What do you mean?"

Yebga took out the document he'd found in Dread Pol's pocket and placed it on the table before Moreau. The inspector leafed the pages of the passport somberly.

"What do you think about this?"

It was an affair between blacks. It was assumed that Yebga must know something about the matter.

"N'Dyaye had an African modeling agency. Each girl more

153

magnificent than the last. The way I see it, he used them as a cover for some kind of smuggling he was in. Maybe Malika got a whiff of this, so they made her disappear."

The three of them remained for a long while going over the facts and details of the case.

When they parted company, the rain had stopped falling. A light breeze blowing through Paris now made Yebga shiver.

Moreau agreed to keep him up to date each day by telephone and left them on the Boulevard Gouvion-Saint-Cyr, in front of the Mini.

"Creep," said Myriam, snuggling up to Yebga after she'd slammed the small car door.

Her hair smelled of straw, the wet forest.

"Stop it, Amos, or else we'll end up back at the police station . . . and for a good reason this time! Come home with me.

Chapter Twenty-Nine

That same night, Ed Smith and W. Jones Dubois made their appearance on the mezzanine of the Pink Toutou, where they had been lured by flashes of golden skin shining through high slitted skirts. Their day had not been wasted. Yebga's assailants were stationed in Neuilly. It would be a few hours before they could size up the neighborhood and draw up a plan of attack that would finally make them internationally famous. Since they had time to kill, they returned to the place of their first Parisian conquests. Something was amiss, however, when they reached the shadows of the bar. When Smith pushed the obscure object of his desire it squealed . . . in terror! Smith clutched her by the hair and led her briskly toward the stairs. A group of onlookers observed two things: The mop of hair stayed in his hand, and the victim did not react in a feminine manner! Dubois followed his companion's lead, and two transvestites ended up in an armchair at the foot of the steps. The Americans rampaged down the steps, cursing everyone in the club and hurling insults. Blind with rage, punching, kicking, they rearranged the painted faces of these shadowy imposters. The unfortunate bartender displayed a slight reaction and Jones grabbed him by the collar, sending him flying over the bar. He landed on the other side, where more victims lay sprawled out on the rug. In one swoop, the two accomplices knocked down the rows of bottles lined up behind the bar. The modest establishment soon took on the appearance of a saloon from a Western. This last display seemed to finally calm them down. In their immaculate white T-shirts, with their flowered boxer shorts sticking out over their belt loops, the Americans looked like a couple of phantoms who had risen from the grave. A thick layer of sweat covered their foreheads and glistened in their hair. They went back up the stairs to collect their clothes, and then returned once more to survey the room below with satisfaction, broken bottles smashed to bits behind the bar. A mildly intoxicating odor emanated from the mixture of alcohols. It was difficult to describe. The figures huddled behind the bar did not dare breathe. When Smith finally glanced over at the door, he noticed two thugs with sunburnt faces blocking it.

"Check this out!" he called to his companion.

Jones glanced over at the exit and saw the two shadows standing there.

"You two Sambos are going to have to pay for this," one of them muttered.

The other held up a switchblade. It made a dry snapping sound as the blade appeared, shining in the darkness. Dubois pulled his hat down over his eyes. Smith stepped forward.

"Listen, niggers," said the man holding the knife. "We're going to do such a good job, you'll be white before we're through with you. Your own goddamn mother won't even recognize you."

"Damn faggot," said Jones calmly. "Get out of my way!"

"Cut the crap," said the man, who assumed he was dealing with some lightweight from the Antilles. "This isn't Harlem!"

"O.K. Let's go for it," Jones signaled his partner.

Smith pushed the tails of his trenchcoat aside, reaching for the forty-five he'd kept with him since the Rue des Abbesses.

"You sons of bitches." Jones cried. He threw off the safety and crushed the bouncer's foot beneath his heel.

"Get lost, buddy," he barked, slamming his fist into the man's jaw with all his might. The second henchman made the mistake of hesitating. Before he knew what hit him, a heavy weight slammed his solar plexus. Jones readjusted his hat. Smith still held the forty-five in his shaking hand.

"You see?" he said when they were in the open air again. "Over here we don't actually have to use this thing. Paris is mellow. The only problem here is . . . when you're in the mood, it's hard to find a real woman." He reholstered the pistol behind his kidneys.

"You're right, Ed. But we'd better be more careful who we deal with. We might end up humping the Archbishop!"

Several bedrooms later, near Mogador, Smith said with the discernment of a drunk, "Man, these white chicks are too tame. Sure, they have technique, but where's the passion? They're in too much of a hurry. Not my style. I like a free-for-all."

Smith burst out in hoarse laughter. The alcohol and the women were beginning to take their toll. A taxi deposited them on the Rue Saint-Denis, where they recognized a girl in a doorway who had satisfied them several days before. She was from Guinea. This time, both men followed her upstairs and there was no extra charge. Back on the street again at eleven o'clock, they were unable to distinguish between the various bewitching fragrances which flitted over their skin. They started out for Halles, with a little sweet-talk for each streetwalker they passed.

Chapter Thirty

"What are you doing in our territory, M'sieur Moreau?"
"I don't think the Forum des Halles is particularly your territory. Anyway, you're hiding some information from me, L'il Georges."

"No. I'm stwaight in my affaiwes." The Antillean swallowed his r's.

"Yeah, I know. Maybe it's just that your affairs aren't too straight. Anyway, that's not why I'm here today. I'm looking for someone."

The passersby glanced curiously at this man wearing a beige trenchcoat seated amidst a group of idle blacks, then turned away quickly, fearing there might be trouble.

"So?"

"Stop playing dumb."

"I'm here to talk with some friends."

The inspector stared straight ahead. A new group of passengers had just arrived on the platform. He watched the obsessive merry-go-round of commuters, some going up, others coming down . . . like life, he thought. A siren sounded, announcing it was time to close the metal curtains on the shops. A pickpocket, whom Moreau had already had the pleasure of arresting, jostled a fat tourist, probably a German. The group surrounding Moreau fell silent. Then the conversation started up again; nothing had happened.

"Do you have a photo?" L'il Georges rolled his eyes wearily.

Moreau dug into his wallet.

"Well?"

"Well, that's N'Dyaye. I'm sure you know him. I guess you didn't find him in his office, since you here. So, you want to know where he lives . . . He's an Af'ican and we from the Antilles. We not part of the same world, we don't hang out together. The Af'icans here are students or businessmen like N'Dyaye. We don't go to the same clubs. They don't want anything to do with us, say we still slaves. What do you think, think we still slaves?"

Moreau didn't answer. He knew he was on thin ice.

"It's not gonna last. We going to rise up too, one day. Then the Af'icans won't laugh in our faces. They say that we have identity cards, but that we get worse tweatment than they do. They right about that. But we don't want anything to do with them, if they going to act like that."

"Are you going to tell me your life story, or are you going to tell me where I can find this guy? It doesn't pay the same, you know!"

"Someone saw him hanging out at a gay club in the sixth," L'il Georges reluctantly confided. "He was looking for a date."

"Are you sure it was N'Dyaye?"

"No. It was my cousin. How much is it worth to you?"

"Well, did he find what he was looking for?"

"I don't know. I don't think so. He wasn't looking for himself. It was for some rich American. He left an address."

L'il Georges dug into his pockets, removing a crumpled calling card. Moreau jotted down the information L'il Georges dictated to him from the card and slipped his notebook back into his trenchcoat. His envelope for L'il Georges had been prepared in advance.

Back in his office at the Halles station, Moreau retrieved the notebook from his pocket and underlined the following address: 102 Rue de Charenton, tower B, sixth floor, apartment 613.

Chapter Thirty-One

Yebga enjoyed a few hours of welcome rest at Faye's place. The American woman needed to touch base more than he did. She needed to experience the minor details one shares with a loved one, like a meal together, details which become precious when threatened. Seated at the table, going through this ritual, Faye felt a sense of comfort, as though their relationship had been restored. She started when the phone rang, addressing Yebga scornfully, "Why didn't you turn on the answering machine, Amos?"

He strolled into the living room and picked up the phone. It was Moreau.

"Hello, Yebga?"

The cop was in high spirits.

"I'm on N'Dyaye's trail. I have a serious lead. His wife knows where he is and how to find him."

"But we were already at his place," Yebga replied in a neutral tone.

"If you were a cop, you poor chump, you'd know that trick. It's the oldest one in the book. Since he wasn't at his apartment when you checked it, the old fox thought he'd be safe there, that we wouldn't dream of going back."

Moreau was obviously waiting for Yebga's reaction. It was a waste of time.

"Well," said the inspector, "I just wanted to let you know. Got any news at your end?"

"Nothing so far," said Yebga, trailing off.

Moreau hung up, disappointed.

Faye stared at Amos. "I don't like the look on your face," she said, sidling up to him. "I've never seen you this way. It's not the way you look when you love me or when you joke around. It's a cold, faraway look. It's like you don't see me. You're frightening me, Amos."

Yebga smiled weakly.

"It would be ideal for you if we were stranded on a desert island, right?"

Faye looked away.

"There are no more desert islands," Yebga continued. "Can't you understand, honey? I thought there were, too. I thought we could live apart from the world, leading our own lives, safe, protected. But we're affected by other people, our illusions are destroyed. Suddenly everything seems to be out of control because we weren't prepared for the shock. I don't know what's going on or why I'm involved in this. I don't understand what's making me go on. At first I knew what it was that I wanted. I understood my slightest gestures, my slightest words. Now, it's as if I'm no longer living inside of myself. It's hard to come to terms with. Don't ask me for explanations. I don't have any. Or maybe there are too many. Some explanations go back generations and generations."

"What are you talking about, Amos? We were happy together. Why do you have to complicate everything with your intellectual reasoning?"

"We were living a lie. It couldn't last. Yes, there are other people. Sooner or later, you have to acknowledge them."

Faye looked into Yebga's eyes with that gleam of imploring distress which illuminates the silence of words. He stared at her blankly. Neither heard the doorbell until it rang a second time.

"There's no use not answering it," he said, shrugging.

He found Smith and Jones standing in the doorway.

"Well, come in. Don't just stand there."

"What are you talking about?" said Dubois, stepping forward. "You're the one who's blocking our way!"

There was something explosive about his breath, a mixture of burnt alcohol and marijuana. Smith followed him into the apartment. The two Americans were drunker than the entire 125th Street police station on Christmas Day.

They reeled into the living room and collapsed into "their" armchairs. Faye had taken refuge in the kitchen when the bell rang. She stood hunched over beside the refrigerator when Yebga cama in to announce the arrival of the detectives. He was unable to ignore the sobs which she attempted to hold back. He drew near to her.

"What's the big deal? Why are you still crying?"

He tried to stroke her hair but she brusquely moved away. Lifting her head, she revealed a swollen face.

"I'm not crying! And I don't need your pity. Go back to your friends! You all seem to get along so well together! You like hanging around with them in their macho world. I thought you were different, Amos. Different from those brutes. They're always coming and going, coming and going. You'd think they lived here. They think they have a right to whatever they please. We don't owe them anything, Amos! Not a thing! We're not responsible for centuries of slavery. Even that doesn't justify it. I want to live in the present. I don't owe anybody anything. They take my car as if it was theirs. Is this what you mean by other people affecting us? If you feel indebted to these people, settle your accounts without me. I shouldn't have to suffer the consequences of your whims and your bad conscience!"

Voices echoed from the living room. Smith and Dubois were talking loud and laughing.

"Anyway, they're completely smashed," Faye hissed.

Yebga leaned back with his elbows resting on the sink. He stared at length, as if seeing her for the first time. He weighed his words.

"You're right, they're smashed. Don't worry. They're not here to take anything away from you this time. They brought *my* car back."

The reporter emphasized the "my." This did not escape Faye.

"Amos!"

"I won't be disturbing you anymore with my whims, baby. I'm going off to wallow in the macho world. I never should have left it. I intend to stay there until I croak, along with all the other people who live there. You can stay safely over here on this side of the fence in your little bubble. Don't open your door, though. Don't ever open it again."

The words came swiftly. Yebga seemed unbelievably calm, gauging the effects of the poison he was injecting. Faye's mouth fell open. She was speechless.

"I'm carrying centuries of slavery, sweetheart. You're blind not to see its marks on my back. But if you're blind, I can't make you see. I can explain things, but I can't change you."

Jones' head appeared in the doorway, his body followed. He planted himself between the couple, facing Yebga.

"Have you forgotten about us, kid? We've been hanging around all alone in this big apartment. We're thirsty. Do you want us to die of thirst?"

Only an innate sense of balance kept the detective on his feet. Yebga glanced quickly at Faye. She was standing up again. She had obviously made up her mind and wasn't about to give in. Yebga felt an irrepressible desire to hurt her. He slipped his arm around Jones' shoulders.

"Excuse me, man. The wine here is acidic," he said, sneering. "If you really want to quench your thirst, I know some places you won't forget. I'm dying of thirst myself."

"Good news at last," said the giant appreciatively.

Dubois was snoring in the living room.

"Get up, you old mule! We're pulling up anchor!"

Smith jumped like a demon, reaching for the pistol in his belt.

"What's going on?"

Jones burst out laughing.

161

"It's only me, man. Save your lead for someone who deserves it."

Yebga rushed through the apartment, shoving books, clothes and scattered papers into a plastic bag. Faye stood backed up against the kitchen door watching him, her eyes flooding with tears, her jaw tight.

Yebga finally rejoined the ex-cops, his arms loaded down with booty.

"Freeze!" bellowed Dubois.

"Hold it right there!" answered Smith, staggering even more now.

Yebga pointed to the statuettes on the coffee table.

"Here, gather up those treasures from the land of our ancestors. My hands are full."

Smith relieved him of several books, while Gravedigger stuffed Malika's souvenirs into his pockets.

"We're off," said Yebga. "Prepare yourselves."

The three men clambered down the stairs in an uproar equal to the charge of the light brigade. Outside on the noisy street, they fell into the bustling city's rhythm. Yebga took a deep breath of the fresh air, hoping it would soothe the lump in his throat. When he reached into his pocket, he noticed he had the keys to Faye's Mini. He thrust his belongings into Gravedigger's arms and ran back to the apartment building. Through the door, he found Faye sprawled out in the entryway.

"I forgot to give you back your car keys."

She didn't move. Yebga jingled the keys. He felt stupid standing there immobile, hesitantly staring at Faye's blond hair. He checked himself, playing back their quarrel in his mind. Was it only a quarrel? What did it matter anyway? It was too vague, too heavy, too ominous. He didn't need this lurid pathos, especially not now.

"You're coming back, aren't you, Amos?"

Yebga slammed the door behind him. What a question! Only a white girl would have asked. Maybe the solution lay in having several women, not just one who was possessive and whined, making you feel guilty rather than silently understanding you, forgiving you when it was necessary.

Coffin and Gravedigger were already waiting in the Alfa

162

Romeo. They welcomed Yebga with thick laughter.

"What took you so long, kid? What were you doing to her? Did you jump her in the elevator, or just seduce her?"

Yebga started the car and drove off. He felt both good and bad. Why should he atone for sins he wasn't even sure he had committed? His father had always scolded him as a child for being too sensitive. "You're like the white man," he'd say. "A romantic."

"Hey," scoffed Smith, who was riding shotgun. "What'd she do, bite you?"

The Alfa turned sharply, thrusting them back into their seats. The silence was briskly restored for a moment, and then Smith started in again, making comments as they raced along. It was as if they were at some sort of match, where the shuffling pedestrians were the losers.

"Good," Smith gloated. "That's the way to drive! Just like in the good old days, remember, Gravedigger?"

The traffic lights paraded past. Paris stretched out before them, immodest as a naked stripper. All they needed was some background music. Dubois pushed in a cassette tape protruding from the car radio, and the plodding notes of Rodney Franklin's piano filled the night with an electric sound, a tune called "The Groove."

The Alfa pulled up in front of the Kaïssa, a famous African restaurant on the Rue des Deux-Gares. For what seemed a long time, the car doors remained shut, and an occasional passerby could glimpse the spectacle of three black men nodding their heads and drumming with their hands, enclosed in a four-wheeled aquarium. Excessive energy without sound.

Inside the Kaïssa, Yebga ordered steamed fish in a strong pimento sauce, sweet potatoes and an *Aloko* plate. The Americans, however, hesitated. Soon the table was covered in successive waves of dishes brought by Jo, the chef. He was a Cameroonian with a skull like a peeled mango. He made it his duty to bring them samples of each item they questioned on the menu. They still had trouble making up their minds.

"These guys are great," said Jo, each time he returned

from the kitchen. "I like people who appreciate my cooking."

With help from the wine and the pepper, Yebga's laughter sounded like a chorus to the concert of other Africans seated in the small square room. Smith glanced over at a few stray whites who stood out amid the bronze fauna. His eyes were reddened by the alcohol.

"What are they doing here?" he roared. This place is for blacks. We don't want any white asses in the way! Amos, tell Jo to throw them out! Tonight's our night. Tell him to get rid of them!"

"Yeah," Dubois shot back enthusiastically. "White folks outside. Go get a tan!"

Yebga glimpsed the horrified expression on Jo's face, then realized that he himself had taken up the tirade in French. What had come over him? He regained composure and winked conspiratorially at the chef. Jo reluctantly winked back. Fortunately the interlopers, already drunk on the house's special cocktail, were by now reduced to the status of burnt-out candles. They prepared to catch a breath of air, and laboriously began to divide the bill. As they left the restaurant, the ex-cops started in on a funeral march. This was quickly stifled by the harmonious arpeggios of a guitarist from Zaire.

The first notes reminded Yebga of the bars in Kinshasa. There were girls lined up with amber thighs, bronze backs, and metallic breasts sculpted by yellow and green neon lights. He had cut the mooring ropes and sailed now. He felt good. The only thing missing was Myriam. He called out to no one in particular, "Let's move these chairs. You've stuffed yourselves enough for one night. Let's see if you can shake it."

Everyone was in agreement, even an old white-haired man from the Ivory Coast, who sat toying with the necklace around his shy young companion's neck.

"Good idea, Junior," he said, removing his jacket and un-bottoning his vest. "Let's move these chairs."

Jo smiled at this decision, which signaled the beginning of a big commotion. The volume of the music quickly doubled and all eyes followed Yebga, who hurled himself out onto the dance floor and expertly executed some opening steps. The ball had begun. Yebga hadn't forgotten how to dance. His ankles weren't even stiff.

"I like that! Show me how to do it! Yeah!"

Smith stood up and, facing Yebga, began to copy his steps. The spectators applauded frantically, marking the beat with loud shouts of "Shebah!" Soon the small improvised dance floor was overrun. With the help of a few women incited by the hot night to join in, the Kaïssa sailed gallantly in pursuit of its glorious ancestors, the Boule Noire and the Cabane Bambou. It was well into the night before the shouts and uproar died down and the dancers began to take their leave. They all thanked Smith, Dubois and Yebga warmly. By now they were regarded as distinguished luminaries of Parisian night life. In fact, they barely knew the city. Alone again, the four men collapsed into their chairs.

Jo shook his head. "Amos, your friends are the real Mc-Coy. I love you," he told both Smith and Jones.

"We love you too," Smith answered with a grin, taking the accolade in stride.

"They're really O.K.," Jo told Yebga. "I want to be just like them. Black Americans aren't like the rest of us. They've done the incredible. Look at Carl Lewis. Ray Charles . . . We're a bunch of dead losers. We don't even come up to their ankles."

"What are you talking about?" Yebga scowled. "These guys are just as lost as we are. Maybe more so. It's hard being black and American. Don't kid yourself."

Jo was not convinced. He scratched his bald head and continued to argue.

"Look at our strivers," he said. "They bleach their skin to look less black. You'd really have to be stupid to do that."

"Yeah. what about Michael Jackson? Didn't he just get a nose job?"

"They've got balls over there. Take for example, 'Black is beautiful.' How many people would you find here who would say that?" Jo said, urging the two Americans to back him up.

Smith and Dubois nodded, although they knew no French.

"They have stars over there. One of their compatriots came here with N'Dyaye last week. You should have seen him, dressed up like a prince. N'Dyaye said he was a big kingpin in the States."

Yebga recovered his lucidity in a fraction of a second.

"What was the guy's name?"

"Hang on a second."

Jo made his way over to the bar and opened a drawer. He returned with a card which he handed to Yebga.

"It's written at the top there: Don Knight."

The two ex-cops gave a start.

"Are you talking about Don Knight?"

"Yes. Why? Do you know him?"

No." Dubois said. "I was just curious. We've heard a lot about him in New York."

Yebga regretted that his mind was in such a fog.

"Did you know that N'Dyaye is on the run?" he asked Jo.

The ex-fisherman's eyes grew wide as a fried marlin's. "But he's prominent, respected, rich . . ."

"He killed . . ."

"Oh, my God!" Jo raised his hands toward the sky.

Dubois, misinterpreting this gesture, proposed a toast. Smith managed to join in, although his vocabulary had long since been reduced to an occasional stomach rumble. It was definitely time to call it quits.

Yebga tapped Jo's shoulder. "Come on, man. Don't sweat it. Just bring the bill. Unless you want us to sleep here."

The bald man stood with difficulty.

"But why?" he stammered. "He had everything: money, women, reputation . . ."

"Who knows?" Yebga replied vaguely. "Come on! Bring the bill, so we can go to bed. We won't need any lullabyes tonight."

"I saw him just last week. Something seemed to be eating him. Now you're telling me he killed . . . The bill? Forget it. This is on the house."

Yebga thanked their host. The two Americans, when told, protested loudly. Before leaving, they extended Jo an elaborate invitation to visit Harlem, and would not relent until he had accepted, although with no precise arrival date.

When Yebga finally slouched behind the wheel, he felt that he would need at least a week to get his strength back, but the Americans, despite their age, seemed to be catching a second wind. They could take stock of the damage in the morning. They were still much too euphoric for that now.

"Hey, kid. do you have any oldies? Something by Nat King Cole or Mahalia Jackson?"

"Check in there," said Yebga, waving as he tried to steer the car.

Jones rummaged through the glovebox and removed an old Otis Redding tape, the immortal "Dock of the Bay." The Messiah's tormented voice filled up the car. Soon the floorboards echoed with their stomping. Clearly these two weren't ready for bed.

Yebga knew an all-night bar in upper Belleville. Behind its curtained glass doors lay the perfect shelter for his indefatigable friends. He drove there at full throttle. Ali smiled when the men walked in.

"Is that you, Amos? *Ya habibi!* I must be dreaming."

They hugged one another, then Yebga introduced his two companions. Ali's cafe was in a big square room with a bar and several tables. It was a meeting place for African immigrants: Senegalese road-sweepers, Cameroonian lawyers, university students from Burkinabés, musicians from Mali, firemen from Zaire. Along with Arabs from every country in the world, they came here to kill nights that seemed too short, before closing a deal or going back to work. Ali took Smith and Dubois by the arm, escorting them to a table in the back.

"Where are your friends from?" he asked Yebga.

"New York."

The little Algerian whistled with admiration. Some people at the next table were playing cards. Shouts and cries of joy and despair could be heard in several languages around the room. Musicians from Xalam sat eating *couscous* across the room. They had come here from a concert. Yebga greeted them with a nod.

"Do you know a lot of places like this?" asked Jones.

"A few," said the reporter with a smile.

Jones turned toward the card playars.

"I'm feeling lucky, Ed," he confided.

"You're not the only one. I think we should have a go. To-night's our night."

Before Jones could rise, Ali returned with glasses and a bottle. He straddled a chair opposite.

"You're going to find this first-rate. So will your friends. Monga brought it back from Douala yesterday."

The reporter eyed the green flask with suspicion, as Ali waved it under his nose. He raised it to the light, then filled three glasses, laughing.

"Aren't you going to join us?"

"I have to stay sober. I'm your host."

Yebga raised his glass. Smith and Dubois followed suit. They wracked their brains for a profound toast, and finally settled on "to Paris." The decibel level made up for its banality. They downed the contents of their glasses in a gulp. The alcohol seared their throats like a hot knife. Then they felt its fire crackling in their stomachs.

"Wow," Smith bellowed. "You wanna kill us?"

"What do you call that?" asked Dubois.

"We call it 'Coat of Fire.' Its alcoholic content is undetermined.

Yebga translated. The two Americans nodded in admiration.

"Does this come from the motherland?"

From the way Dubois said "motherland," Yebga sensed that he wanted to talk about Africa.

Smith said, "You know, we have to go there one day, Gravedigger. Even if it's just to drink this great rot-gut."

It was almost five o'clock in the morning when they left Ali's. Yebga felt reduced to a string of reflexes. The ex-pression on his face was like a mummy's. Smith and Dubois, showing some signs of fatigue, still found the strength to hum a Manu Dibango tune as they staggered to the car.

Yebga could not recall why he had surrendered himself to this strange pilgrimage. By now it didn't matter. Neither did Faye. Each glass he had emptied was like a hammer which drove the wedge in deeper between them. By now the wedge itself had disappeared, and Faye with it.

Yebga returned to Saint-Germain-des-Prés with all the car windows open.

Chapter Thirty-Two

Black coffee for N'Dyaye, warm milk for Don Knight and tea for Coetzee. Spoons clinked in china cups, but Don Knight's noisy chewing was the only sound which disturbed the calm of their breakfast. Knight hadn't taken time to study proper etiquette in the course of his inexorable climb toward the summits of American business. He viciously attacked his third croissant. They were in a spacious room with high ceilings. The walls were hung with large royal-blue tapestries. Thick Persian carpets covered the floors. The doors were decorated with the characteristic carving of 18th-century French nobility. (All this contrasted wildly with the interior design of Don Knight's kingdom: aluminum-framed, remote-control beds covered in fur; desk/bars made of teak, containing stereos and sheathed in leather.) When one of the doors opened, a broad-shouldered man entered the room wearing a satin robe, looking as if he'd just awakened. N'Dyaye, appearing skimpy in his civil servant's suit, ran over to greet him. "Good morning, Minister."

The man replied with a disdainful gesture. "Spare me your *salaams*, N'Dyaye," he said.

He walked to an empty chair. N'Dyaye's companions, profiting from what they'd heard, addressed the man with discreet hellos.

"Let me pour myself a coffee before we begin," he said, filling his cup.

He took a sip and then surveyed them one by one.

"Is everything ready?" he asked Coetzee.

"Yes. The weapons arrive tonight."

"Perfect. And you, Knight, do you have the money?"

"I sent a telex. Everything should be ready by this afternoon."

"Good. Working with professionals is such a pleasure,"

169

he said, applying butter to his toast. "And you, N'Dyaye, as soon as this deal is closed, I suggest you take a brief vacation. Your name's coming up a little too often around here. You *have* sold off what we had left, haven't you?"

"Yes, Minister. The last shipment went out a week ago."

The broad man gobbled down his toast and wiped his lips. This was a sign that the interview was now over. He walked to the French windows and threw them open. The sun was high. The lawn stretched out smooth before him to a small forest which surrounded the mansion. There were guards posted throughout the garden and between the trees. Security would have to be reinforced tonight, he thought. Coetzee stood up.

"Well, I'm going to make sure everything's ready."

The large man turned to leave the room, but stopped briefly beside N'Dyaye, who stood in the middle of the room, staring at the figures in the rug.

"The girl you found me was superb, N'Dyaye. You're a connoisseur." He spoke into N'Dyaye's ear with a strong guttural accent. "I'd really like to introduce her sister to a friend, if it's at all possible."

"Certainly, Minister. I'll make a note to contact you as soon as I have arranged things."

"Thank you, N'Dyaye. Now go on."

When N'Dyaye offered his hand to Don Knight taking his leave, he felt it had been seized by a fist of iron.

"Do you remember what I asked you?"

N'Dyaye grimaced.

"Yes," he answered wearily. "It's not really in my line, but I asked someone to find what you're looking for. I'll stop by soon and see what he came up with."

"It's kind of you," said Knight, stroking his ruby signet ring. "But you seem put off. Why? It's not forbidden by Islam."

N'Dyaye walked off. "These Africans are really uptight," Knight thought.

Chapter Thirty-Three

Yebga woke up late. Myriam lay stretched beside him reading. She had dressed already. Yebga felt acutely aware that he was naked. He surveyed the strange bedroom he was in, but could not connect it with his antics of last night. The young mulatto gently kissed his face. So he hadn't done anything to compromise this new relationship after all! He regretted leaving his memory beside a green bottle at Ali's, but he was happy.

It was already past noon. Yebga had no appointments to keep, and yet he had wakened feeling late for something. He could not explain why he felt so pressed for time.

"Can I use the phone?"

"Sure," smiled Myriam, as though she had expected him to ask. "I'll just make breakfast."

Yebga rolled over and reached for the receiver. On the pillow he smelled Myriam's perfume. It was new to him. He wondered, was this the beginning of a new chapter in his life? He liked the fragrance in any case, and the bottle too, for that matter! When Glenn's voice boomed at the other end of the line, Yebga held the receiver at an angle to save his eardrum.

"Amos! Are you crazy? What is going on? What do you think this is, the unemployment office? You show up once every two weeks!"

After his editor's tirade, Yebga briefly explained the situation.

"Nothing is really clear yet," he said. "But I'm doing some cross-checking. For instance, there are a few knots in the N'Dyaye–Don Knight connection. I'm looking into it. These things take time. And then I have my Americans to look after. In the end, they'll supply me my material, whatever it turns out to be. There ought to be an entire book about them. So just take it easy. I'm working. I don't have any answers yet, or even a title for the article. But before

171

too long I'll have enough for a lead story and a follow-up."

Rather than lose face, Glenn at first refused to sound convinced, but by the time he asked Yebga to stay in closer touch, his voice had mellowed. Yebga knew he had won the round when they hung up. Still in bed, he devoured his breakfast, then leaped from the covers, naked as a jaybird, and dashed for the shower. Myriam burst out laughing.

"No, darling. It's over here. That's the kitchen. I don't want to scare the neighbors. Try the bathroom," she said, pointing to a closed door with a smile, as though she'd seen others make this same mistake.

Yebga filched a few aspirins from the medicine cabinet and dressed quickly. He didn't feel up to making vows or explanations to Myriam. She understood. She made no mention of last night. She didn't try to kiss him in the doorway. Instead she handed him the statuettes that he had now forgotten. He shrugged and stammered that he'd call her later, when things were clear. She nodded weakly. When he went out, she sat down on the bed. She was still staring at the crumpled sheets a long while after Yebga had disappeared down the stairs.

Yebga soon arrived in the Rue Casimir-Delavigne.

"You just missed them," said the receptionist. "They left less than a quarter of an hour ago!"

Yebga thanked her and ran back to the street to hail a taxi. He was bathed in sweat when the driver dropped him in front of the *World*. In the hall, he came across Mukoni loaded down with heavy files. Despite his burden and his penchant for ignoring any problems but his own, Mukoni stopped today to ask if everything was all right. Yebga suspected his exhaustion must be showing. He stammered a few general remarks. Before the man could press him, Yebga asked, "Was that Tchad? Is Glenn here?"

"I don't know. See for yourself," Mukoni said.

Yebga felt relieved to get away so simply. Then a flash of inspiration overcame him.

"Does the name Don Knight mean anything to you?" he asked.

Mukoni's eyes grew wide. "You've never heard of Don Knight?"

"Just answer the question," Yebga said.

"O.K., O.K.," said Mukoni. "I can see which side of bed *you* got up on this morning." Mukoni took his time, straightening a cuff, then turned to Yebga with the weary look of an instructor about to administer the baccalaureate exam to a group of mentally disabled students.

"Don Knight is one of the richest black men in the States. He owns a string of beauty supply houses and he only employs blacks to operate them. That's the official version, anyway. The IRS suspects he's been fencing stolen merchandise, running gambling houses and heading an agency of pimps, though people say his taste runs to young boys. There's been talk of him setting up some foundation here. I guess that covers it. Oh, if you're interested, he also organizes boxing matches."

"What would a guy like that be doing in Paris?"

"You mean he's in France?"

"Are you deaf?"

The elevator clanged to a stop on the third floor and the two reporters strolled across the editorial room to Glenn's office. The editor-in-chief was out. Yebga settled into an empty armchair. Mukoni perched on a corner of the desk.

"How do you know that Don Knight's in France?"

"Listen," Yebga said, exasperated. "Let's just drop it, O.K.?"

"Funny, the press association didn't tell us about it. Knight is a bigshot in black American circles. He's not the type to disguise himself as a pushcart vendor." Mukoni rubbed his chin.

"Do you remember Salif Maktar Diop's accident?"

"Yeah, sure."

"I think Knight had something to do with it."

"Are you crazy? What would a man like Knight stand to gain from bumping off some two-bit dealer?"

"It's a little more complicated than that, Rodolphe. Something strange is going on in this city. I haven't put my finger on it yet, but I can sense it. I'm beginning to dream about it. I can feel it in my bones. It's something bigger than us, but it's somehow tied in."

Mukoni walked over to the window, gazed down at the street below, then turned back to Yebga.

"Hey, what are you anyway, a reporter or a clairvoyant? Give me one of your Davidoffs," he said.

Yebga thrust a hand into the pocket of his jacket and encountered Malika's two small statuettes. He recalled Myriam handing them to him just as he was leaving her. Beads of sweat broke out on his forehead; then, like a robot, he searched another pocket and exhumed the white box of cigarettes. Mukoni stared intently, like a cat eyeing a bird. He ignored the box that Yebga offered him.

"What are those things?"

"Souvenirs," he said mysteriously.

"Can I have a look at them?"

"Yeah, sure. But be careful. They mean a lot to me. In this whole farce, they're the only link I've turned up to Malika. It's almost as if she gave me them herself."

Mukoni disregarded Yebga's comments. He seized the objects and took them to the window.

"Where did you find these things?" he whispered.

"I told you, Rodolphe. They belong to a girl I haven't even met, Salif's sister. One of her friends gave them to me."

"What's her name?"

"If you're looking to get laid, you'll have to wait. She's traveling at the moment."

"Damn it."

Yebga could see that Mukoni wasn't joking. The man paced back and forth before the window like a panther in a cage.

"I'm not sure yet, but if I'm right, you've got a time bomb on your hands. I see now what you meant about this thing we're all connected to," he said. "I don't know where it comes from, or where it's going, but it's out there. I can feel it too."

"What are you talking about?"

"Do you remember the case I was working on about six months ago?"

The Cameroonian thought hard for a moment.

"You mean your story on the million-dollar museum heist?"

174

Yebga stopped abruptly, staring at the statuettes in Mukoni's hand. His eyes grew wide.

"Do you mean these . . ."

"I can't be positive until I check. I still have the photos of the rarest pieces. They're in the archives."

Yebga lit a Davidoff. The pungent smoke felt soothing to his throat. Mukoni eyed him with amusement.

"You really ought to take a shower," he chided. "You're getting careless. If you think you're going to keep your girl like that . . ."

Yebga ran a hand across his face. A scruffy growth of beard grated his fingers.

"I am clean, you know, unshaven, yes, but clean. And I promise you, some women like . . ."

"You had me worried," said Mukoni.

"I broke it off with Faye."

Mukoni felt too off guard to comment. Yebga cuffed him on the shoulder.

"You don't have to pretend you're at a funeral, you know. Quite the contrary." He grinned, looking abstracted, then abruptly changed the subject. "Mukoni, do you think that Chester Himes invented his two detectives, or do you think someone inspired him?"

He exhaled a thick stream of smoke. Mukoni coughed.

"You're working much too hard," he answered wryly. "You've got too many headlines going all at once. Why don't you take a few days off. The sea might do you good. Go to the seashore. I'll hold your statuettes for you. I'll be here all day if you want to know for sure about them."

Yebga waved impatiently and left the office. His ears were no longer ringing, and he enjoyed the few rays of sunlight which trembled from the sky. He slowly made his way to the Metro entrance. It seemed like an eternity since he'd last made this descent into the center of the earth. He observed the world around him with amazement. At the Halles station, three cops accosted him and asked to see his identity papers. It was the first time he'd been harassed like this in the fifteen years since he had come to France. "I really must look like a molester of old women," he thought, removing the green papers from his pocket. The cops examined these at length from every angle, then returned them, looking sheepish. "Monsieur," one muttered. Yebga grinned at him triumphantly.

He hung around the fountain at Innocents for a few minutes, then headed toward the Rue des Lombards.

Samba's brother-in-law opened the heavy black door. There was nothing friendly about the look he gave Yebga. His face still showed traces of his recent treatment at the hands of Dubois and Smith. He pointed with his chin toward the stairs in the direction of Samba's office nook. The reporter groped his way down darkened stairs into the coolness of a cellar. A faint glimmer of light filtered under the door of Samba's den like a fog beacon. Yebga knocked twice softly. He heard muffled male voices through the door. He knocked again, then heard a chair and footsteps. The door opened, and Yebga stood facing a man he'd never seen. Samba sat facing the door, his back to a small table. He didn't bother to stand up.

"Come on in, Amos. I've been waiting for you. I was about to send someone to look for you. This man here has a few things to tell you," he said tersely. "It's not important that you know his name."

Yebga turned to the mysterious informant. He was wearing a beige linen suit, rather light for the time of year, a sort of safari ensemble. The reporter studied the contours of his scarred face; it was as though the man never smiled. Behind the eyes there lay a dead expression. Yebga guessed the man was from Zaire.

"I know what N'Dyaye was up to with the girls he looked after," the stranger offered in a heavy accent. Then he fell silent.

Yebga glanced quickly over at Samba. The old man seemed lost in thought, as if what he was hearing did not concern him.

The Zairean continued. "French customs officers aren't hard on objects, they're hard on men. But if your papers are in order when you come into the country, no one bothers to search your bags. They really only search them when you leave. N'Dyaye was a middle man. He used the girls to transport merchandise. That's why he always kept them on the move. And if one got nabbed, she just said the masks or statues she was carrying were gifts. I took them to the airport. I filled their suitcases. I bought their tickets."

Yebga stared at the man's curved lips, which quivered like the beating wings of a butterfly. Suddenly he started. Samba's voice cracked the still air.

"That's enough," he ordered. "Now get lost. Get the hell out of here, and don't open your trap ever again. As for you," he said, turning to Yebga, "I'm sure you didn't understand it all, you couldn't. There are some things people your age just can't grasp. I'm even beginning to lose track. There's someone behind N'Dyaye, Amos. Someone with enormous power. Someone who can sow life just as easily as death."

"What difference does that make, if men are murdered on the way? The ends don't justify spilled blood. The means aren't moral."

"Don't interrupt. You don't know what you're saying. Morality has nothing to do with it. We're living in times of great confusion. Schoolboys call this history. I call it life. It moves blindly forward and carries us away with it. N'Dyaye isn't responsible for anything. Life is pushing him. He isn't strong enough to go on alone. Look for him. I know you'll find him. But you won't find out what's going on from him. You'll find a man made of flesh and blood. A rich and powerful man. But there will still be someone else behind him. I'm worn out. The keys my grandfather entrusted to me don't open any doors now. I'm going back to Ziguinchor. I'm selling out and leaving. I knew this day would come. It will come for you too. Meanwhile, don't get yourself in debt. It's better to be poor and to have your dignity. Look at Youssouf. Deep down he's not a bad guy. He's just been sucked into a whirlpool. He has family back home waiting for money. If you tell them life here is difficult, they think you're being selfish. Youssouf had to find money. He would never accept money from a white man. The man he's working for is African. Youssouf N'Dyaye and I grew up together. His father died in the war, fighting for the French. His brothers followed. N'Dyaye himself almost died in Algeria. No. He never would accept foreign money.

"You've got to find him, and you can help him, Amos. We have to help each other. We can't allow each other to be tried in white men's courts. We can't let them humiliate N'Dyaye. I could give you names, lists of names, businessman, ministers, even presidents. They all knew Youssouf. What's the point? There is none. Names won't help you find Youssef. By itself, a name doesn't stand for anything. I'm Samba Diouf Demba. What does that mean?"

He blew his perfumed breath in Yebga's face.

"What will you do if you find him before the police?"

Yebga hesitated.

"I'll make him tell me everything. Then I'll write an exposé to show the whole mess up. It is still a scandal!"

"And then what will you do?"

"He has nothing to fear, if he's innocent. But a man was killed. N'Dyaye is a key witness."

"What you mean is, you're going to turn him in. You're going to turn on your brother, do the white man's police work. What gives you the right, Amos? Is it because you went to school? Or because your father's not around to tell you who is good and who is bad?"

Samba looked away.

"Times are changing. I would never have betrayed my brother, Amos."

"N'Dyaye isn't my brother."

The club owner looked helpless.

"The word 'family' means nothing to young Africans in France. You want to forget where you came from. You want to lock yourselves up between four walls with a woman and some children. That's where your family stops. You don't have any brothers or fathers or grandfathers or uncles or aunts or cousins. How do you manage to live alone like this?"

Yebga stood, enraged with shame and anger. Many years ago he had decided to make it on his own here; to make a place for himself in a world where black was one race among many. His mirror reflected a clean image, a landscape chosen freely, where he survived thanks to the skills he had acquired over the years. Now that image had begun to fade into the shadow of a continent he mistakenly assumed did not exist. He felt a need to cling to something solid, to stay afloat. The newspaper . . . perhaps Samba was trying to upset him, to prevent him from doing his job. Maybe it was nothing more than that. Maybe Samba had even joined in with the dealers.

Looking somber, as if he were digesting the elder's lesson, Yebga promised the old man he would come back.

Chapter Thirty-Four

"Are you the new editor-in-chief?" Mukoni laughed.

Yebga had found Glenn's office empty and sat down there to organize his notes. He finished the sentence he was working on, then raised his head.

"Where have you been hiding?"

"I was working for you. Imagine that."

Mukoni's arms were loaded down with files. He sat down in a chair facing his colleague.

"Are you writing already?"

"How could I be writing? I have my hands full just sorting out the details."

Rodolphe set his files down on a corner of the desk and grinned at Yebga.

"Look at this: photos of the major pieces pinched from the museums in the past five years."

The folder bulged. Yebga quickly sifted through the photos. There were more masks and ivory sculptures than he could count. Eventually he came upon the lot Malika's statues once were part of. Half the girl's heritage had vanished.

"Every country in the world has these photos," Mukoni said. "Africa may not have a Mona Lisa, but we do have these. And if they're ripping this off too . . ."

"Stop whining," Yebga countered. "You don't give a goddamn about your culture."

"What's eating you, Amos?"

"Let's just drop it. What else did you find out?"

"The local investigations haven't turned up anything. Not one lead. Can you imagine how worthless the Maka-linese police must be."

"Well, you seem to know everything. Who's in charge of the police down there?"

"The minister of defense, supposedly. But if you look at the police reports, you'll see they've all been signed by the same person. And he's not really the chief of police."

Yebga picked a file from the stack and reexamined it. He saw the same name scrawled across the bottom of each page in black ink: Mathias Mfalane.

"Who is this guy?"

"He's the minister of defense's brother-in-law."

Samba's words echoed in Yebga's head. That raw, deceitful force which fragmented and deformed everything was emerging from the mud. Yebga was not afraid, however. He experienced a feeling more subtle than fear, as if something were giving way inside of him. He had wanted to shed light on things, and now this light only exposed more darkness. The sound of scraping feet dispelled his mood. Glenn entered the office, trailing an odor of tobacco in his wake. He removed his glasses and stopped short in front of the squatters in his office.

"Oh, excuse me, Yebga! I forgot to knock. Don't mind me. Just pretend I'm not here."

He took a few steps forward and stood opposite Yebga. Gauging the Cameroonian's haggard face, his growth of beard, his bloodshot eyes, his humor softened.

"Where were you this time? Even the best of serials has an end. Aren't you going at this a bit too long?"

"I feel like I'm drowning," Yebga answered.

Mukoni intervened, "He's exhausted, but we've both been working hard."

Glenn was silent for a moment, then sighed.

"Sorry if I disturbed you." And he slammed the door behind him as he left.

He thought you were putting him on," Mukoni said. "We'll be in for a little trouble when this is over."

Yebga stood and walked around the desk, getting back to business.

"I'll need all of this illustrious minister's addresses in Paris. And I'd like you to explain everything to Glenn. I just can't do it. I'm going for a little walk. Don't leave till I get back."

Yebga waved a hand, then disappeared. Mukoni leaned back in his chair and propped his long legs on a corner of the desk. He shuffled through the photos. Then he sighed, closing his eyes.

Yebga wandered aimlessly. An old three-beat jazz tune, one his father used to sing, ran through his head. He soon forgot about the buildings all around him, the sad gray Paris crowd. He started singing softly to himself, until the ground beneath his feet felt not like concrete but baked mud, like the floors of the big house back in Douala. He remembered a large table, where at night the whole clan gathered to palaver. Yebga walked along now with his eyes closed, apologizing when he bumped into a passerby. He remembered his happiness as a child too, playing blind man, fists clenched against his lids, the clucking of startled chickens, the feel of mud walls, and his mother's gentle scolding. He held his hands in front of him, fingers spread, and felt the sun's warmth dazzle him, flooding his eyelids. What would happen when he opened up his eyes? He knew he was in Montparnasse. The tower would stand out from here, a dark mass in the fog.

Yebga stopped, he opened his eyes wide and found himself before a building made of glass and steel in the Rue du Commandant-Mouchotte. He glanced up at the address. His efforts had not been wasted, after all. Chester Himes had lived here in May of sixty-eight. So, he *wasn't* all alone! His intuition had not abandoned him. Neither had his energy. He had found a landmark in a foreign land. To the astonishment of onlookers, Yebga laughed until he was out of breath.

In the basement of the *World*, Mukoni welcomed Yebga back. He leaned against a filing cabinet in the archives.

"You'd better call Faye. She phoned here earlier and we had quite a chat. You're even dumber than I thought, you know that? Some other chick named Myriam called too."

"Keep your nose out of my private life, Rodolphe. That's not what I need help with. I don't want to hear another word about it."

"Look at yourself, man. You imagine you're Don Juan but really you've been acting like a bum since you dropped Faye. The role just wasn't written for you, man."

"If you want a shot at her, the lane is clear! It's none of my business."

"What do you have against her?"

"She's white, and she acts like it."

Mukoni stepped between the dusty shelves and shoved a folder into Yebga's jacket. Then he made his way around a bookcase, ducked down an aisle and disappeared.

Chapter Thirty-Five

In the basement of the police station, the hands on the round aluminum clocks were sweeping toward seven, when Moreau was summoned to his desk by the ringing telephone. By the time he reached it, a masculine voice on the line was finishing a sentence:

". . . you asked me to call back at seven o'clock."

"Yes," came the reply. The inspector recognized the voice of N'Dyaye's wife. "Be at the entrance to the Porte Dauphine Metro at seven-thirty. Bring what my husband asked for. A car will be there to pick you up."

She hung up the telephone.

Moreau thanked the wire-tap technician for his help, then radioed the squad cars he had mobilized for the operation. He grabbed his gun and hastily made off to his own car, a white Renault 5, parked in the courtyard. He found his driver there, immersed in a maintenance manual.

Mukoni's handwriting was so small and tight that the piece of paper he had given Yebga looked almost blank. He finally managed to decipher four addresses: one in the sixteenth arrondissement, one in the Marais, one in the eighth and one more in Neuilly.

This guy probably never gets bored, Yebga reflected. At least I won't be driving into ghettos. I bet the hand that signed Diop's death sentence is well manicured. This was not the time for sociological reflections. If he wanted to wrap this story up, he would have to get to the heart of the matter swiftly. Yebga telephoned Sam, an old Cameroonian cabbie and a man he had entrusted with tricky errands for the newspaper before. The cab dispatcher patched the call into Sam's taxi radio and the old man's nasal voice came on the line. He bellowed with laughter, making his fare anxious.

"Amos!" he shouted. "Where you been?"

Yebga pictured Sam Mbida with a microphone in one hand and the wheel in the other, an enormous cigar plugged between his teeth.

"I need you, Sam" he said.

"Just a minute," replied Mbida. Then screeching to a halt, he bellowed, "Twenty-five francs," in the direction of his fare.

"What? But I'm going to Avenue Rapp!" squealed the elderly lady seated behind him.

The taxi was parked near the Opéra. Mbida, grasping the headrest behind him, whispered confidentially.

"Yes, madame, I know. But I have to go somewhere. It would be better if you didn't come along. Just give me twenty francs."

Mbida picked up the microphone, paying no heed to the woman who by now stood clutching her purse and shouting insults from the edge of the sidewalk.

"Hello, Amos?"

"Sam, I hope I'm not bothering you."

"Don't be ridiculous. Where are you?"

"I'm at the *World*, Rue de Vaugirard. Meet me on the Boulevard du Montparnasse."

"O.K. Ten minutes."

Mbida set down the microphone and turned the taxi into the dense afternoon traffic like an enraged Mamelouk pushing enemy cohorts back to Berezina. He drove like a lunatic. He had obtained a license several decades ago, thanks to a helpful cousin in the government and with the aid of bureaucratic bribes. He pulled up short at the curb outside the *World*, startling Yebga, who automatically climbed into the front seat.

"Hang on," said Mbida, shutting off the engine. "If you sit in front, I'll have to cover up the sign. Cops take these small infractions seriously."

"Don't tell me you're turning chicken."

Mbida rearranged things on the roof, took his place again and drove off.

"Where are you going, kid?"

"Place des Vosges, my man."

The taxi made an abrupt U-turn back onto the boulevard, as if the traffic had been halted just for them. Yebga sat up in his seat. Sam watched him from the corner of his eye.

Chapter Thirty-Six

Smith and Jones paced in front of the mansion gates like two grizzlies in a cage. They had agreed to make a stake-out of the place, to play it safe, but they would need to be prepared in case of trouble. Smith noted several points of entry to the grounds. The gate itself was not too high to scale. Since there would probably be a welcoming committee, they resolved to wait till nightfall to break in.

They hoped their mission would permit them to cast off, once and for all, their phony alter egos, without embarrassment or loss of face. To succeed would make them heroes in their own right. Himes could roll over in his grave for all they cared. Alone, on foreign soil, on their own, without Captain Brice's fictional support, or Lieutenant Anderson's literary cover, they planned to make these rich men pay in blood for using petty henchmen to kill blacks.

The forty-five from Pigalle would hardly offer sufficient protection from the adversary troop. Smith and Jones recalled the offer of that famous doctor of Mentaloscopic-Kinesis, Zigaman Fâ.

"Do you remember his redhead, Gravedigger?" whispered Smith.

"What a horny broad! I knew another chick like that. We locked ourselves up for an entire weekend, I didn't even have time to take off my socks."

On the Avenue de Clichy they made their way through towering swells of Africans in *boubous*, then shorter waves of tourists from Japan. They skirted islands of crap-shooters. They strolled aloof through rows of peep-show sirens, who sang to them and shimmered as they passed. The light on the Soleil d'Agadir shone like a beacon on the concrete sea below. Coming down the walk, a black man, tall and gaunt as a yam, lured them over, waving a piece of cardboard in Smith's face. Carefully ironed pant legs protruded from beneath his black *djellaba*. A knitted purple cap adorned his head.

"What do you want?" roared Smith.

The man broke into the quick pitch used by sellers of salvation. "You've got troubles. It's written on your face. Come with me to Doctor Zigaman Fâ. He can fix everything. Come with me."

Smith and Jones looked at each other in disbelief.

"Isn't that the guy we're looking for?"

"Yeah, that's his name."

"O.K." Smith said. "Let's go." The panderer's face lit up at the suggestion. He led them a short distance to the Soleil's entrance, turning frequently to make sure they hadn't left him. They crossed the cafe in single file, until they reached a soiled cloth partition. The messenger coughed twice, then pulled aside the curtain to let them pass. The room they entered was about four feet square. Save for a candle burning on a soapbox in the center, the room was bare. Beside the crate, a man in a large white robe sat meditating, cross-legged, with his arms folded before the dancing flame. He didn't blink as the Americans came in. For a moment, they thought he might be a dummy. An odor of spicy fish lay on the air. Smith glanced over at Jones. In the dark, he caught his partner's eye. There was something else behind him.

"Freeze!" bellowed Smith, clapping his hands.

"Hold it right there!" echoed Jones.

The phony monk jumped at the noise, then plunged his right hand deep into his robe. Smith was stroking the butt of the forty-five tucked in his belt before the robed man raised his eyes. Thinking better of it, the man stood up and reached to flip a wall switch. Light poured from the ceiling. The spiritualist smiled, radiant.

"My old chaps!" he cried. In his hand, he held a recent model of a small automatic.

"Zigaman!" Dubois shouted. "What's all this nonsense?"

"One has to live," he sighed, stepping toward them. "Being a doctor isn't enough. You need patients."

With his fingertips, Jones pushed away the gun in disbelief.

"Is that the kind of pill you give your patients?"

Zigaman Fâ looked limply at his pistol.

"Sorry," he said. "In my profession you never really know."

He set the gun down on the altar and laboriously freed himself from his holy garments.

"I don't need all this crap for you," he told them, smiling faintly.

Beneath the robe, he wore a loosely knit black pullover with jeans and Stan Smith tennis shoes. He blew the candle out, turned off the light, then pushed aside the curtain.

"I didn't think I'd see you two again! I'm glad you're here. Is something the matter?"

Dubois nodded.

"We going outside?"

The doctor's gaze followed Dubois'.

"Yeah, outside," he nodded.

They quietly made their way to the Barbès Metro station. Zigaman Fâ extracted a dirty cigarette from the pocket of his jeans. He began to puff on it dreamily.

"We need some guns," said Jones, as though he were asking for twenty dollars.

The doctor of Mentaloscopic-Kinesis stopped dead in the middle of the sidewalk, then had to run to catch up to the men.

"Guns? What for?"

Neither man replied. Fâ got the message.

"Forget I asked." he said. "When do you need them?"

"Tonight," Smith said.

The good doctor from Goutte-d'Or ran a hand over his scalp.

"That's short notice," he said. "That's really short notice! But maybe I know someone who can help you. What do you need?"

Smith and Jones agreed without discussion.

"P-thirty-eights with nickel-plated barrels are the best."

Zigaman stared at them in surprise.

"Are you crazy? Sylla may be able to help you out. But you'd better forget your nickel-plated popguns."

The man assumed a more decisive air and headed down the Boulevard Barbès at a military gait. The two Americans were right beside him. There were no hordes of tourists in the Rue de la Goutte-d'Or when they arrived. This part of Paris was a ghetto. Here and there small groups of Arabs stood talking in low voices or smoking *kif*, indifferent to shouting children playing games around them. Brilliantly colored clothing hung from the windows of dilapidated buildings.

"I knew there'd be some place like Harlem in this city," Smith told his friend with satisfaction.

Doctor Fâ broke in. "I'll take you to Sylla's place and wait outside. I can't talk to him. We're rivals and there's a little water in the gas these days. He speaks a bit of every language, though. Just ask for guns. He'll give you what he has. But they sure as hell won't be those pre-war things. And watch him with your money, he's a thief!"

The party filed into the tottery stairwell. The lightbulb there had burned out and they missed the first few steps, clumsily ascending five flights to a dingy landing. Once these, Zigaman Fâ knocked on a door; then before it opened, he plastered himself back against the wall.

Smith and Jones, still panting from the climb, were flooded with bulk memories of Harlem: underground gambling dens, knife fights, weird religious sects, abortion doctors. Fâ left behind, they stepped into a room littered with large blue iron trunks and animal skins. Mysterious flasks lined up on shelves filled the back wall. The man who let them in stood with his eyes closed and raised his arms up in a pompous gesture, throwing back the sleeves of his *gandoura*, his hands turned up toward the sky. His fingers were covered with gold rings.

"You American," he blurted out, nodding his head, blinking pale blue eyes for the effect. "You looking something and Master Sylla help you."

Smith plunged his hand into his trenchcoat and the forty-five appeared in the bare light. Startled, Sylla soon regained composure. Smith scrutinized the pale eyes, gleaming now with curiosity.

"We need guns."

The man drew near, trying to touch the pistol, but Smith stepped back.

"Not my job," said Sylla. "Hard."

Jones pulled a wad of bills out of his wallet. Sylla's eyes grew narrow, then his neck craned.

"Dollars," said the American. "We have dollars. I guess you like our money?"

The green bills looked crisp, almost alive. Sylla licked his parched lips.

"I try," he stammered.

"We need thirty-eight nickeled," said the ex-cop, defying Zigaman Fâ's advice.

"Yes, yes." said Sylla, looking away. "Moment."

He rang a small copper bell with a carved handle and a roguish boy of about twelve materialized in the doorway, amid the din of a television.

"Ibrahim," the marabout announced, "He get guns. Two guns."

"We're in a hurry."

"Quick be he. Not long."

The old man spoke to his grandson in Arabic, then sent the boy off with a snap of his fingers. He returned to his prayer rug, and picking up a rosary, rotated it before himself as he spoke.

"You need potions for future? You want I look your sex? To give you much power in love! I know good prayers for that," he added gravely.

"No thanks," said Jones, and glanced down at his fly unconsciously.

"Why you need guns?"

Smith frowned at this. The man turned quickly to his prayers, singing endless verses from the Koran.

"I think he's a Black Muslim!" Smith whispered.

"That could be," Dubois agreed.

They sat for twenty minutes, suspiciously eyeing their surroundings. At a muffled sound behind them, the two leaped up. Sylla smiled mysteriously.

"Not afraid. My grandson Brahim with the guns."

The child handed his grandfather a blue plastic bag, then disappeared.

Sylla set about emptying the bag of several small white boxes in various sizes. Smith grabbed them all. There were three small square cartons containing cartridge clips. Two others, flat and longer, held the guns: two brand-new Smith and Wessons. The ex-cops weighed the pistols in their palms, disassembled them, then checked the ammunition. Clicking the breeches, they towered over Sylla from a height.

"How much?" asked Jones.

The man scribbled a figure on a scrap of cardboard: 500.

Smith, unimpressed, counted out three hundred dollars in tens and tossed the bills onto the prayer rug. Nothing disturbed the stillness in the room as they walked out.

Zigaman was waiting in front of the building to guide them through the alleys of Goutte-d'Or. The appearance of a taxi cut short their farewells, but not before reminding Fâ of the torrid redhead with the *deux-chevaux*.

Chapter Thirty-Seven

It was three minutes past seven on the dot. Moreau's Renault 5 sat parked at the bottom of the Avenue Foch, where he could keep an eye on the entrance to the Metro. He radioed the squad of cars around him, making sure that everything was in order. Leaning against a Guimard column, Bienvenu Gratien, known simply as "Willy" to his friends, stood waiting for a car to pick him up. The white slacks on his adolescent frame were still visible in the growing darkness. Barely twenty, Willy was fresh off the boat from the islands. A first voyage to Senegal had taught him that one could earn money at an inverse proportion to wasted time and effort, provided one showed up at just the right moment in just the right place. Willy had become a prostitute much as some people undertake to study engineering or the law. He wanted to succeed, in short. Still, it was the first time he had taken on this sort of rendezvous. He usually worked familiar territory, reducing the risk of meeting lunatics or being beaten. This seemed like an adventure to him. His friend, L'il Georges, had told him it would pay well, very, very, well. He swallowed hard, as a long Mercedes glided past him. An electric window silently rolled down. A large black head, on an impressively thick neck, stuck through the door. The driver gave Willy the once-over, then waved him to the car. Bienvenu Gratien leaped into the limousine like a gazelle. Breathless, his heart pounding, he squeezed into a corner, a fragile misplaced creature in a cave of leather and wood. The car made a U-turn and headed back toward the Place de l'Etoile.

Moreau waited until the Mercedes had turned into the Avenue Foch, then ordered his driver to follow. The Renault slid anonymously into the traffic. Microphone in hand, Moreau stared through the darkness, eyes glued to the taillights of his prey. The Mercedes continued on at an easy pace past the Arc de Triomphe, onto the Avenue de la Grande-Armée. Moreau's grip tightened on the mike.

"All Maillot units: The car is a black Mercedes limousine, license plate number 15 FSG 75. Heading in the direction of Boulogne. Over."

He gave his call number and the radio crackled.

"Moreau."

"Maillot patrol. We've spotted the vehicle."

Yebga rushed down another set of steps at a well-to-do residence. The man was not here either. No lead. No trace. A cleaning woman here had just informed him that the minister was in Africa. Her tone sounded so sharp one might have thought he had inquired about her sex life. Yebga spotted the 504 pulled up at the curb on the Avenue Mozart, where Mbida had managed to find a parking place.

"Well?"

"Same thing again," Yebga answered.

"Don't look so down," Mbida said. "This is only the third address we've been to. As long as there are addresses, there's hope!"

"They aren't addresses. There's only one left."

Samuel Mbida shrugged his shoulders and stepped down on the clutch. The final destination was Neuilly.

Smith and Dubois stepped out of a taxi on the Avenue Charles-de-Gaulle and continued on toward the mansion on foot. There were only three other residences in the cul-de-sac. They were old buildings and offered the partners convenient vantage points. Here they could observe the movements around the mansion. They nonchalantly walked to the end of the street, then retraced their steps. The street was deserted, their maneuver proved a waste. They slipped back to the nearest observation post. It was about sixty feet from the entrance they'd been watching now for hours. They turned up the collars of their trenchcoats, shielding themselves from the fine rain, and went into hiding.

Moreau was on his way down the Avenue de la Grande-Armée when his radio crackled.

"Moreau."

"Maillot patrol."

"Where are you?"

"Neuilly. We're easing up into the small streets."

"Good. I'll be right there."

Samuel Mbida had more stories than Paris had alleys. There was one about a Dutch woman looking for a nightclub where they had black men listed on the menu; another about an old American lady who wanted to marry him because he reminded her of a dear departed Texan who also reeked of alcohol, smoked cigars and drove like a maniac.

191

Then there was the one about a woman from Thailand who paid her fare with shudders and moans, hard cash, in a grove in the Bois de Vincennes. Mbida always had stories about women, stories about ass, wantonly seasoned. Once he got started on them, he couldn't stop.

Yebga was mildly disgusted by his driver's life-long march across a land of fleshy hills and oozing grottos. When Sam stopped talking briefly for a moment to suck on his saliva-drenched cigar, Yebga tried, but failed, to change the subject. Pauses were rare. The car was old and slow. Yebga was forced regrettably to listen to endless tales of Sam's encounters with white women.

In Neuilly, when they reached their destination, Yebga climbed out of the taxi, gazed up at an imposing set of gates, then quickly pressed a recessed button. He heard a man's voice through the intercom: "What is it?" Yebga felt distinctly that he was being watched through the latticed grill.

"Amos Yebga, from the *World*. I'd like to see the minister."

"The minister is not receiving today," barked the voice. Then communication was cut off.

Yebga returned clear-headed to the cab. So, the minister was here. He ordered Mbida to take him back to the Avenue Charles-de-Gaulle. As he climbed into the cab, Moreau drove past.

"Follow that guy over there," the inspector told his driver. Then into the mike, "Who did you say this fortress belongs to?"

"The minister of the defense of Makalina-Busso," said a voice.

Chapter Thirty-Eight

Mbida's Peugeot drew up at a cafe near the Pont de Neuilly, tailed by Moreau's unmarked Renault. Mbida had finally stopped his ribald memoirs. Yebga stewed in silence at Sam's side.

"I'm going to get some cigars," he said, pointing at the bar. "You need anything?"

192

"Same as you but bigger," said Mbida, following him into the cafe.

The driver beached himself in a booth of Formica and imitation leather. When Yebga handed him a fistful of Cuban cigars the size of bazookas, the old bandit exposed a gap-toothed smile.

"You young folks know how to live. Yes, sir."

Yebga wasn't certain anymore. He needed to go back to the beginning. It seemed to him he pierced a veil of official lies and dubious excuses only to face the impregnable walls of a small Neuilly fortress. He had taken risks, he had followed leads, he had struggled, and come out empty-handed once again. The minister still held all the cards and the heavy iron gates around his mansion were like the borders of of a taboo Africa.

"So what are we going to do now, kid?" Mbida wondered, blowing a cumulo-nimbus at the ceiling.

"I don't really know. It's another dead end. I've run all this way for nothing."

Mbida wracked his brain for an appropriate reply and turned up nothing.

"Hello, gentlemen," said Moreau, sitting down at the Formica table. "If I'm disturbing you . . ."

How had this man found him, Yebga wondered. Had the minister sent him? Did it matter?

"It's raining," Yebga said. "The last time we saw each other, Inspector, it was drizzling just like this. Do you believe in signs? Of course not. You only want one thing. You want to be through with this whole affair as much as I do, but not for the same reasons. Drop this investigation. If it suits you, nab a fall guy. Kids disappear but it isn't the blacks who are eating them. It's you with your shitty proceedings."

"I have a warrant out for N'Dyaye's arrest," Moreau broke in before Yebga went on.

"Sure," Yebga laughed. "You can do all sorts of amusing things with official warrants. But it's too late for N'Dyaye. N'Dyaye is in hiding. And when he comes out, cops in white gloves will escort him to the airport. They'll probably drive him in the paddy wagon. Do you see who's fucked here? Or do I have to draw you a diagram? Samba was right. I should have split before . . ."

"Who's Samba?" asked Moreau.

"What does it matter? Let's go, Mbida. Let's get out of here. I just want to forget everything. Come on!"

Chapter Thirty-Nine

Ed Smith and Jones Dubois pulled their hats down low over their foreheads. The minister's neighbors were nowhere in sight, probably too busy, thought Dubois, tasting the soup, or amusing themselves with the maid, to pay attention to the sidewalk. Even if one of these trust funders took his dog out for a pee, he would probably take Smith and Jones for thieves, rousing the indigenous population to safeguard his wife's pension, his son's security, his daughter's dowry, Aunt Clarisse's silverware. If he should see these huge hands tightened on the newly purchased guns beneath their coats, he would dive straight through the first breach in the box hedge, running even faster than his hound.

A long Mercedes zoomed up to the sidewalk. As the driver leaned out of the car to activate the gate's remote control, he found himself face to face with the nose of a Big Bertha in working order.

"Go man, go," Smith hissed, as the heavy metal grills began to open.

Crouching forward, the two men rushed around the limousine, passing through the iron gates which marked the mansion's boundaries.

"Looking for someone in particular?"

The voice had come from very near, behind a thicket hiding a glass look-out.

Smith stood up.

"Freeze!" he cried.

"Hold it right there!" Jones shouted.

"Get the bastards," said a man behind the glass. "They've got pistols."

Jones ran as fast as he could toward the steps. Smith rolled to the ground, scraping his elbows on the gravel. His hat sailed forward, landing at the feet of a silhouette emerging from the darkness.

A shout followed so closely on the shots, that it seemed to have preceeded them.

"Ed!"

"Gravedigger!"

Alone under the gold light that splashed off the stone steps, Smith cocked his revolver and began shooting at gray shapes floating toward him through the mist like ectoplasm.

He moved forward without aiming, his arm stretched out in front of him, a few feet from the body of his partner, two steps away, now one. Smith felt almost nothing. Only a slight burning like the match one forgets to blow out. A searing match that burned into his back, just below the shoulderblade, then lower. The black man smiled as his legs gave way, like a performer in an old ancestral dance. Blood flowed in thin streams at his feet, yet he was dancing, as though his heavy frame no longer touched the ground. He spun around a few more times, and then collapsed onto the cement, free at last.

He'd better watch out up there, that old spade Himes. From here on in, Coffin Ed and Gravedigger Jones would have all of eternity to dictate their adventures to their Maker. They finally had him in the palms of their black hands.

BLACK LIZARD BOOKS

JIM THOMPSON
AFTER DARK, MY SWEET $3.95
THE ALCOHOLICS $3.95
THE CRIMINAL $3.95
CROPPER'S CABIN $3.95
THE GETAWAY $3.95
THE GRIFTERS $3.95
A HELL OF A WOMAN $3.95
NOTHING MORE THAN MURDER $3.95
POP. 1280 $3.95
RECOIL $3.95
SAVAGE NIGHT $3.95
A SWELL LOOKING BABE $3.95
WILD TOWN $3.95

HARRY WHITTINGTON
THE DEVIL WEARS WINGS $3.95
FORGIVE ME, KILLER $3.95
A TICKET TO HELL $3.95
WEB OF MURDER $3.95

CHARLES WILLEFORD
THE BURNT ORANGE HERESY $3.95
COCKFIGHTER $3.95
PICK-UP $3.95

ROBERT EDMOND ALTER
CARNY KILL $3.95
SWAMP SISTER $3.95

W.L. HEATH
ILL WIND $3.95
VIOLENT SATURDAY $3.95

PAUL CAIN
FAST ONE $3.95
SEVEN SLAYERS $3.95

FREDRIC BROWN
HIS NAME WAS DEATH $3.95
THE FAR CRY $3.95

DAVID GOODIS
BLACK FRIDAY $3.95
CASSIDY'S GIRL $3.95
NIGHTFALL $3.95
SHOOT THE PIANO PLAYER $3.95
STREET OF NO RETURN $3.95

JIM NISBET
THE DAMNED DON'T DIE $3.95
LETHAL INJECTION $15.95

AND OTHERS . . .
FRANCIS CARCO • *PERVERSITY* $3.95
BARRY GIFFORD • *PORT TROPIQUE* $3.95
NJAMI SIMON • *COFFIN & CO.* $3.95
ERIC KNIGHT (RICHARD HALLAS) • *YOU PLAY THE BLACK AND THE RED COMES UP* $3.95
GERTRUDE STEIN • *BLOOD ON THE DINING ROOM FLOOR* $6.95
KENT NELSON • *THE STRAIGHT MAN* $3.50

AND ALSO . . .
THE BLACK LIZARD ANTHOLOGY OF CRIME FICTION edited by **EDWARD GORMAN**. Authors include: Harlan Ellison, Jim Thompson, Joe Gores, Harry Whittington, Wayne D. Dundee and more $8.95

Black Lizard Books are available at most bookstores or directly from the publisher. In addition to list price, please send $1.00/postage for the first book and $.50 for each additional book to **Black Lizard Books, 833 Bancroft Way, Berkeley, CA 94710.** California residents please include sales tax.